"I genuinely haven't wanted to be the guy who makes the precious time you have in the city about me. It's just that…well, you've messed me up in the head quite a lot… I can't believe all this hasn't been obvious."

"Well, I don't know, Thomas," I replied, finally regaining my voice. "I'm not exactly used to men telling me that they don't want to date me but expecting me to know that they really do."

"That's fair. And all of this is new to me, too, to be honest. Even up to just now, when you asked me that question, I wasn't sure if I was going to say something, because I didn't…"

"Because you didn't want to ruin what we have?" I offered, again understanding him more than I cared to admit.

"Yeah. Exactly."

We turned the corner onto my block, and Thomas stepped toward me, closing the gap between us once again.

"So, now that you know how I feel, are you really going to tell me it's just me?"

Dear Reader,

Growing up, I always bristled at the saying "Want to make God laugh? Tell him/her about your plans." Maybe that's because I love a good plan. It's something about the linear nature of it—if all goes right, it can be the simplest and most satisfying thing in the world. Yet when I look over my life, many of the best things that have happened to me have been entirely unplanned. Weird, right?

Well, this is exactly what Olivia Robinson is facing in *Her New York Minute*. In the fourth book of my Friendship Chronicles series, the British native goes to New York with one goal in mind: become the youngest head of her company's portfolio division. She never expects to also meet a charming attorney who shows her what it's like to be loved just as she is—and to be honest, she struggles with that disruption.

With the help of some of your faves from the rest of the series, however, Olivia eventually realizes some of the best things—even the dreams she stopped believing could ever happen for her—come unexpected...out of the blue...and in a New York minute.

Hope you enjoy!

Darby

Her New York Minute

———

DARBY BAHAM

HARLEQUIN
SPECIAL
EDITION

HHARLEQUIN®

**SPECIAL
EDITION**™

ISBN-13: 978-1-335-59451-8

Her New York Minute

Copyright © 2024 by Darby Baham

Harlequin Enterprises ULC
22 Adelaide St. West, 41st Floor
Toronto, Ontario M5H 4E3, Canada
www.Harlequin.com

Printed in U.S.A.

Darby Baham is an author and storyteller on a mission to make women like herself feel seen and believe that love is possible for them, yes them. The former *Washington Post* contributor often uses her doubts, hopes and fears to connect with her readers and inform the themes in her Harlequin romance series, The Friendship Chronicles. This series is a love letter to female friendships and offers an intimate look into the dynamic love lives of Black women.

Books by Darby Baham

Harlequin Special Edition

The Friendship Chronicles

The Shoe Diaries
Bloom Where You're Planted
Her New York Minute

Visit the Author Profile page
at Harlequin.com for more titles.

To the unexpected blessing who came into my life and knocked me off my feet—thank you.

Part 1

"There is no force more powerful than a woman determined to rise."

—Bosa Sebele

Chapter One

This is going to be my year.

That was all I kept thinking as my plane began descending into JFK International Airport, carrying hundreds of passengers and all my hopes and dreams of kicking ass and taking names in the most limitless city on Earth…plus my year's worth of luggage.

In just six months' time, I'd gone from being the portfolio manager of a team that had shocked our global investment company when we'd raised $500 million for a little social impact fund that no one but us had really believed in to being offered the opportunity to go to our New York office to duplicate my efforts in America. So, I bloody well knew the impact I could have in a short amount of time, and I was ready.

Like I said, this was going to be my year.

Never mind that I didn't really know what I was in

store for—all that mattered was that I had a grand plan and I was going to execute it to perfection. On my agenda? Show up, flawlessly polished stilettos in tow, wow the US office with my ideas for taking what we'd learned so far and expanding on it, and prove to everyone that I was even more than the superstar they maybe imagined I might've been. I'd already started to establish myself in the UK office, having overseen multiple million-dollar portfolios since, but it still sometimes seemed as if people were waiting for me to take my next step up. And even if they weren't and it was all in my head, I'd certainly put enough pressure on myself to excel that it made up for at least ten people at once. Either way, I knew one thing to be true—I couldn't just succeed in London if I wanted to move up the ladder at my investment management group; I also needed the C-suite brass in America to see what I could do up close and personal before they, hopefully, eventually gave me the thing I really wanted: head of the portfolio division.

So, there I was, on a flight headed thousands of miles away from the only home I'd ever known, taking on a new position that they hadn't fully described to me other than saying, *New York needs you, and we think this can be a great opportunity.* Not exactly a detailed job description, but I had decided to bet on myself. And as long as everything went according to my plans, I expected that this time next year, I'd be flying right back to the UK, a year older, perfectly positioned for a promotion to senior portfolio manager at thirty-six and in line for my dream job soon after. What more could a girl from Brixton really ask for, yeah?

I closed my eyes and waited for the plane's wheels to hit the ground so that my new adventure could begin, allowing the smooth sounds of Tems's voice to calm my nerves as "Free Mind" played softly in my ears. About two songs and five or six minutes later, one of our flight attendants turned on her mic and announced what we'd all been waiting for after sitting around for eight hours on a plane.

"Ladies and gentlemen," she began. "Welcome to New York City, where the local time is 5:25 p.m. For your safety and the safety of those around you, please remain seated with your seat belt fastened and keep the aisles clear until we are parked at the gate. Be careful when opening overhead bins as items tend to move during flight... On behalf of all of us here at JetBlue, thanks again for choosing us. For those of you from New York City, we'd like to be the first to say welcome home. If you're visiting, we hope you enjoy your stay, and we look forward to seeing you again soon."

Welp, I thought as I readied myself for the eventual dash off the plane, *this is it*. And as my friend Robin would say, *Here goes nothing and everything all at once.*

Once I heard the familiar ding letting us know that we could unbuckle our seat belts, I began packing up all my items in an attempt to have my ducks in a row before I inevitably had to wrestle down my heavy luggage from the overhead bin. Down into my knapsack went my bottle of water, the snacks I'd been noshing on the whole flight, a book I'd ambitiously thought I would read and hadn't and, of course, my trusty earbuds only after I'd reluctantly turned off my playlist. Each item had its own place in the gray-and-teal backpack that served as both my carry-on and purse for the day, meticulously plotted out during the weeks prior to my trip to ensure I didn't leave anything I really needed in London. The plotting and planning also helped me to make sure I could magically fit everything I might need in a year into what I could only bring with me on the flight: my backpack, a carry-on and two checked pieces of luggage.

As soon as I saw the rest of my row begin to move, I dutifully slid out of my seat, stood up tall and turned to face my luggage nemesis that had already given me a struggle when I put it in the overhead bin. But I was also me, Olivia Robinson, a badass woman on a mission, so I wasn't about to let a bit of heavy luggage stop me from starting things off just right. Fully determined, and with a deep breath conjuring up all my strength, I resigned myself to the struggle I'd ultimately overcome and then reached my right arm up and pulled on the top handle with all my might, tugging it with proper force…only for it to not move even one tiny little spec.

"Okay, that's all right," I whispered to myself. "Even Beyoncé has to do things twice sometimes, yeah."

I prepared myself for my second attempt, this time rising onto my toes in my white low-top trainers and using both hands to try to wrestle the carry-on out of its home. I jiggled it. I tugged at it. I even grunted while I pulled. But again, no such luck. To make matters worse, the frustrated sighs I had been worried might come if I didn't stop holding up the progress in the aisle began loudly making their way to my ears, causing me to not only feel completely embarrassed but also wholly upset with myself that I couldn't just will this thing to work.

This was not how I'd planned my year to start. Not staring down a stupid little heavy carry-on trying to make me second-guess all my beliefs in a matter of a few minutes. The fact of the matter was that the way I'd lived my life for years now was pretty simple: you put your all into something, you believed in yourself fully and the results you desired would come. *Why didn't this carry-on understand basic physics or whatever?*

I was two seconds away from going down a nasty rabbit hole in my head when I heard a deep-toned voice behind me, offering what felt like the nicest gesture known to man.

"Can I help you out here?" he asked, startling me out of my thoughts.

With a heavy sigh of relief, I answered with the only thing I could utter in that moment: "Yes, please."

Then, swiftly, I came off my tippy toes, closing my eyes briefly in thanks, and turned toward my knight in shining armor.

"I would really appreciate that," I added, running my hands down my dark blue skinny jeans as I laid my eyes on the kindest smile staring back at me.

It was one of those full smiles, where the joy permeated on every part of the person's face, showing up not only in the off-kilter upturn of his lips but also in the fullness of his cheeks and the glow in his eyes. His teeth, white like a Colgate ad, sparkled in contrast to the dark brown hue of his skin, set off perfectly by his low-cut beard and the goatee that traced along the indented curves of his mouth. But it wasn't just his smile that caught my attention. His chuckle—just as deep-toned as his voice and probably stemming from my less-than-stellar attempt at trying to compose myself in his presence—revealed a playful nature underneath the suaveness of his gentleman persona. And his beautifully sculpted arms, covered only by a long-sleeved white shirt that left nothing to the imagination, only served to add to my now very persistent desire to melt back into my seat so I could watch him work his magic in full view.

Resisting that particular urge, I simply stepped aside to give him full access to my luggage in hopes that he could quickly rescue me from being the embarrassed woman holding up an entire international flight of people from deboarding their plane. With one hand and one full swing of his arm, my handsome knight snatched the luggage down from the overhead bin as if it were the lightest piece of paper on a table. Then, with his eyes stayed on mine, he delicately placed it on the ground, lifted the handle and put it right next to my hand so I could easily grab it and wheel myself off the flight.

"Wow," I uttered before I could stop myself. "Thank you, honestly."

"It's no problem at all," he replied with a wink and a gentle head nod toward the exit. "I was a little worried the eye daggers you were getting were going to turn into real ones, so I couldn't leave you to fend for yourself too much longer."

"Truthfully, I was, too."

Taking his cue, I turned toward the exit, gathered myself and tried my best to walk as fast as I could down the aisle. To my absolute horror, this only served to embolden the crowd behind me, which proceeded to give me a loud round of applause for finally moving out of their way. It wasn't exactly the first impression I'd planned, but I had my luggage, so I was back in swing mode. Plus, as recently as two days before, I'd experienced something far worse than a bunch of strangers mocking me—I'd maybe, kind of, sort of broken up with my boyfriend of two years, except it had gone about as well as my attempt to pick up my luggage, so I really wasn't quite sure.

All I did know was that despite any mishaps that had occurred between now and then, I was in New York. And so, if nothing else, I was going to hold my head as high as the top bun that my waist-length, brown-and-blond passion twists were tucked into as I walked off that plane. I also vowed to myself not to look back at anyone behind me until I got to baggage claim. The last thing I was going to do was let these strangers see me sweat. Not after I'd fought through all my fears to be right where I was.

My handsome knight, however, didn't seem to get my telepathic memo that I was avoiding anything and everyone from that plane experience—a fact I soon realized as I heard him calling from behind me as we stepped into the gate area of the airport.

"The clapping might have been a little unnecessary," he said, falling in step with me as he quickly caught up to my five-foot-four stride.

"Ha. Oh yes, a bit," I replied, a little flustered that he wanted to keep talking…to me.

"Though you were giving *'damsel in distress who refuses to ask for help'* vibes, so maybe they felt you needed some encouragement."

Ah, so he was a funny guy, too, I realized. *Just my luck.*

I paused my steps and turned to directly face him, wanting him to see clearly that while I'd appreciated his help, I wasn't exactly in the mood for his jokes. Unfortunately for me, as soon as we locked eyes, I completely lost my train of thought. The devious and kid-like smirk on his face somehow took hold of my very brain process, causing me to simply—and almost uncontrollably— smile back at him, which then led to us both tumbling into a series of giggles that only we understood.

"It wasn't that I refused," I replied, trying to contain my chuckles and suddenly feeling like I needed to plead my case. "No one offered until you did."

"Fair point."

He dipped his head slightly to the side in acknowledgment, all the while keeping his eyes trained on mine in some sort of hypnotic force that demanded I stare right back. The wild thing was I didn't even think he was actively trying to seduce me, but in the brief period of time that we'd stopped walking, I'd had to catch my breath on at least three different occasions in his presence. Maybe this captivating effect was something this guy was used to, I theorized. After all, the man had the makings of every picture-perfect model that my friends and I would cut out of our *Right On!* and *J-17* magazines to hang on our bedroom walls when we were preteens.

Standing at what looked to be about five foot ten, with gray eyes so deep they matched his baritone voice, he also had the kind of broad shoulders every heterosexual woman dreamed of holding tightly on to when she was in the throes of passion with her man. His hands were also impeccably manicured and looked like they were both soft and moisturized to perfection but also might have a slight gritty texture on the back side, as if he might have been a former athlete who now only used them to get someone's attention in a restaurant. And his body? Let's just say I imagined even Broderick Hunter would be envious.

I shook my head and all the arresting thoughts of

this man who I didn't know out of it, reminding myself that I was barely single and not at all in New York to meet new men, let alone captivating ones in airports. Plus, I wasn't starring in anyone's romantic comedy film last I checked, so I quickly put aside any foolish notions of some sort of meet-cute where the slender, brown-skinned woman from London met the dashing American with an intoxicating smile, and brought myself back to our conversation at hand.

"Also, maybe if they had, the whole ordeal wouldn't have lasted as long as it did," I opined.

"Or…and don't try to tussle with me on this…you could have asked for what you clearly needed, and that also would have resolved your problem."

He tilted his head to the side again and held back what looked like another smirk, betraying how much he was enjoying our banter as the single dimple he had on his right cheek poked out from behind his beard.

"I guess I'm not used to asking for help," I admitted in a slight whisper—and then almost immediately regretted being that open with someone whose name I didn't even know.

"I gathered. Which is why I stepped in."

For a split second, he allowed himself to look at me sincerely, and the eyes that had once shown me kindness and then turned playful were suddenly relaying that he understood what I'd meant on a foundational level. That I didn't need to explain to him why everything in my body resisted asking anyone for help; he already knew. Thankfully for my weak knees, he just as quickly returned back to his jokes, because I was fully unprepared to have someone read me that well in a matter of seconds.

"You know, to rescue you from your damsel ways," he added, winking at me again before going back to his insanely hypnotic stare.

"Well, I do thank you kindly, sir," I replied, and then mockingly curtsied before him. "Whatever would I have done without you?"

"In my head? I imagine you would have eventually climbed onto the arm of one of those seats, grabbed that suitcase with all your might and forced it to bend to your will. It might have taken you another five to ten minutes, but you would have gotten it."

"I don't know if I should take that as a compliment or an insult," I said, still smiling.

"Definitely a compliment. You seem like a woman who doesn't back down from a fight and who usually gets what she wants. I like that."

Stuck standing in front of each other as if our feet couldn't move if we tried, it felt like he was waiting to see which route I would take our fairly innocuous conversation. As if he were silently asking me: Are you going to choose to be even more vulnerable with a perfect stranger in the airport, or should I keep up our surface-level teasing rapport until we part ways?

The answer seemed pretty obvious to me, of course, especially as more people piled off the airplane and rushed past us on their way to Passport Control. Door Number Two was what normal people chose in airport interactions. They went about their business, and if they actually spoke to anyone, it was surface-level chitchat that they'd forgotten by the time they jumped into their Uber and headed home.

As obvious as my choice should have been, there was something about this guy that made me want to choose

Door Number One. I wasn't sure if it was the way I kept losing my breath every single time he hit me with one of his bloody intense stares or if it was the fact that he was quite literally stunning or if something behind his eyes just made me want to know more. Whatever it was (and maybe it was all three), the temptation was strong. Any normal woman would have already melted right into his arms, really, told him all her fears, hopes and dreams, and plotted out how their chance encounter would evolve into a marriage proposal within the year. But I...try as I might...had never once been accused of being normal, at least not by any of my exes. Of being a founding member of #TeamTooMuch? Sure. An incessant planner who didn't know how to let life come to her? Mmm-hmm. Unemotional, coldhearted and only focused on winning? Yes, yes and yes. But never normal. So, it was pretty clear what my choice was ultimately going to be.

"Well," I said, clearing my throat. "Once again, I find myself saying thank you to you, so th...thank you, genuinely."

I fumbled my way through my words as I started trying to walk away, hoping to end our impromptu conversation as soon as possible so that I could go on pretending like I didn't notice the little crinkle on his nose as his smile grew wider while watching me squirm.

"Is that a Brixton thing?" he asked, seamlessly matching his steps with mine as he once again caught up to me.

"Is what a Brixton thing?"

"Overly thanking people."

"Oh, well, I didn't know that you could thank someone too many times," I replied. "Plus, how do you know I'm from Brixton?"

"It's hard to miss the accent, love. And I've spent enough time in London that I'm starting to learn the differences."

"Oh, well, good on you, babes."

I caught myself right before I winked at him in some sort of instinctual effort to mimic his demeanor toward me even as we continued walking in step.

"But…to answer your question, no, I wouldn't say we are overly generous with our thank-yous. And to prove it, I take mine back."

I lifted my eyebrows to show him that I could join in on the teasing, too, when I wanted.

"Well, that's not how it works," he retorted with a big smile on his face and that damn crinkle catching my attention again. "Once it's out there, you can't take back a thank-you."

"Oy, you say that, but I believe I already have, innit. *Thankyouverymuch.*"

"And…you just thanked me again."

He burst out laughing, bending forward as he proudly chuckled to himself and causing me to stop walking again as I protested my point.

"That doesn't count! You know what I meant there."

"Doesn't matter what you meant, love. It's what you said."

I sighed loudly.

"Fine. Well, now that you've added to my embarrassment from the plane, th—"

This time, I caught myself before finishing my sarcastic thank-you in response. The grin on his face showed me I didn't catch it soon enough, however.

Ugh. How had my knight in shining armor so quickly turned into someone who I wanted to shake—and maybe kiss, but mostly shake—that fast?

Really, it didn't matter. I just knew, as I'd known all along, that I needed to get out of his presence as fast as I could before I succumbed to whatever chemistry we seemed to have that had me equally intrigued and frustrated since it was more than I'd ever once had with the man I'd been dating for the past two years.

"You know what?" I asked rhetorically. "I think it's time for me to head to Passport Control. I assume we're going in different directions, yeah?"

His once bright smile faded upon maybe, finally, realizing that I really was trying to end our airport banter.

"Wait, wait, I'm sorry," he replied sincerely. "I'm not trying to embarrass you further, I promise. I was just having a little fun."

"At my expense?"

"I'd like to think not, but if I really have offended you, please let me know."

The look on his face was genuine and probing as he waited for my reply, almost as endearing as the first time he'd slipped his cool and had shown how caring he could be. So, as much as I wanted to play coy and get him back for all his teasing, those deep gray, thoughtful eyes wouldn't dare allow me to let him think he'd actually hurt my feelings. He'd pulled me in yet again.

"No, you definitely didn't offend me," I admitted with a smile. "Though it certainly has been an interesting welcome to a new country. I'd been told that New Yorkers weren't this talkative, so already you've managed to throw everything I believed out of the window."

"Hmm," he said, stepping in closer to me. "Well, that might be because I'm not originally from New York."

"No?"

"Uh-uh. I mean, I've lived here for almost a decade, so it is home. But I'm actually from Philly."

"Philadelphia, Pennsylvania?" I asked to clarify.

"Yep, born and raised."

"On the playground is where you spent most of your days?" I joked, using the follow-up iconic line from *The Fresh Prince of Bel-Air*'s opening theme song.

"Hold up. Y'all were watching Will Smith in London, too?"

"Don't do that. London's not on an entirely different planet, you know."

"No, I know. But to be honest, it's not like we grew up thinking about what anyone outside of America watched or listened to, so that's kinda interesting. Makes me want to know more."

He shrugged casually as he said his last statement but also drew his eyes back up to mine with that familiar probing look that had almost made me choose Door Number One before.

"We had our own stuff, too, yeah," I replied. "But especially among us Black Brits, we definitely paid attention to what Black Americans were doing. You know, diaspora and all. Beyond that, however, *The Fresh Prince of Bel-Air* was just bloody popular in the UK. It shaped a lot of what I thought about America when I was a little girl."

"You are aware now that it's very different, though, right?"

"Ha ha, yeah. I've seen a lot more shows since...oh and

rap videos, too. Very important," I teased, and watched him stare at me wide-eyed in horror.

Finally, I had *him* on his toes, which I took great pleasure in, biting my lower lip and playfully raising my eyebrows before I continued.

"I also have actual American friends now, too…so that's probably helped the most."

"Oh, good," he said, breathing a sigh of relief. "For a moment I thought I was going to have to give you a breakdown of Black American culture, complete with my top ten movies you have to see, a nineties-music playlist and at least one full-season watch of *A Different World*."

"Just not the first season!" we said in unison, laughing like we'd known each other for ages.

Locking eyes with me once more, he moved in a few steps closer so that I could just barely make out the cologne that seemed to perfectly complement his entire essence. Again, a different woman, a normal woman, might have inhaled deeply to take in his full scent, but I resisted. I didn't have the luxury to get caught up in some fairy tale with a guy who was likely just a big flirt.

Remember, Liv, I reprimanded myself, *we're only here in America to improve our chances at a promotion. Handsome, charming, irresistibly sexy men are not in our plans.*

"How long are you in town, by the way?" he asked, wrestling me out of my thoughts again.

"A year," I said with a wistful sigh.

"Wow, okay, that is not what I expected you to say."

"Not even with my heavy luggage?"

"Oh, true, that could have been a giveaway. Or you could just be a bad packer."

"I think maybe quite the opposite, or at least I hope. I've had to pack up a year's worth of luggage for this flight, so fingers crossed I got it right."

"Something tells me you made damn sure you did," he replied, sending chills down my spine again as he caught my attention with yet another bloody intense gaze. "Can I ask—what are you doing for the next year?"

"Well," I said, clearing my throat again, "my job is interested in seeing if I can pull off some more big portfolio wins for them, this time in the States. And I'm using it as a chance to kick ass and take names, so that they have to give me the promotion I want."

"Well, all right, Ms. London. Welcome to America, then."

I smiled as I recognized his admiration for my ambition. It was a nice change from what I'd been dealing with in my relationship with David, where it felt like any big win that I'd had at work made him more and more resentful of me.

"Ha ha, thanks," I replied sheepishly, realizing I'd done it again but hoping he didn't take the bait and call me out. "What brought *you* to New York, by the way?"

"So, actually, I came here after law school, but I didn't always know that I wanted to be a lawyer. Before that, I worked in tech sales for a little while, stacked some money, and then decided to try something new— law. After that, everything just fell into place—I knew where I wanted to work and that I loved to travel. New York law firms offered me the best chance to practice law in the US and overseas, so it was kind of a no-brainer for me. Once I passed the bar, I started working for my current firm, and now here we are."

"Wow, that's really cool," I said, genuinely impressed

by him and, frankly, myself for correctly assessing that his current job wasn't one that was physically labor intensive. I could totally understand why he wasn't intimidated by my ambition, too; he had his own with some to spare, it seemed.

"Yeah, guess we're both doing our thing, right?"

He raised his right hand up toward mine and stared into my eyes as he waited for me to meet his hand in return. After a short hesitation, I lifted mine as well, meeting him for a high five as I also realized that my cheeks were starting to get heavy from cheesing so much. Then, the two of us stood in front of each other, not knowing what else to say but simultaneously not quite ready to leave…our right hands falling down together and moving into something of a handshake that neither of us wanted to end.

In truth, I probably could have stood there forever now that I finally experienced what it was like to feel the touch of his skin, but that would not have been a smart move on my part. Just as I'd presumed, the texture of his skin was soft with just a hint of roughness underneath; what I hadn't counted on was the electricity that had flown through us as soon as our hands collided.

With another quick breath, I slowly began to untangle my fingers away before I lost myself and never wanted to let him go.

For better or worse, he took the hint.

"Well, it's been nice meeting you," he said as he took a step back from me.

"And I *thiiiink* it's been lovely meeting you, too," I replied, still smiling but inside realizing this was definitely goodbye. "At the very least, us meeting helped me get my luggage off the plane."

"At the very least, yeah."

My shining knight took another step away from me, and with one final wink, he turned to his left and walked out of my life. Well, it was to go to the American Passport Control entrance, but for my purposes, that was the same thing. I grabbed my earbuds again and started my playlist back up, falling right into the achingly apropos "Yebba's Heartbreak."

ily had been so happy that finally, in my thirties, I'd brought home a man who'd seemed respectable and ready to settle down. And for a while, I'd been happy, too! Never mind that, together, we'd had the passion of a toad on a log; I'd had an attractive and successful man who liked me, and for most of my family members that was all that mattered. There was just one problem: when I was truly honest with myself, whenever I stopped to think about what I really craved from my partner, I had to admit that there had always been something off about us despite how much we'd tried to make it work.

I mean, I was a woman who liked over-the-top everything, and David had really never appreciated that. He'd loved me—I thought he still did—but in his heart of hearts, I also believed he'd always thought *it just doesn't take all that* whenever he'd look at me and how I operated in my life. But that place where it seemed like an extra step might be too much? Well, that was where I thrived! It was why simple girls' nights in with my friends included sparkly decorations, balloons and champagne. And why I'd made my company millions of dollars in less than a year. Because when someone else thought they'd done enough, I was just getting started. Maybe in relationships that could be too much for some people to deal with—there was a reason I was staring down thirty-six and single again, yeah—but it had always served me well in my career...so the lesson I'd learned from him was clear: my career was bloody well where my focus needed to be.

On the bright side, my brother and Robin had made up for everything David hadn't done. The two lovebirds, who quite literally owed me for putting them together after serendipitously meeting at my flat, had pulled out all the stops and showed up to my flat the next day with three bottles of bubbly (one for each of us) and plans for a farewell tour throughout London. For a full day, we'd traipsed our way through the city, drunkenly giggling at all my old haunts and finishing off in Brixton with a surprise dinner hosted by my family. Craig, who was an accomplished photographer, had even taken a ton of photos while we'd been out—one of which I'd posted on Instagram with a *Goodbye, London* caption right before boarding my flight.

Now that's how you send someone off like a boss, David. Tuh!

Right as I could feel myself getting upset again, I saw out of the corner of my eye the first of my matching gray-and-teal luggage pop out of the carousel shooter and make its way toward me.

"Yes," I whispered under my breath, and ran toward my bag, catching it by the side handle and dragging it toward the rest of my things.

What a relief. I double-checked the tag to be sure my name was on it and then lifted it onto the cart that held all my luggage together so that I could easily wheel them out when I was ready.

Now there was just one more to go.

I fixed my eyes back toward the carousel in anticipation of seeing my next one come around the corner.

"Now, what's in *this* bag? The UK army?"

As soon as I heard that unmistakably deep voice to the left of me, another smile I couldn't control instantly grew on my face. If I was going to keep running into him, I would need to work on that for sure.

"We really must stop meeting like this," I said, turning toward him. "One might begin to think it's on purpose or something."

"To be fair, it's not a huge leap that we would see each other again at baggage claim," he said, correcting me slightly with that same smirk he'd had when he'd called me out about not asking for help.

I guess he'd had a point both times.

"But also," he continued as he snaked his fingers through his luggage handle for safekeeping, "I was kind of hoping I'd run into you again."

"Oh?"

His words caused my heart to skip just a beat faster than normal, but I steadied myself in time to not let him in on that little secret.

"Yeah, well, I realized after we parted ways that I never got your name. And I…"

Before he could finish his thought, I saw my last piece of luggage come bouncing around the bend from the corner of my eye. Without hesitation, I dived toward it in a feeble attempt to catch it before it went back around, and then I'd be stuck waiting for it again for God knew how long. Unfortunately, because of my impromptu dive, I caught ahold of my luggage in a weird position and once again found myself struggling to wrestle it down—that was until I felt my kind, handsome stranger's hands on the left side, helping to pull it off with me.

Together, we yanked it down from the carousel and then stood the twenty-three-kilogram bag up onto its wheels, the dynamic duo having once again conquered what felt like my ongoing luggage wars.

"Apologies," I whispered, catching his eyes. "I didn't mean to interrupt you, but…"

"Please. There's no need to explain. It's important you get your suitcase. I get it."

"Thank you," I said with a chuckle, knowing full well that would make him smile.

I wheeled my last bag over to my cart to add it to my ever-growing pile before turning to him again.

"You were saying?" I asked once I'd connected my bag with the others.

"Oh right, I was just going to finally ask you your name."

"Oh, of course," I replied, raising my hand to meet his again. "It's Olivia. Well, Liv is what most people call me."

"Okay, well, hi, Liv. I'm Thomas."

The way he grabbed my hand, keeping his eyes fixed on mine, if I'd been a betting woman, I might have actually thought the man *was* trying to seduce me this time around. But I knew better; in London, I'd hardly ever had anyone approach me out of the blue. So, while I'd dated my fair share—mostly men who I'd met at get-togethers—I'd long realized that I wasn't the meet-cute kind of girl. And yet second after second passed by with our fingers intertwined before Thomas and I let go, only prompted by the sleeve on my mid-thigh-length sweater falling down to my wrist and breaking my attention from his gaze. Finally, I did us both a favor and loosened my grip, similar to our last handshake, eliciting the ripple effect of him parting from me again.

"Hi, Thomas," I said, stepping back from him just a tad. "I feel like I already said this, but it's lovely meeting you."

"Technically, the last time you didn't seem all too sure."

"That's true. But now you've helped me twice with my luggage. I can't deny it anymore."

He chuckled to himself, turning his head slightly away from mine in what seemed like an attempt to regain his composure.

"Duly noted," he replied, shifting his intensity as he returned his eyes to mine.

"You know," I said, looking back at him, desperately holding on to the last remaining bit of willpower I had to not "accidentally" fall into his arms so he'd have to put his hands on me again, "I could actually use your help with one more thing."

Thomas raised his thick eyebrows at me as he waited for me to continue.

"You mentioned you've lived here for a fairly long time, yeah?"

"Yes."

I could see his smile growing again, betraying whatever cool pretense he was trying to give off.

"Well, I'd love any recommendations on anything I should do or see while I pretend to be a New Yorker for the next year."

"Recommendations, huh? Hmm."

He stepped back and looked at me quizzically, very obviously trying to read me. Unfortunately for him, I couldn't afford to let him see how much he'd captured my attention in just our three short interactions, so I wasn't exactly making it easy. And to his credit, he didn't try to push me to give more than I was comfortable divulging, either. He just simply...observed.

"Where are you staying?" he finally asked.

"My company put me up in a flat... I'm sorry,

apartment—I have to get used to saying that—in the East Village."

"Okay, okay. Nice area, but can I be honest with you?"

"Please do."

"Actually, first let me ask you something else. Where did you last live in London? Was it Brixton?"

I laughed, having a thought of where his line of questioning was going.

"Uh, no. I was born and raised there, but my last flat was in the City. It was easier to live in London's financial centre when I started working for investment firms."

"Sure, that makes sense."

Thomas paused and looked at me again before proceeding forward, almost as if he was still trying to determine how honest *he* would now be with me.

"So, I'll say this… The East Village has a lot of character, so I don't think you'll ever be bored there," he began. "But it's not exactly known for being a bastion of Black cultural experiences, if you get my drift."

"I sort of expected that, yes. Hence my question to you."

Once again enjoying my rare position of being the one to slightly tease him, I finally let my wink fly and laid it on thick so he knew it was my version of "get back" toward him. My clumsy attempt at teasing, however, only seemed to embolden Thomas instead of embarrass, as it had done for me. For all at once, his eyes lit up, and I could almost see a streak of joy run across his face, even as we both began walking toward the doors to leave the airport.

"Well, then my recommendation for you, Liv, if you want to find something in New York that's a little different…you gotta check out this Everyday People day party happening in Brooklyn next Saturday. The music's going to be lit, they'll have all kinds of food vendors—everything from Jamaican to Dominican to soul food from Mississippi—the people are going to be cool as hell, just trying to dance and have a Black-ass good time before the weather turns too cold here, and…"

Thomas paused and let his lips curl up slightly in that now signature smirk of his.

"I'll be there, too, of course."

What woman could resist all of that, normal or not, right? Especially the way his eyes twinkled as the last part of his argument floated out of his mouth.

Okay, I thought, *maybe I'm not being ridiculous and he is actually flirting with me.*

"Is this your way of telling me you want to see me again, babes?" I asked, hoping for some clarity and, even more than that, a simple yes.

He licked his lips before responding, which only served to draw my attention to how kissable they seemed.

"I'm a little more straightforward than that, Liv. If I wanted to ask you on a date, and I'm assuming that's what your question really meant, I would."

He never took his eyes away from mine even as he shattered the little dream I'd begun to let sprout up. Served me right. I knew better than to think this guy, of all guys, was into me and not just being a genuinely nice person who just so happened to have a proper dangerous smirk.

"Don't get me wrong—you're very beautiful," he continued. "But you just moved to a new country, so

I'm not under any mistaken impression you're looking for anything more than what you already told me…"

"To kick ass and take names," we said in unison, eliciting another round of laughter from us both.

"Exactly," he continued. "And I don't want to get in the way of that. You really just seem like cool people, so I think you'd have a good time there. Plus, it wouldn't be a bad thing to run into you again without having to help with your bags."

"You're right," I replied, feeling some sense of relief that once again this stranger got me in a way no one else had seemed to do so before. But also a little sadness because in understanding me, he somehow intrinsically knew he wasn't part of my plotted-out story. And yet he appeared content to be a fun witness on the sidelines, which I kind of really appreciated.

"And that's not a bad proposition," I continued. "I'll be sure to tell my girl about the party, and maybe we'll see you there."

"Oh, so you have friends here already? The American ones you mentioned earlier?"

I couldn't tell if he was shocked that I knew other people in the city or disappointed to not be the sole source of my New York recommendations, but there was a bit of a curious tone in his voice. I shrugged it off so I wouldn't start overthinking it.

"One. And sort of," I explained. "She's a friend of my friend who moved to the UK earlier this year, but she's already been very kind to me. She and her boyfriend are even picking me up from the airport today."

"Ahh, well, that's great, Liv. I'm glad to know you won't be alone in the city."

Thomas's eyes dipped between my eyes and lips as

he stared back at me. It seemed like there was so much more he wanted to say, but from our brief interactions, I understood something about him, too—he was used to thinking everything out so that he always presented as cool, calm and collected. That meant he certainly wasn't going to allow himself to come across flustered in any way, at least not in some feeble attempt to, what, woo *me*? Doubtful. After all, he'd already said if he wanted to ask me on a date that he would, and he hadn't. I guess he'd chosen Door Number Two as well.

"I hope I see you both there," Thomas continued. "And I can guarantee you one thing—you won't re- gret going."

"Well, you certainly make a compelling argument. So, chances are good."

"I'd rather the chances be great, but I'll take it."

I stood in front of him for just a few seconds more, cheesing like I had a high-school crush, until I eventu- ally gathered myself again, took in one last breath and said my goodbye.

"Until we meet again, dear Liv," he replied, holding my attention until I stepped back and made the left turn to walk away from him this time, maneuvering with all my bags on my cart.

Before I walked through the exit doors, I glanced be- hind me once more and saw him heading to the Uber/ Lyft pickup area, carrying only a small duffel bag and rolling a piece of luggage that could have been a carry- on if he'd desired. We couldn't have been more differ- ent, and yet there was something about him that felt oddly familiar…like home. I'd have to unpack that on another day.

For now, I had a friend to find in the pickup area. And

maybe thanks to Thomas, I had one piece of clarity about my big adventure to the Big Apple—nothing about this trip was going to be boring or go as I expected. But I was ready for every minute of whatever it was going to be.

Chapter Three

"Liv, oh my God, I'm so glad you made it, *cher*!"

As soon as I walked outside, I saw Reagan and her boyfriend, Jake, standing next to their car, waiting for me to arrive. Reagan, whose friends called her Rae, was, as I'd said to Thomas, actually one of Robin's close besties, so not even really someone who I'd had a direct relationship with for very long. And yet as soon as she'd heard I was moving to New York, she'd graciously offered to be my city buddy. She'd only just moved to New York herself within the past year, having grown up in New Orleans and lived in Washington, DC, since college. So I think she was intimately aware of what it felt like to move here after having lived somewhere else very comfortably for so long. Plus, as she'd said to me at the time: "New York can be magical, yes, but it can also be a place where a lot of lonely people lose their way because of its vastness and the millions of people often looking out for themselves."

I hadn't realized back then that she'd meant even showing up to pick me up from the airport and shepherding me to my new flat. But in the eight weeks since I'd said yes to my interim new job, I'd learned that Reagan's kind of attentive friendship was not just reserved for Robin and her other best friends—it had been for me, too.

All of this was some kind of fated connection, really. Robin, who everyone at work had told me about before we'd met but who'd happened upon me in the kitchen of our office just a few days after she'd moved to London for *her* new promotion, had become one of my closest friends in less than a year's time…and not for nothing, my brother's girlfriend. And because of that friendship, I now had someone in New York waiting for me at the airport as I embarked on what I hoped to be the trip that would put me on a direct path for *my* next promotion. If that wasn't kismet, I wasn't sure what was!

"Oh," I exclaimed, enjoying the friendly embrace of Reagan's arms. After *the breakup that wasn't* and all my anxious thoughts about whether I was making the right decision, it was nice to have someone excited to see me, no strings attached. "Reagan, babes, you are a sight for sore eyes."

"Liv, please. I think we've long moved past the formalities of full names. Call me Rae, *cher.*"

The remnants of her Louisiana Creole accent dipped in and out as she spoke, especially when she used colloquial nicknames like *"cher"* that were common French derivatives down there. Mixed with what I considered to be a typical American accent employed by journalists and TV hosts alike, Reagan's interesting tone to her voice was equally soothing and could be used to cut someone down if necessary. That said, if it was possible, I maybe appreciated this statement from her, laced with her dual accents, even more than her hug, because Robin's friend group—amazing as they all were—hadn't exactly been easy to penetrate at first. That was never more evident than with their nicknames.

I could remember like it was yesterday, meeting Robin's friends for the first time at our favorite pub, Dirty Martini, and making the grave mistake of calling her by the nickname they'd endowed her with, "Rob." She hadn't let me in on the fact that only three people in the world called her by that name (Reagan, Jennifer and Rebecca, to be exact). So I'd walked right into an incredibly awkward situation as they'd all looked around to see where I'd purchased my audacity from when I'd casually used it. I'd later learned that there had been one other friend who'd used that nickname— Christine—who they'd all been close with and who had passed away after fighting a long health battle. That had helped me better understand their instinct to close ranks and want to make sure some random stranger wasn't encroaching on something they all considered fairly sacred.

Thankfully, we'd recovered from that mishap and they'd each, in their own way, proven to be incredibly helpful as I'd prepared for my new adventure. Still, I'd never dared to use any of their nicknames since—Rae, Jenn and Becs, respectively—for fear of the death stares I'd received the first time around. Reagan's explicit permission—no, encouragement—to do so felt like a big step toward me actually being her friend and not just Robin's workmate who she'd agreed to show around.

Reagan shook me in her embrace one last time. Holding her hands still on my forearms, she then positioned me an arm's length away so she could see me in full and smiled. "You look good, girl. I'm especially loving the new hair!"

"Thanks, Rae," I replied, and then chuckled to myself, thinking of how Thomas would have almost certainly made fun of me just then if he were with us. "You know how it is—I wasn't quite sure how long it would take me to find a new hairstylist here, so I thought it better and easier to get my hair braided for the time being."

"Oh, I totally get it. That's my go-to for any extended trip—that or a cute wig I can plop on and off as needed."

"Mmm, I didn't think wig, but that's a good idea, too."

"No, but I love these passion twists you have going on. Keep that," she replied, swinging her head around my shoulders so that she could get a full look even as she held me tightly. "And when you're ready to take them out, I'll bring you to my girl uptown. She does a mean silk press. Don't worry—I got you."

"You are the best, truly."

"Please, I wouldn't be a good friend if I held out on you like that. How was your flight, by the way?"

Reagan dropped her hands from my arms and motioned to Jake to begin off-loading my luggage into his trunk. Without any protest, he winked at her, mouthed a quick *Welcome* to me and pulled my cart toward his car. I was curious to see how he planned to get everything in there, but he didn't look at all concerned, easily grabbing the largest of the luggage first and sliding it into the left side of his trunk.

"Honestly, the flight was pretty unremarkable, which is just what I needed," I said as I followed her to the right side of the car. "My anxiety has been on high alert, really wanting to make sure I do everything right while I'm here. I can't afford for this to be a waste of time, you know? So it was nice to have several hours to zone out, listen to my tunes and be still for a bit…give my mind a short break from all my plans."

"Liv, that's great. I'm genuinely happy you took that opportunity on your flight over here. I can't express enough how necessary that was, especially coming here, where life can be so *go, go, go* if you're not careful. But what am I saying? I'm sure London is no different, right?"

"Time will tell, I guess. London can be pretty fast paced, but it's also home, and my guess is that there will still be some adjustments I have to make."

Reagan stared back at me with one of her signature smiles that started at her eyes and somehow permeated throughout her whole face. It was yet another comforting thing I'd grown to love about her as she and Robin had both turned into my risk gurus, delivering various reminders, exactly when I needed them most, that change could be scary but was worth it.

"Oh, of course," she said, seamlessly jumping into her latest "you got this" spiel. "But the main thing to remember when you're questioning if you made the right decision—and you will question it, that's just kind of the nature of taking risks—or when you're wondering if you're doing things quote, unquote 'right' is that we get to decide what's right for us and what's wrong for us. So, if you're here in the middle of it, doing your thing like I know you will be, then already, it's right.

At least for now. And that's all you need to know in the moment, okay?"

I took in a deep breath while listening to Reagan speak, hoping to somehow soak up everything she was saying and have it ready in my arsenal during those quiet moments when I'd inevitably be wondering what the heck I was doing. I'd had more than a few of those already before arriving, but I'd managed each time to remind myself that I wasn't going to get what I wanted by playing safe. Hearing Reagan's reminder that I wasn't going to get it by worrying whether I was doing things the right way or not, either, was also important because I knew what it meant for her to be saying it, especially as she used her fingers to emphasize her belief that there was no such thing as "right" by putting it in fake air quotations.

For years, Reagan had been the one stuck in a job she hadn't wanted, dating men she hadn't wanted and living her life by a bunch of strange notions of what she'd thought perfect success looked like. But two years ago, she'd admirably decided to stop waiting for everything to be perfect before she'd gone after what she'd wanted. Since then, she'd quit her coveted online political-journalism job, started a vertical at a women's magazine, taken a chance on her ex-boyfriend from college who at the time hadn't lived in her city, and moved to New York after convincing her new job that they needed a New York office and that she was the best one to make it happen. If anyone understood my internal struggle of wanting to always get things "right" but also secretly just wanting to be okay taking a risk that was worth being wrong, she did.

"You're totally right, babes. I'll use that as my reminder over the course of the next year. I'm sure I'll need it a few times."

She winked at me as Jake closed the trunk, having finished putting all my bags inside with zero problems. The three of us then climbed into his black BMW 7 Series and headed to the East Village—my new home away from home.

"So, tell us, Liv, what are you most excited about?" Jake asked as he drove us through the streets of Queens to get onto the motorway.

"Mostly I'm just thrilled to have the chance to shine in a new country. I know what I can do for our investment firm, and I know what I have done, yeah? This is my chance to show *them* it wasn't a one-, two- or three-time fluke."

"I know that's right," Reagan chimed in, snapping her fingers in agreement.

"But also, I just met this guy when I was deboarding the plane and…"

"Oh, a new guy? Already?" Reagan interrupted.

"Yes." I chuckled. "But it's not like that, and that's not the point of the story. Yes, he was quite dreamy, but he also made it bloody clear he wasn't interested in anything. He did, however, pique my interest in learning more about New York and even mentioned that there's this day party happening on Saturday in Brooklyn. So I am slightly curious and excited about that. Have you heard of it?"

"Oh, the Everyday People party?" Reagan asked.

"Yes, I believe that is precisely what he called it."

"Yeah, of course, we know that one well," Jake chimed in. "We've been to it a few times, right, Rae? Good vibes."

"Definitely good vibes and great people," she replied. "Are you trying to go?"

Reagan contorted her body so that she was looking directly at me from the front passenger seat, waiting for my response.

"I was considering it, maybe. But I also don't want to lose focus while I'm here. I feel like by next weekend, I'll probably need to be studying whatever first set of portfolios I'm going to be handed when I get to the office this week, so…"

"Say less," she interrupted again. "We're totally going. But I think this needs to be a girls' outing. That all right with you, hon?"

Jake threw his right hand up briefly to show his relief in being let off the hook. I imagined that the last thing he had in mind was taking a perfect stranger to her very first American dance party, so I didn't blame him at all. Of course, Reagan was the exact opposite— all too excited to make it a thing.

"Perfectly fine with me, Rae. You all go and have your fun."

She delicately kissed him on the cheek in appreciation and then turned her body back toward me.

"Then that's settled. I'm going to invite my girls Keish and Gigi. We'll make a day of it and still get you home in time that if you want to do some investment work on Sunday, you won't be so exhausted that you can't," she continued. "Deal?"

"I don't know, Rae."

Her enthusiasm was intoxicating, and there was a little part of me that wanted to maybe run into Thomas again, but I still wasn't sure if it was the best decision given all I wanted to accomplish in such a short amount of time. Did I have time to play around and day drink and dance all day when I had really important work to do?

Reagan certainly seemed to think so.

"Listen, Liv, I get it. You came here for a very specific reason, and we're totally going to support that. I'm never going to be that woman that isn't here for another Black woman and all her ambitions. But girl, you're in New York for the next year, so you might as well *liiiive* while you're here. I promise you that you can do both."

She paused her speech and stared me down, refusing to turn her body back toward the front windshield until I'd acquiesced to her.

"And besides, I'm not taking no for an answer," she finished.

"Okay, okay," I replied. "I guess we're going to a day party next weekend."

"Yes! Ugh, Liv, you're going to have so much fun. I think this will be your real welcome to the city."

I smiled in the back seat and resigned myself to the fact that I'd definitely met my match in Reagan, even though she was four years younger than me. Where I'd been accused of being #TeamTooMuch by people in my past, known for planning and plotting out everything meticulously and had worried maybe they were right, Reagan didn't seem to care. In fact, before I ever moved to New York, she'd warned me that she had made good with herself about her little quirks, like being the friend who had no qualms telling her friends what to do. She hadn't been lying.

"Now, tell us more about this guy who you met," she said as she finally positioned herself comfortably in her seat, facing forward. "You said he was dreamy?"

"I don't think Jake wants to hear about this kind of stuff," I demurred.

"Oh, please, men love this kind of stuff," she said, laughing. "Don't you, Jake?"

She took her left hand and cupped his chin in a joking manner, causing him to roll his eyes and chuckle a bit.

"We don't like to admit it," he said, his eyes still on the road. "But yeah, I do enjoy hearing all of Reagan's friends' dating stories. If nothing else, they're never boring."

"See?" she asked me rhetorically. "So go ahead. Spill the beans."

Damn, I just knew Jake would have been on my side on this one, but I'd forgotten one hard and fast rule: healthy couples actually did tell each other a lot, so he was likely quite used to hearing about all her friends' escapades. That was something David and I had never done now that I thought about it.

"Well," I began hesitantly, "we're not dating, so this won't be a fun dating story for you, but yes, he was quite dreamy. And funny, too, actually."

I sat back into my seat and remembered the way Thomas had me giggling even when he'd been making fun of me. Also, the way he'd shown up twice and helped me out of a jam without ever having to be asked.

"But he had multiple opportunities and never even asked for my phone number," I added.

"Hmm," Reagan moaned aloud, betraying the fact that she was pondering the information she was receiving. "But he did invite you to this party. So, maybe he's shy?"

"No, I didn't get *shy* from him at all. In fact, he seemed pretty confident and aware of himself."

Reagan paused again as she took in the latest bit of information.

"I guess we'll just have to see what happens at the party, then," she finally responded.

To my left, I heard Jake laughing to himself and caught his eyes in the rearview mirror.

"I hope you know that means she's plotting, right?"

"Yeah, I'm picking that up right now," I said.

Reagan twisted herself around so that we could both see her raised eyebrows and her face filled with glee. Then, without missing a beat, she turned to face the windshield again and declared, "Make fun of me all you two want, but this is going to be really good!"

She turned around to face me once more. "You know, dear Olivia, everything can change here in a New York minute."

"Is that so?" I asked.

"Yep. That's part of what makes this city so magical. Just you wait and see."

Reagan turned back to face the front of the car, leaving me in the back seat alone with my thoughts to ponder the future. In the quiet of the moment, as we zipped through the motorway, I felt my heart beat just a smidge faster than normal. Something about what she said had me excited, a prospect that was both scary as hell and exhilarating all at the same time.

Chapter Four

A couple days later, I found myself walking into my firm's building in New York's iconic Financial District, clad in my deep chocolate-brown trousers and matching blouse with my favorite pair of Christian Louboutin heels—the medium camel-brown So Kate 120 mm leather pumps. From outside, the building mirrored many of the others around it: towering skyscrapers either adorned with tons of glass or aluminum or art-deco remnants from the 1920s.

Inside, however, it was an arborist's dream sight to behold, featuring almost a maze of rows and quadrants of stone and wooden benches flanked by the greenest, most plush bushes and potted trees I'd ever seen not in an actual park. In an area of town that surely leaned into the mystique of the concrete jungle, this green oasis was a stark disruption from the sidewalks filled with more people than plants.

Finally, set off to the back of the atrium and flanked by a row of lifts was the concierge desk, there for any guests who needed to be checked in or, in my case, employees who had yet to receive their entry badges. With a quick glance at my watch to check the time, I sauntered my way to the back, received my guest pass and walked to the nearest lift that would carry me to my new office. By the time I arrived on the twenty-second floor, I'd steadied my breathing enough to walk through the doors of our firm with my head held high and ready to meet all the top players in America.

I stepped toward the receptionist's desk and noticed that the clock had just struck 7:30 a.m. *Good job, Liv*, I thought, patting myself on the back in my head. *Way to start this new adventure off right.*

One thing I had vowed when I'd said yes to New York was that these new people I'd be working with would never be able to say they saw me slacking off, ever. Showing up just as the sun rose in the sky, even as I was still trying to adjust to the time difference, was step one in my plans. Now I just needed to meet the man who would hand me my first American portfolio, set up shop in my new office and hopefully find my own version of Robin when I inevitably made my way to the kitchen for some coffee.

"Cheers," I said, walking up to the receptionist, a young woman who looked to be in her early twenties and rocking the cutest little short bob of red hair. "I'm Olivia Robinson, and I'm here to meet with Walter Cody."

"Oh, hi, Olivia! It's very nice to meet you," she greeted me in return. "Walter just walked in as well, so let me call him back here for you. It'll probably just be a minute."

"Sure, thank you!"

I watched as she dialed Walter on the phone, waited for him to pick up and then politely explained I was waiting at the front desk for him. I could only barely make out his end of the conversation, but it sounded like he was a bit floored and hadn't expected me to get there around the same time as he did. Little did he know this was the very least of the surprises I had in store.

"He's coming now," she said, hanging up the phone and turning her attention back to me.

"Thanks! I guess he wasn't expecting me?"

"To be honest, it's usually just me and him here for the next hour," she replied with a shrug.

"Hmm. Well, go ahead and count me as number three. I might be here with coffee, but I'll be here."

"Ha ha, good to know. We have tea in the kitchen, too, if you prefer?"

"I do enjoy a cuppa tea," I replied with a wink, letting her know that I caught her attempt at trying to make the new British woman feel comfortable. "But not for early mornings. That requires French roast, dark, with a few teaspoons of sugar."

"Noted," she said, laughing. "For what it's worth, I agree."

"I can see we'll get along swell. What's your name, by the way? I apologize for not asking before."

"Oh, that's okay. It's Wendy!"

She paused and watched me gather myself as I was sure my face completely gave away my very tickled reaction. Then, after a beat, she shrugged her shoulders, patted the bottom of her bright red hair and said, "I know, it's funny."

"There are worse ways to make an impression," I replied.

"I'll remember that the next time some weird guy on one of the dating apps makes a joke about loving their four-for-four deal with a junior bacon cheeseburger."

"Oh, no, Wendy. No."

Why are some men on dating apps so weird? I wondered. *Ugh.* If nothing else, I was glad at least to not be worrying about that at all. No need for dating apps when you weren't planning to date.

"Oh, yes," she replied. "And I wish that was the worst joke I've heard."

"Wendyyyy!"

I moved closer to the front desk and grabbed her hands in horror for what else she could have possibly endured simply because her parents must have seen her red hair and thought, *Wouldn't it be cute or funny to name her after the little fast-food girl?*

"I know, I know. Commiserate with me!"

She held my hands tightly and dropped her head onto the desk, inciting one of those guttural laughs from us both that helps to fully wake you up in the morning. Since the floor was so quiet, with no one else around to mask them with the natural noise that came from a bustling office, our outcries reverberated through the walls of the lobby just in time to practically slap Walter in the face as he walked up on us.

"I see you've met Wendy," he said with a straight face and his hand outstretched to meet mine. "I'm Walter."

I dropped my hands from Wendy's and turned around slowly to properly greet my new boss. "Hello, Walter. It's nice to meet you."

"Likewise," he replied, straightening out his posture

even as he spoke. "I apologize—I didn't realize you'd be getting here at this time, or I would have had everything ready for you."

I watched Walter closely as he ran his hands through his blond hair in what seemed like a sort of nervous fidget. He was certainly dressed in what Reagan had warned me was the typical New York–finance guy's uniform—dark blue suit, light blue button-down shirt underneath and camel-brown hard sole shoes—but I wasn't getting the arrogance from him that she'd said usually came with it. Straitlaced demeanor that indicated he would never be caught dead laughing with Wendy in the lobby? Yes. But outside of that, he seemed, well, fairly normal.

"Do you need more time? I'm in no rush," I said, deciding to give him an out and to let him know I wasn't judging him. Technically, he was my supervisor, so if anything, I should have been the one looking nervous while meeting him. "It's just that when we spoke, you said that you normally arrive around this time, so I figured I should, too."

"No, you're fine. I appreciate the initiative, I do. And we're all very excited to have you with us. We've heard some pretty amazing things, haven't we, Wendy?"

It was the first time he'd acknowledged her since walking up to us, which seemed to catch her off guard as much as it did me.

"Hmm," she said, looking up and trying to restrain a small giggle. "Oh, yes. Lots of great things."

Walter ran his hands through his hair some more, his now telltale sign that things weren't going according to his plans.

"Right," he said, looking off to the side. "Why don't

I show you where your office is, let you get settled and then I can come by a little later and give you the full tour. I think you'll find that the layout is pretty similar to what you're used to in London. We have four floors in this building—a trading floor, C-suite floor, this one's for us in portfolio management and then, of course, there's a floor for the RFP and marketing teams."

"Perfect—I'm looking forward to learning my way around," I replied. "Just one small request? Can you also point out the kitchen to me? I'd love a French roast sooner than later."

"Oh, of course. Not a problem."

Walter paused as if he was waiting for me to ask him something else. When I didn't, the look of relief on his face was palpable.

"Well, shall we?" he asked, pointing me in the direction away from the lobby.

"Sure."

I turned to Wendy once more and waved. It was obvious Walter seemed concerned that he hadn't been waiting for me in the lobby when I'd arrived, but truthfully, I was thankful she'd been the first of the two I'd met. She wasn't going to be the Robin to my Liv, but I had a feeling we were going to get along a lot better than stiff ol' Walter.

I'll meet you in the kitchen in ten minutes, she mouthed.

"Deal," I whispered before turning back around and nodding my readiness to Walter.

Step-by-step, I followed him as he walked me into the rest of the floor, past the sea of tall cubicles for the junior staff and over to the surrounding walls of glass offices reserved for senior employees. As we turned to our right, I caught a glimpse at what looked to be his office in the corner, immaculately bland except for the multiple stacks of papers on his desk. That seemed about right.

We walked by another four offices before we finally got to mine: pristine, empty and cold.

"And here we are," he said, motioning toward it like my own Vanna White.

I stepped into the space and scanned it quickly, immediately contemplating how I could give it my own flair and make it more *me*. I'd need to get a painting for the main wall at least—something vibrant that reminded me of home—or maybe I could even convince my brother to send me a canvas of one of his photos. Then, I might also bring in some framed pictures of friends and family and even a plant I'd try to keep alive for at least a month.

As I strode in further, I noticed a coat hanger in the corner and a double-screen monitor and MacBook on my desk, plus a sticky note with a few predetermined passwords I could use and then tailor to my own. The tech items were each positioned so that, while seated, the window facing outside would be on my right and the glass doors looking back into the rest of the floor would be on my left. I'd need to see if that worked for me once I got a little more settled, but for now, it would do. No need to really freak Walter out and start moving furniture on my first day in the office. He already clearly didn't quite know how to be a normal human being around me.

"So, this is it?" I turned back to him, wondering if he had more information that he wanted to detail for me.

"This is it," he replied with a shrug. "But I can still show you the kitchen and where the women's restroom is, of course."

"That would be great—thanks."

"And then we'll have our first meeting in the main conference room at eight thirty, so I can introduce you to everyone there and give you the full tour afterward. Maybe, if you're comfortable, you can talk about some of the lessons you and Frank learned from such a successful fundraising effort with your social impact fund. I think our teams are eager to see how we can use what you both did as a model."

"I'd love that," I replied, realizing this had been the most words Walter had used with me yet. "And I'm totally comfortable talking about our experience launching that fund and the multiple others that have been successful since."

The last part of my statement was a small addition to his, but I needed Walter to understand he wasn't getting a one-trick pony here. The recognition on his face as he took in my words let me know that he understood what I was saying—we'd done so much more than that first social impact fund, and I was prepared to talk about it all. Before we stepped back out of the office, I hung up my cherry-red coat with its wide, turned-down collar and belt at the waist, placed my workbag onto my desk and grabbed my mobile phone. As we made our way to the kitchen, I took my opportunity to quickly text Reagan.

Me: Hey, Rae! I know I was on the fence about it before, but on second thought, let's definitely go to that party this weekend.

She responded before I had time to even black out my screen. Thankfully, Walter wasn't exactly what one would call a Chatty Patty, so I was able to read her response and text back without him even noticing that my attention wasn't solely on him.

Reagan: Well, we were always going, but I'm glad you came around instead of me having to drag you out there, ha ha. What made you change your mind, though?

Well… I replied hesitantly. I just got to my job, and girl, I don't think I'm going to find my Robin here. I did meet one young lady who seems nice, but I get the feeling I'm going to have to really connect with my people outside of the office.

Reagan: I hear you, sis, loud and clear. And don't worry, I got you. Just one question: What size shoe do you wear?

I looked up from my phone just in time to catch Walter silently pointing out the women's bathroom and mouthed a quick thank-you in reply. A few moments later, however, he finally perked up as we made our way into the kitchen, looking at me with an awkward but distinct grin on his face. I hadn't had a chance to respond to Reagan yet, but I had a feeling that I'd have plenty of time to do so once I was back in my office. I locked my phone and slid it into my pants pocket just as Walter realized he needed to say words to me again.

"And here we are…at the kitchen."

He was nothing if not succinct. Walter outstretched his arm and waved it around to emphasize where we were, which all came off just as clumsily as when he showed me my new office. Off to the side, I peeped that Wendy was also in the kitchen, standing near the single-serve coffee machine and trying to hold back her giggles from our interaction. That only made it harder to keep a straight face, but I knew I needed to try. After all, *he* was my new boss, not Wendy.

"Thanks again, Walter. You've been incredibly gracious this morning," I said. "I know you weren't expecting me here so early, so if you want to head back to your office, you can. I think I can take it from here now."

"Thanks, Olivia," he replied.

I wasn't sure whether it was relief that shone on his face or if he was genuinely touched by my response, but something about what I'd said produced the first relaxed smile from him I'd seen all morning. Either way, I was going to happily take the win.

"Great. Then I'll see you at 8:30 a.m."

And with that, Walter turned on the heels of his brown shoes and quickly disappeared out of the shared kitchen. It took Wendy just about thirty seconds—enough time to make sure he was out of earshot—before she burst out laughing.

"God, he's so weird," she said, passing me one of the office mugs from the cupboard. "I often have to remind myself that just because you can make a company a lot of money, that doesn't mean you're not a super self-conscious nerd."

"Well, I'm hoping that it's just jitters about meeting me for the first time. I need this next year to be a lot less stiff than the past ten minutes."

"Don't worry, sis. You got this."

For some reason, Wendy's "don't worry" didn't give me the same confidence that Reagan's had. In fact, I kind of bristled at her use of the term "sis" so soon after meeting me, but I *had* just been joking around with her, so I shook away any thoughts of her being a bit too familiar, rinsed the mug in the sink and turned to my new-found, much younger friend and asked her possibly my most important question of the morning.

"So, Wendy, how do I make coffee in this contraption you all have?"

"Oh, it's super easy," she said as I watched wide-eyed while she pressed what looked like eighteen buttons before the steaming-hot liquid began to pour into my cup. That would be something I would need a greater tutorial on eventually, but for today, I was just happy to see coffee coming my way soon.

"You need anything else?" she asked.

"No, but thank you. This right here, when it's done, will be more than enough for now."

Another twenty minutes later, I'd changed what felt like fifty passwords, made sure that my email and files were all synced from the UK and onto my new laptop, and desperately tried not to second-guess my decision to leave the job I'd only started less than a year ago to come to America as part of some foolish plan to wow a bunch of people in a country I'd never been to and convince everyone I deserved a senior-level position. If my interactions so far were any indication, I was going to have my work cut out for me. While Wendy wanted to be my best friend before she even knew my middle name, Walter could barely look me in my eyes, and I'd yet to see anyone else even show up in the office yet. *Bang-up job so far, Liv.*

After some slight pouting, I took in a deep breath and refocused myself, determined to do what I set out to do.

Kicking ass and taking names wasn't always going to be awkward-interaction free, I reminded myself, but it was still the ultimate goal. I also recalled that I'd yet to text Reagan back, so I scooped up my phone and quickly tried to rectify at least that one mistake.

Sorry, sorry! I typed as fast as I could. I didn't mean to go that long without responding to you.

Once again, she texted back immediately.

Reagan: Please, there's no need to apologize. You are at work.

And so are you, I responded. That's no excuse.

Reagan: Negative. I never get to work this early. It'll probably be another hour and a half before I stroll into my office. But also, give yourself a break, Liv. Again, I know you're at work, so I'm not stressing over here like why didn't she respond to me? That would be ridiculous.

Me: Wow, must be nice...and okay, thanks for that reminder.

Reagan's comments reminded me of my brother's, who was always saying that I put a lot of pressure on myself to show up perfectly for everyone all the time. I was sure he would have agreed with her in this moment.

Reagan: Well, on the flip side, you all make far more money than us writers, so I think it evens out lol

Me: Fair!

Reagan: Back to the important topic, though. Shoe size, please.

Me: Oh, I wear a size 6.

Reagan: Wow, really?! I didn't realize you had such small feet! lol

Me: Wait, shoot, I forgot it's different here. Umm...

I paused to remember the conversion in my head.

Me: I think it's an 8 in the US.

Reagan: Okay, Liv, you just won over my heart. I, too, am a size 8. This is going to be so good!

Right after Reagan's text, she also sent over a GIF of Steve Harvey as a judge on his daytime TV show repeating her last words, which made me laugh a lot louder than I'd expected it to. And because my luck was what it was that morning, I finally saw a few people walk toward their desks just as I realized they probably heard my outburst. I quickly stood up, went to close my door and sat back down before replying.

Me: Okay, well now I'm excited, too lol

Reagan: Oh, you should be. This means you totally have to come over to shop in my shoe closet before we go to the party.

Me: Wait, you have a shoe wardrobe...in New York City?

Reagan: Well, I have something I made into one. Don't worry, you'll get to see it.

Me: Of course you do. And okay, I'm looking forward to it.

I looked up again and noticed it was a few minutes to eight thirty and I should start heading to the conference room. I already had my spiel ready to go in my head. Now it was time to do all the wowing I'd been planning on when I'd first arrived.

Me: All right, babes, I need to head to this meeting. But thanks again for everything! Talk soon.

Reagan: Have a great day, girl. And btw, has anyone ever mentioned you thank people a whole lot? Don't answer. Just think about it.

Ha. Well, Reagan didn't know it, but she was the second person who'd said as much in a few days' time. Maybe they were both onto something, but remembering the first person to call it out only served to bring back flashbacks of Thomas's deviously dangerous and dimpled smirk. And there was no way that I needed that kind of distraction on my mind.

I took in another deep breath, stood up, straightened out my back and gave myself one last internal pep talk before grabbing my laptop and heading toward my glass office door.

This was it.

My moment.

And I wasn't letting Walter's awkwardness, Wendy's

overfamiliarity, Reagan's incredible shoe wardrobe or visions of Thomas's grin get me off my game.

With my renewed sense of confidence, I stepped out of the office and strode past the gaggle of cubicles that lined the walkway to the main conference room on our floor. To my left, I heard people as they began shuffling their belongings around their desks, as they greeted their colleagues "Good morning," and even as they click-clacked away on their computers. I could see a few of them also begin to gather their laptops and pens and paper, presumably preparing to head to the same meeting I was off to.

By the time I arrived at the glass-enclosed office space, decorated with only a large cedarwood conference table in the middle and rows of ergonomic office chairs flanking it plus one lonely side table with a plant on top, only two other people were seated. I casually glanced at my watch to see if I'd had the time wrong before greeting them. Nope—according to my clock, at least, it was 8:28 a.m.

"Oh, you'll see everyone pile in here in a few," the first woman said, likely noticing the concerned look on my face. "Most people here believe in being on time but not necessarily early."

"Good to know," I replied, and immediately realized how that correlated with Walter's consternation about my early arrival this morning. "I'm Olivia Robinson, by the way."

I stuck out my hand to shake hers as she returned the favor.

"Julie," she said, gripping my hand firmly. "It's nice to meet you, Olivia. Walter has told us a lot about you."

"Really?" I asked, perplexed.

For someone who'd barely spoken more than a hundred words to me this morning, I had a hard time grasping that he'd been over here extolling my efforts prior to my arrival. And yet Julie was the second person who'd said as much. There seemed to be plenty I needed to better understand in America. For example, in my very Jamaican family, if you were just on time, you were late. Basically, the exact opposite of what seemed to be the culture in our New York office. Then again, my parents and their siblings were trying to combat decades of stereotypes about Black people in the UK as part of the Windrush generation. No one in this office, from what I'd seen thus far, came from anything close to a similar background or understanding.

True to Julie's word, people began strolling into the office less than a minute later. So, with no real guidance about hierarchy, I made a quick decision to sit in the chair that seemed the least likely to cause any issues— definitely not at the head of either side of the table, but also not too far away from at least one of them. The one I chose—third on the left from what I guessed was Walter's seat, the head of the table on the right side of the conference room—was a gamble, but I figured it was better than sitting smack-dab in the middle or off to the side in the chairs that were the stepchildren of the room.

Luckily for me, my gamble paid off. Because just a few moments later, Walter also arrived and plopped down right into the seat I'd guessed was his. Once he settled in, opening his laptop and adjusting into his seat, he looked around to make sure everyone else was seated, scanning the room until he landed on me. And then, in yet another surprise, he smiled, nodded his head and mouthed *Welcome* to me once again.

It was as if the person I'd met an hour earlier had been some sort of off-brand clone and this was the real Walter Cody, commanding all the attention in the room, not seeming to be at all awkward and, oddest of all, helping to welcome me into the office among a room full of strangers when he barely even looked me in my eyes while we were by ourselves. Maybe he was just really good at rising to the occasion when he absolutely needed to, I thought. I certainly hoped I had that in me as well—but without the opposite-clone part.

"Good morning, everyone, and happy Monday," Walter began, quieting the room without raising his voice. "I know we have a lot to cover today, but first I want to introduce you to the star of the UK, the person I've been telling you about for weeks, Ms. Olivia Robinson. Olivia, as you know, will be joining us for the next year, and while she'll probably start off with one or two portfolios at first, I want to have her eyes on all of them by the time she leaves. I think we'll all be able to benefit from her perspective and her expertise, and if we can't convince her to stay—because that is also a goal of mine, Olivia—then we can at least send her off in the best way possible, with several millions of dollars raised under her watch."

Walter's break in the middle of his speech, wherein he spoke directly to me, completely threw me off and, just for a second, threatened to distract me from what I'd been planning to say. But he had on his best "command of the room" mask, so come hell or high water, I was going to as well.

"Hi, everyone," I said after clearing my throat just a bit. "I'm really so excited to be here. And thank you,

Walter, for such a gracious introduction. I hope to live up to those lofty words."

"You will," he replied with a nod. "Olivia, I know we talked about this earlier, but I'd love it if everyone could hear from you on how you have grown multiple funds in the UK from ones that were pretty niche to multimillion-dollar investments."

"Sure. I'd love to," I said, adjusting myself in my seat to make sure that everyone around the table could see and hear me clearly. I noted that he'd changed his language from just being that I'd succeeded with the one investment fund, so at the very least, he was really good at listening and taking notes.

"Before I dig in, however, let me just start by acknowledging that nothing Frank and I have done this past year is revolutionary, really. What you are going to hear me talk about, and what you'll hear me preach every day that I'm here, is that we listened to our clients, we worked very hard to identify the pieces they didn't realize they were missing and we executed on that with creative ideas. Nothing more, nothing less. For one portfolio, that amounted to us getting one hundred thirty percent of the investors we were expecting and exceeding our fundraising goal by one hundred fifteen percent. I'm here today with you all, however, not because we did that once but because we have reached at least those metrics eight times since."

I paused and looked around the room to get a gauge of my audience and saw that, to a person, they were each staring at me wide-eyed and eager to learn more. Maybe I'd misjudged how things were going to go this morning after all because what I now knew to be true was that as much as I was looking forward to making a name for myself this year, they all needed me here, too. And that wasn't exactly a bad position for this expat to be in.

"So, let's jump in to talk about how we did that."

For the next fifteen minutes, I explained my approach to life and how it had seemingly resonated in our investment world: I always went the extra step, yes, but more importantly, I studied my clients, my friends, my colleagues...and learned them to a T. I had literal folders upon folders of background information on each client, which I painstakingly pored through before I ever offered even a morsel of advice. It was how I'd known that first social impact fund had needed high-quality photos and a dynamic website to really resonate with our target audience. And it was what I wanted everyone in my new office to commit to do at least while I was there.

When I paused to see if anyone had questions, I looked around the room and saw each person taking notes, even Walter—whether on their laptop or in their notepad—meticulously jotting down all that I was saying so they wouldn't lose any of it.

Maybe these were my people after all, I thought. Things were certainly trending in a better direction— that was for sure.

Chapter Five

"Reagan Lorraine Doucet, when you said you'd created a shoe closet in your apartment, I could never have imagined this is what you meant."

My eyes scanned her bedroom with equal wonder and glee as I processed what I was seeing before me: a meticulously decorated bedroom split in half to where she had her queen-size bed, rug, dresser, nightstand, full-length mirror and bedroom bench on one side, and the other side was lined with what looked to be custom floor-to-ceiling shelves, a second complementary rug and an ottoman chair in the middle. Separating the two sides of the room were a decent-size window on the wall that faced her bedroom door and a natural walkway on the floor between the two rugs. Finally, in the corner when you first walked in was the most elegant pearl-white ladder I'd ever seen not in someone's bookstore, presumably for Reagan to reach the shoes that were positioned beyond what her five-foot-three stature could muster with outstretched arms.

To say I was in shock would have been an understatement, but really, I shouldn't have been. The reason we'd gotten along so well thus far was because we were both the good kind of extra…planners who were going to make sure that what we wanted was executed perfectly. So, honestly, the more accurate phrasing would be to say that I was in awe, not that I was at all surprised.

"You thought it was just going to be, like, a second room turned into a closet, right?" she asked, her eyes betraying her excitement.

"Maybe! To be honest, I didn't bloody know, but whatever I thought it was going to be, this is beyond that."

I stepped my bare feet closer to her shelves, noticing how the shoes were organized by not only color but shoe style, too, ranging from red stiletto heels on one side to faux-snakeskin mules on the other. It was almost like being at a shoe-store showcase but tucked away in a flat uptown.

"Now that you mention it," I said, turning back to face her, "why didn't you just rent a two-bedroom and convert one of the rooms into a wardrobe? This is gorgeous, but I'm sure that would have been a lot easier."

"Easier, but not cheaper. We may be uptown, but the rent is still expensive. The only difference is if you're lucky like me, you can find a place up here that's more than six hundred square feet and has enough room in the bedroom for me to get creative."

She paused and chuckled before spitting out the rest of her words.

"Well, that and it's slightly more Black people uptown, but don't get it twisted—that's not what it used to be, either."

"Still, I'd wager a lot more than what I see in my East Village neighborhood."

"Oh yes, that's not even a question," she replied, laughing again. "Okay, enough of all that, though. Let's get into the good stuff. We have to find you some shoes for today."

Reagan jumped up and down like a little kid who'd just been told she could have some candy and let out a tiny squeal before her face turned dead serious. Raising her right hand to her chin, she circled me, checking out the outfit I'd chosen for the day party we were going to attend in Brooklyn that day: a loose-fitting denim long-sleeved shirt, unbuttoned to right above the small amount of cleavage my 32B breasts could form and tucked into my ripped and distressed fitted jeans of the same color. Both my sleeves and jeans were rolled up, with the sleeves stopping halfway to my elbows and my jeans hitting right above my ankles. To tie it all together, I'd pulled my passion twists into a half-up, half-down look with a loose topknot so that my big gold hoop earrings could be seen.

"Hmm," she said finally, as if she were a doctor assessing the scene before giving a diagnosis to a patient. "I think I have the perfect pair of shoes for this."

"Wait, really?" I asked, completely caught off guard.

I'd guessed when she'd said I could come over and shop through her wardrobe that we were going to be pulling out a ton of shoes until finally, after partially destroying her room, one emerged as the winner, the exact right one for the occasion. That was what happened in all the films, yeah?

"Oh, did you want to pick out something yourself? Because you totally can. I just have a feeling that these will be perfect."

"No, I mean, it's your shoes, babes. We can do whatever makes you feel comfortable."

I spoke with some hesitation, not wanting things to get awkward with the one friend I had in America—and especially not over a favor she was offering me.

"Are you kidding me right now?" she asked incredulously. "Liv, I wouldn't have invited you over here if I was worried about my comfort level. When are you going to believe we're actually friends?"

She stared me down and waited for a reply, but I was too busy processing how quickly she'd read my reluctance for what it truly was—a mistrust in our friendship—but deeper than that, a mistrust that anyone really wanted to be connected to me who wasn't obligated to like family or indebted to me like my colleagues.

"Sorry," I responded sheepishly. "I guess you can only be told so many times that you're 'too much' before you start to believe everyone thinks the same thing."

"Olivia, look at my bedroom. How could I ever think anyone else is 'too much'?"

I panned my eyes across her room again and began to chuckle from some place deep inside my belly. She was right. I might have been over-the-top for some, but at the very least, I'd met my #TeamTooMuch crew through Robin and her friends.

"Better question, though—who is the jerk that made you think you were too much?" she asked as she pointed for me to sit down on the ottoman and grabbed her ladder from the corner.

"Jerks, plural, you mean?"

"Ugh, okay. Well, yes, jerks, plural."

"Well, David certainly thought so…"

"David—your ex David?"

"We're not exactly exes…actually I don't know what we are right now."

"Wait, how are you not?" Reagan turned back toward me, interrupting me and sliding her ladder to the shelves at the same time. "Y'all aren't doing the long-distance thing, right, *cher*? Because that might change my plans for you and ol' boy at this party today."

"Plans?" I asked, narrowing my eyes at her.

"Never mind all that," she said, waving off my suspicious looks. "Tell me what's the deal with you and David."

"There's no deal."

Reagan was mid-climb on her ladder when she looked back at me again as if to say *Girl, please*.

"There's no deal!" I protested. "We just didn't end things on a great note before I left. But we talked later and decided to press pause while I'm over here, and then we'll see where things are when I get back."

"Pause. As in the relationship?"

"Mmm-hmm."

"With a man who said you were too much? On what sounds like multiple occasions?"

"To be fair, he may never have said those exact words, but…"

"Okay, give me an example of his words. I know you remember them vividly."

She wasn't wrong about that. I remembered every bloody word David had ever said that had made me feel small, whether he'd meant to or not. I also had an uncanny ability to play them over in my head late at night when I should have been sleeping.

"All right, so for example, on our last night together, we got into a little tiff because I wanted him to show me that he was going to bloody miss me. It was like he had no emotion about me leaving whatsoever, despite the fact that we'd just spent the last two years together. So I asked him, 'Do you even care that I'm going away for a whole year? Like, has any of this meant anything to you at all?' And his response was very classically David. He said to me, 'I should have known you would blow this out of proportion. It's not like you're dying, Liv, so what do I need to be sad about? Plus, you made the choice to take this job, to choose your ambition over us. You didn't *have* to, so don't get upset with me for being okay with your choice. And I mean, really, Olivia, if it's what you want, who am I to stop you? I could never stop you even if I wanted to. I learned that a long time ago.'"

"Wow, I hate him," Reagan replied as she stepped down her ladder with a clear container in her hand.

"It wasn't great, that's for sure."

"And you're on a *break* with this guy?"

"I… I know it probably sounds dumb, but we have been together for a while, so… I don't know. There's a part of me that thinks we've never been a great fit, and then the other part doesn't want to end a two-year relationship because of one bad conversation, especially when I probably wasn't being very fair questioning his feelings for me in the first place."

"But you said it was *classically* David, right? That would mean it's been more than one bad conversation."

I didn't know what to say in response. David and I

weren't always compatible, to be sure. Where I was the hopeless romantic, he just wanted simple. And where I believed in dotting every *i* and crossing every *t* at all times, he would rather me just have been more chill and go with the flow. But that didn't mean there hadn't been good times between us. And I wasn't sure I was ready to give all that up on the chance I might meet someone new who fit me better. I was also afraid that if I kept trying to explain myself, my eyes would start watering and I'd have to redo my makeup soon. Thankfully, Reagan understood my silent response and pivoted slightly as she handed me the clear container.

"You know what? It's okay—you don't have to answer that. I'll just say this—I don't believe in breaks. As Monica said on *Friends*, a break is a *breakup*."

"Haven't you and Jake been on a few breaks yourselves?"

"Absolutely not." She chuckled. "We've totally and completely and fully broken up more times than I can count, yes. But there was no mistaking when we weren't together what the deal was. I was single AF when Jake and I were off, and I enjoyed every moment of it, you hear me?"

"I hear you," I said, joining in with her in a round of giggles.

"Luckily for him, though, no one in this world gets me like he does. So, despite all our messiness and our actual breakups, I wouldn't trade my worst days with him for my best days with anyone else. Can you say the same about David?"

This question elicited my second silent reply mixed with only a heavy sigh this time, a response that was probably all Reagan needed to hear to know that my answer was *no* yet again.

"Then, no offense but screw David," she replied. "I'm Team Thomas anyway."

"You haven't even met Thomas yet." I laughed in response, rolling my eyes at her.

"And I don't need to! I've seen the way you can't control your cheeks when I mention his name, *cher*. That's enough for me!"

"He is a very attractive man," I said, agreeing partially.

"Mmm-hmm, and you like him."

"I don't know him."

"You *want* to know him."

"I want to…pick out a pair of shoes and have a great time with you and your girls today. Honestly, that's all I can focus on wanting right now."

"Lies! But I'mma let you have it because we don't have much longer before we need to meet up with Keish and Gigi, and I might need time to revive you after you see these shoes."

With one last bashful giggle and another playful roll of my eyes, I finally opened the container in my hand and saw before me a pair of velvet dark olive green pointed-toe mules with a big faux-fur pom-pom situated on the top of each. I'd never seen anything like it before and was quite possibly in love.

"Reagan," I whispered.

"Oh, I know."

"These are…"

"Too much?" she asked with a wink.

"Ha! I was going to say 'exquisite,' but yes, that works, too."

"Well, I think they're perfect for you, your outfit and

your time here in New York—where we don't believe in 'too much,' okay?"

"Okay," I replied, failing at holding in a huge smile yet again. "I really do love them."

"I knew you would," she said smugly. "Now, try them on and make sure they fit so we can get on out of here. We've got a cute boy to find… I mean, fun party to get to."

About an hour later, the four of us walked into the Everyday People party like we were the original members of Destiny's Child. Alongside my Canadian-tuxedo 'fit and Reagan's beloved olive green mules, stood Rae herself, with gray distressed jeans that had a slight fringe at the ankle and a long-sleeved white textured blouse, which she hadn't buttoned at all but simply tied at her natural waist. Miraculously, she managed to keep her double-D breasts lifted up and tucked inside of this blouse but had also strategically used her long, barrel-curled hair as a second barrier, draping her tresses just inside the boundaries of the shirt. She then paired her outfit with scarlet-red pointed-toe slides from Anthropologie that included three rows of tassels on the top. Standing next to her was Keisha Edwards, who often simply went by Keish—a five-five beauty with thick thighs and bee-sting boobs. She had on a pair of ripped, acid-washed jeans with a white fitted T-shirt tied at the front, some white Chuck Taylor trainers and her signature leopard-print glasses that set off her short hair that was slicked to the side just right. And finally, Giselle Lewis, aka Gigi, was rocking quite possibly my favorite outfit of the bunch—a pair of royal blue jeans with rips at the knees, a yellow-and-black crop top that said *Girl*

Power, black lace-up oxfords and her shoulder-length jet-black twists practically glistening under the sun.

One might have easily thought we'd coordinated our outfits so that they perfectly complemented each other without matching, but they would have been wrong. In fact, Reagan and I hadn't even seen Keisha and Giselle until a few minutes before when we'd joined them in line to show our tickets to the bouncers. And yet I was very happy to say that just like our clothes, the connection between myself and the other ladies was almost immediate. This was something I should have assumed being that I'd yet to meet anyone even tangentially related to Robin who I didn't get along with, although I continued to be pleasantly surprised by it. I made a mental note to tell her this the next time we caught up on WhatsApp.

"Liv, I hope you are ready for some good drinks and dancing," screamed out Giselle as we walked in. "This is one of my favorite parties to go to."

Once inside the venue, which was actually mostly an outdoor spot with a covered vendor area surrounding it, the volume increased exponentially, so our voices had to match the intensity to hear each other. Not only were we trying to speak over the sounds of '90s music blasting through all the speakers but we were also competing with the laughs and conversations of at least a thousand other beautiful, golden-brown Black people all around us.

After a full week of being the only Black woman on my team, this felt like heaven. So much so that I found myself gazing, starry-eyed for a bit, completely missing my cue to respond to Giselle.

"Oh, she is," Reagan replied for me with a wink.

"Do you have a drink preference?" Giselle followed up quickly, thankfully not giving me enough time to wander back into my thoughts.

"I'm guessing a martini is a long shot here, yeah?" I asked.

"I think that's a good assumption. I would stick with something more typical, like a liquor plus a chaser."

"In that case, I'll get something with gin…maybe a Tom Collins?"

All three women stared at me blankly so long that, at first, I thought they hadn't heard me over the music and the crowd, so I repeated myself but louder.

"No, no, we heard you," Keisha chimed in. "We just have no idea what the heck a Tom Collins is. Is that the British version of a gin and tonic?"

"Oh." I laughed. "Sorry! It's just basically gin, lemon juice, soda water and simple syrup."

Giselle chuckled to herself before responding to me. "All right, well, I think that will work—they should definitely be able to make that. I'm just so not saying the name!"

"Fair," I said, shrugging my shoulders.

She turned to the other two ladies and confirmed their drinks with them as well.

"I already know whiskey ginger for you, Rae. And, Keisha, do you want a vodka tonic today?"

"Sure do," Keisha replied enthusiastically.

"Okay, great."

I watched as Giselle then swung herself around and squeezed through the crowd gathered at one of the vendor bars, the three of us following close behind her so that we could be there to grab the drinks as she passed them back to us. I was also fascinated that she'd barely even had to ask what the other women had wanted; she'd just known. That alone wasn't shocking—friends tended to know what their friends liked to drink—but Reagan had only moved to New York earlier in the year, so I hadn't assumed she'd connected with Keisha and Giselle so quickly. Plus, I always associated her with Robin's crew, so it was pretty cool to see she'd formed a close bond with another group of friends in her short time in the city and hadn't lost the closeness with her original friend group. That was definitely inspiration for me—I wanted to make sure I kept my friends and family back in the UK close but certainly wanted to take this time away to branch out, meet new people and make even more friends along the way.

"How long have you all known each other?" I asked, turning to Reagan while we waited for Giselle to send the drinks backward from the bar.

"I went to high school with Keish, so we've known each other a pretty long time. Back then, it was me, her and Christine that were unstoppable, but then she went to the University of Southern California for undergrad while Chrissy and I went to Howard, and we didn't stay as in touch with each other as we should have. We reconnected at Christine's funeral, though, and I found out then that she lived in New York, which, you know, definitely came in handy some months later."

"So she was your Reagan when you moved here, essentially?"

"Kinda, yeah. I mean, I had Jake here, too, of course. But it was good to have someone else I knew here other than him, so I wasn't just relying on him and his friends for any sort of connection outside of work."

"Totally," I replied, not really knowing but presuming sort of what she'd meant. I'd never experienced anything like what I was doing now—moving thousands of miles away on my own and knowing just a couple people who I could call if I needed them. I'd traveled around the world, but in the thirty-five years I'd been alive, I'd never lived more than thirty minutes from home.

"And Gigi, she is a friend of Keisha's from college," Reagan continued. "They both moved here about six years ago and were roommates until they could afford their own places. When I got to town, Giselle and I clicked super quickly, too. It was like I'd known her just as long as I'd known Keish."

"That's awesome," I said, trying to hold back my face from showing how much I was gushing about their connection. "I hope this year is like that for me."

"There's no hoping about it, *cher*. I already know it's going to be."

Just then, Giselle caught our attention as she began passing the drinks back to us one by one, sending the overflowing plastic cups our way. By the time we received the third one, she was making her way toward us with her own drink as well, dancing through the crowd like a woman on a mission.

"Y'all ready to really get this party started now?" she asked, staring directly at me.

"Oh, yes, very much so," I replied, this time making sure I did so myself.

"Then let's get it!"

Giselle dragged out her last word in glee as she grabbed my waist. Then the four of us strutted our way onto the outdoor dance floor just as the DJ started spinning the iconic remix to Brandy's "I Wanna Be Down." That was just the cue I needed to truly let my hair down as I proceeded to rap every bar like I was onstage, seamlessly flowing through each verse from MC Lyte to Yo-Yo to Queen Latifah and using my cup as the perfect fake microphone. The girls could hardly contain their glee as they joined in, singing Brandy's chorus and egging me on as I continued on my one-woman show.

"Okay, Liv, let me find out we need to give you a rapper nickname!" Reagan screamed out as she bounced along to the '90s beat.

"No, for real—you didn't tell us you knew nineties hip-hop like this," Keisha chimed in, agreeing. "You betta get it!"

I shrugged my shoulders playfully and kept rapping, not wanting to mess up the flow on my favorite verse from the Queen just to explain that we often listened to the same songs in the UK as they did; we simply had some extras they probably didn't know.

Just as the song was ending, I realized I needed to capture this moment as our first real bonding experience, so I pulled my phone out and started snapping photos of the three ladies singing Brandy's last notes like their lives depended on it. One by one, I clicked the camera app on my phone, snapping them in various positions and capturing all the fun we were having in our own little pocket inside of this massive venue. It wasn't until they each started making googly eyes, nodding their heads in rhythm to the beat and pointing at me that I realized something else was happening, too.

"What's going on?" I asked, laughing and confused.

It took maybe another few seconds for it to dawn on me that they weren't pointing *at* me, they were directing me to turn around and look behind me. As I swung around to see what they were staring at, everything came into focus all at once. Because there, in all his charming and handsome glory, was Thomas and those extremely dangerous dimples acting as if he was also posing for my camera. Maybe the ladies had figured out it was him without me ever having to even tell them what he looked like. Or maybe, like me, they were just drawn in by the orange aura he seemed to carry around with him wherever he went.

"Thomas!" I screamed out before I could contain my excitement. Luckily, I caught myself before I acted on the sudden urge to throw my arms around him.

"Heyyy!" he replied, revealing his excitement and maybe, I dare say, a tiny bit of embarrassment. "My bad—I thought you were taking a selfie at first, so I was trying to photobomb you until I realized you were actually taking pics of your girls."

"Oh, ha ha, so that's what was going on behind me. All I saw were their giggles and figured I needed to turn around."

I paused awkwardly, not knowing what else to say just yet, and then let my mouth simply blurt out the next thing that came to mind.

"But yeah, it was just of them…not me."

Honestly, I could have kept that inside.

It was hard to think straight with him suddenly standing in front of me, however—clad in an all-black outfit that accentuated his beautiful skin tone under the brightness of the warm October sun. He wore a crisp black T-shirt that looked as if he'd steamed it to perfection for at least ten minutes before putting it on, matching joggers and a simple gold chain that landed at the top of his chest moving in sync with him as he breathed in and out while staring at me. Truthfully, it was less about the clothes and more about the way they fit on him as if they'd been constructed simply to entice poor souls like mine, dipping in and out in concert with his muscles and showcasing all the ways that his body was molded over time. It was also his deep gray eyes that I could never turn away from whenever he set them on me. And that smile—the same one that had lured me in on the airplane and the same one that was now trying to take me out in front of a crowd full of people.

It was enough to make a woman swoon right there, out in the open, with no shame at all. Somehow I resisted, but what I couldn't avoid was the annoyingly enticing thought running through my head that with all the people crowded into this venue, he'd still found me.

"You know what? It's good to see you," I said, trying to start over.

"Same, Liv. I'm glad you actually came."

"Well, you did make a very compelling argument in the airport."

"Oh yeah?" he asked, drawing closer to me, presumably so we wouldn't have to scream as loud to hear each other.

His new proximity to me had a dual effect, however; while I could hear him more clearly, I was also perfectly positioned to catch the faintest scent of Le Labo Santal wafting off his body.

"What part was most persuasive?"

"Umm, I think it was the 'Black-ass good time' part," I replied with a smirk, desperate not to take in a deep breath so my knees didn't buckle in his presence.

"Ohhhh, okay."

Thomas nodded his head in understanding, and yet

the look on his face was one of playful suspicion as he stepped even closer to me, barely leaving enough room for air between us.

"Well, it does look like you and your friends are having exactly that," he replied.

"Yeah, we are! So I absolutely have to thank you for the recommendation."

"Seeing you this happy is good enough for me, love."

I felt the smile on my face growing exponentially. Then, despite my best avoidance efforts, Thomas's eyes caught mine in a deep and penetrating stare before he expertly dragged them down to my lips, subtly licking his at the same time.

Yeah, that certainly isn't going to help me not feel all swoony around him.

Thankfully, the DJ became my saving grace as he switched up the tunes and began playing yet another one of my all-time favorite songs, "Creep" by TLC. He was most definitely in a '90s-music zone, and I loved it. So much so that my legs began bouncing to the music even as Thomas and I fixed our eyes on each other. To keep the little bit of composure I had remaining, I took the playful tone of the song as my chance to change the vibe between us and began mouthing the lyrics as I started my two-step.

"Oh, so this is your jam, huh?" he asked, bouncing his limbs in step with mine.

"Yesss! I mean, how can you not love TLC, yeah?"

"You're not wrong. All-time classic female group right there."

"Exactly!"

I continued swaying my body to the beat as we talked, inciting more and more smiles from Thomas—a fact that I didn't exactly mind as a side effect to my love for the song.

"Well, don't let me stop you," he said, nodding in the direction of my friends as if he was reluctantly giving me permission to go back toward them.

I had another thought in mind, however. I didn't know if it was the swagger of Left Eye creeping into my bones or the idea of him walking away again that propelled me to push past my fears, but before I could second-guess myself, I grabbed Thomas's hand and pulled him back toward me. As soon as his body was close enough that I could practically feel his heart beating, I turned around so that my back now faced his chest, wining my butt and torso in a circle as T-Boz's raspy vocals intermixed with the trumpet and drums on the song. To his credit, Thomas barely skipped a beat, pressing his frame into mine and mimicking my dancing style in a perfect rhythm.

It was almost as if we were created to melt into each other, the way our limbs seamlessly moved together, his hips meeting mine in a move that felt so sinfully amazing.

"So you're sure I had *nothing* to do with you choosing to come here today?" he asked, whispering into my ear as we continued grinding to the song. "It was just for a good time?"

I leaned my body into his and turned my head slightly backward so that I could see his eyes in my periphery as I replied, "Well, you know, in London, we have a right to silence, yeah, if a person is on trial and thinks that their answer may incriminate them. Sort of like your Fifth Amendment."

"I'm aware," he responded with a deep chuckle in my ear.

"Good. Then you'll understand when I choose not to respond to this line of questioning."

"And you can certainly do that, Liv. But just know that means I'm exercising my right to assume it was all me."

I didn't respond; there really was no need to because he knew—and I knew that he knew—he was right. Instead, I continued dancing to the sounds of TLC as the DJ began blending in the melody for "Red Light Special," automatically grinding our moves down to a sultry wine. Thomas took the opportunity and wrapped me in his arms, forcing our bodies to move as one in a rhythm likely only intended for dance floors with no lights, or private bedrooms. Instead, there we were, out under the illumination of a 3:00 p.m. sun, slowly letting our bodies do all the talking we'd had difficulty accomplishing with our mouths. Exposed for anyone and everyone to see if they wanted, including Reagan and her girls, who I'd yet to return to.

I didn't care, though. In that moment, and with that man, I'd managed to forget all my rules. And instead of continuing to fight it, I finally closed my eyes, took in the deepest breath and let him and his Le Labo cologne sweep me away.

Chapter Six

Bun-bun! Bun!

Phew. One verse and chorus into TLC's "Red Light Special," the DJ let off the definitive horn sound that always signaled to the crowd that the vibe was getting ready to change. This time around, it also literally saved me from descending into a mush of a woman whose body was ready to be at Thomas's beck and call.

I snapped my eyes open as the horn reverberated in our ears.

"Nah, nah, nah—y'all not quite ready to go there just yet," the DJ shouted into the microphone in response to the round of awws drawing loudly from the crowd.

"Don't worry, I got you. But it's too early! It's too early," he continued protesting. "So let's pick this vibe back up, all right. You're rocking with the best of the best today, baby. So let's gooooooo!"

With that, he jumped us from 1994 to 2019 as he

dropped the staccato beat of City Girls' "Act Up," immediately getting the crowd back on his good side. All around me, the women soon became their own personal rap stars, joining in on JT's classic first verse and informing all the men that they didn't care about them unless they were doling out Birkin bags on a regular.

For my part, I took the opportunity to loosen my body from Thomas's grip and showcase my skills again, jumping into Yung Miami's superfast rap flow with ease.

"Oh, it's like that now?" Thomas asked as I playfully pushed him off me so I could have the space I needed to wave my hands and bounce my body to the new beat.

He watched in awe as I continued, the both of us staring each other down but unwilling to let either win in our unspoken game of chicken. Two more seconds of TLC and I might have lost, but with the City Girls? Tuh! I was up again.

Reagan, Keish and Gigi must have realized this, too, because just as Yung Miami started flowing on the second verse, they bounced right up to us, rapping alongside me with all the fervor that part of the song required.

"Ayeeee," I shouted out, excited to have my girls around me.

Now that they were there, I could see clearly again, too, and very quickly reminded myself of what I'd known to be true since the moment Thomas had helped me lift my luggage off the plane: yes, he was cute and could charm my pants off without trying, but I didn't have time to be falling for him or his dimples, despite what the parts of my brain and body inspired by Left Eye might've thought.

"Oh, so y'all are like a crew of female rappers, huh?" Thomas asked jokingly.

"Nah, that distinction is only for our little London fairy Liv, here," Reagan chimed in, raising her voice so we could all hear her over the music. "But who can resist a verse by Caresha, right?"

"I could see how that might be difficult, especially when you've got your own version of Monie Love in the building," he replied with a wink toward me.

"Ugh, I stan her!" I shouted back.

"I had a feeling you did."

I took in a deep breath and shook off the sensation that quickly ran down my spine. It was an incredibly small detail, but the fact that he'd assumed my love for her just added onto the *He Gets Me* pile of examples building up between us, and that was sexier than I wanted to admit.

"By the way, these are my friends, Reagan, Keisha and Giselle," I shouted out, pointing to each one as I called their name.

"Nice to meet you! I'm Thomas."

He raised his hand to shake each of theirs, and I watched in horror as they gleefully made it known he'd been the topic of previous conversations.

"Oh, we know who you are," Reagan replied through a fit of giggles.

"Yes," added in Giselle. "In fact, we heard you recommended the party to our girl, right?"

"I did. I did," Thomas replied, nodding and simultaneously raising his eyebrows toward me. "None of you have been before?"

"No, we all have…plenty of times actually. Liv is the only newbie," said Keisha.

"Ahh. Okay, well, I'm glad she's in good hands, then."

"Meaning yours?" Reagan asked, quickly boomeranging the conversation to what they'd all been obviously thinking as they'd watched us a few steps away. "Because, I mean, we weren't trying to interrupt earlier, but…"

"Ahh." Thomas grinned bashfully. "You know, it's easy to get a little carried away around this one."

He absentmindedly scratched an itch on his right ear and then bumped the side of my torso playfully, giving me a knowing look that told me I was going to hear about this discussion later.

"But no, I actually meant with you all. That way you can navigate her through the ins and outs of the whole party since you've been before."

"Oh yeah, that's a given. We got our girl's back, ain't that right?" Reagan replied, soliciting a round of "mmm-hmms" and "yeps" from Keisha and Giselle.

She also nodded her head toward me with a similar knowing look. Clearly, everyone had intentions of replaying this conversation with me afterward.

"Well, that's real good to hear, Reagan. Real good. Because this lil' dangerous ass twerk that she seems to have could get her into trouble, you know."

Thomas laughed out loud, bumping me in my side again as he talked *about* me to my new friends but was clearly directing his comments with the intention of riling me up.

"One might argue you're the dangerous one," I chimed in, unable to resist the need to defend myself.

"Who, me? Nah, I'm a literal angel when I'm not around you, love. You can ask anyone."

Thomas punctuated his sentence with his now patented smirk that threatened to snap the very feeling out of my knees. It also managed to miraculously quiet down my City Girl squad, who simply watched in awe as he lured me into another concentrated stare. Powerless to his desires, all I could do was stand there, biting the inside of my mouth to keep from responding or smiling back too hard…a fact that he clearly noticed and replied to with another wink.

"Now, tell me again how you came here just for a Black-ass good time and not for me," he whispered, bending his torso and neck toward me so that his lips were perilously close to the nape of my neck.

"It may have been a combination," I admitted.

"Mmm."

"But to be fair, you did tell me you weren't interested in me. So…"

"That's definitely not what I said."

"I'm bloody sure that's not something a girl forgets, yeah."

"Well, Olivia, I'm pretty intentional with my words. So, trust me, I know that's not what I said."

His eyes kept mine in a trance as he awaited my next reply, somehow admonishing me and encouraging me to be a better spar partner all at the same time. When I didn't say anything in return, his eyes lit back up, like he was a man who knew he'd finally won our game of chicken.

With his symbolic championship belt in hand, Thomas turned his head back around to the other girls and offered up his hand again for a goodbye shake.

"Ladies, it has truly been a pleasure meeting you," he said. "I know you probably came out here to have a good time with your friends, so I'm going to leave you to that. My apologies for monopolizing Monie Love's time for a while, but she seems to have some kind of an invisible hold over me where that just happens."

They each stared back at him, clearly charmed as much as I had been when we'd first met (and still was, despite my best efforts). I also recognized that he was once again using a conversation with them to speak to me indirectly.

"Do me a favor, though?" he asked playfully. "Don't let her in on that secret, okay? I told you she's dangerous— she might try to take advantage of me."

"Don't worry," Keisha replied, now fully hypnotized by the dimples and the charm as well. "We got you."

"Umm, I thought it was 'we got Liv,' remember?" I interrupted.

"Of course," Reagan replied, playing cleanup man. "We got you, too, girl. Always."

Too. Tuh!

Thomas finished shaking each of their hands and turned back to me, with now four championship chicken-game belts under his wing. He'd somehow silenced me and impressed my friends, and I could see in his face that he knew it and was quite pleased with himself.

"Are you happy now?" I asked.

"I told you earlier I was happy just seeing you happy."

"But you're even happier now. I can tell."

He tilted his head to the side and gazed at me with a mischievous grin that made me want to jump up and kiss it off of his face. I shook away the thought and instead attempted to pivot the conversation once more before he said his final goodbye. It was all I had left to help me keep some kind of composure.

"By the way, before you leave, we should still take that picture from before," I offered.

"What was that?" he asked, slightly perplexed.

"The picture! You know, the one you were initially going to photobomb? I was thinking we could just take it together instead."

"Oh! Yeah, we should definitely do that. You're right."

Without another word, Thomas reached out his left arm and wrapped it around my waist as he expertly maneuvered my body next to his, positioning me right into the nook of his five-ten frame, our bodies sinking into each other like magnetic forces we couldn't control. In response, I focused my attention on the mechanics of the photo. I unlocked my phone, turned the camera to selfie mode and raised my right arm high, trying to get us the perfect angle. And it would have been—perfect, that is—if not for the fact that I was six inches shorter than him and thus was not doing a very good job of getting us both in the picture.

"Why don't you let me do that," he asked, gently taking the phone out of my hand and lifting it into the sky before I could reply. "This is your side, right?"

"Ha ha, it is, yeah."

"Good. Then let's do this, shall we?"

Thomas held my attention with his eyes until he received the silent yes that he was waiting for: a simple nod from me. Then he pulled me into him even closer and, with the flick of his thumb, snapped seven photos in succession as the two of us stared into the camera with the widest smiles ever on our faces. When he was done, he promptly returned my phone back to me and waited patiently as I looked through my gallery to see if he'd done a good job or not.

"There's got to be at least one cute one in there that you'll like," he said, drawing my eyes to his again.

"Oh, I'm sure! I mean, look at us. How could there not be?"

"Exactly. When the woman's not wrong, she's not wrong, ladies and gentlemen."

Leaning toward each other, we both fell into a fit of giggles. I even had to grab his arm to steady myself, a mistake I soon realized once I felt another powerful shiver crawl down my spine as our bodies connected again. I quickly removed my hand and cleared my throat.

"You should, uhh…take my number," he said with a slight stammer that made me wonder if he'd felt the electricity that had flowed between us, too. "So that you can send me whichever one you like best, you know. It's not fair if you get to just have it, right?"

"That's very true," I replied, maybe a little too eagerly, at once happy for the logical excuse he'd given us both as for why I needed his number but then instantly wanting him to betray that reasoning and tell me something else. "Is that the only reason you want me to have your number, though? So I can send you a picture of us?"

He smiled in response, clearly enjoying the fact that I'd rejoined our banter game better late than never.

"No, it's not," he admitted. "But I wasn't lying in the airport, either, Liv. I get that you probably have a lot going on just having moved here and everything, so I'm not trying to jump in and be that guy who asks you on a date before you've even finished unpacking. Plus, I remember what it was like when I moved here. I want you to take the time to enjoy all that the city has to offer before you go back to the UK."

"That's fair, and I appreciate you understanding my priorities."

And the thing was, I really did; the fact that he wasn't

trying to get me to choose him over my plans for the year was not only refreshing, it was also comforting. I hadn't realized how nice it would feel to be around someone who didn't seem as if he needed me to be less than myself to like me. At the same time, it was still a little disappointing to hear that same person once again say he didn't want to date me. Try as I might, I was sure it showed on my face.

"Of course. I'm a man with my own as well. That said, I wouldn't mind us spending some time together," he added, looking at me earnestly, his head tilted to the side again. "Whenever you're ready."

"Soooo…a date but not a date?"

Thomas smiled at me again and moved in closer. "How about we just say I'll let you decide what it is. That work?"

"Okay. We can do that."

I handed him my phone again, feeling as if I was getting sucked into a vortex that I wasn't sure I wanted but also wasn't sure I didn't want. It was the strangest feeling I'd ever had.

Is this what American women have to deal with on a regular basis? I wondered. *Because it isn't for the faint of heart.* I made a mental note to talk about this with Reagan and Robin later. My girls Nneka and Tracy— my besties since primary school—were certainly going to want to hear the play-by-play, too, but I needed my American friends to tell me if I was losing my mind or not.

Thomas dutifully typed his number into my phone and then, just as he had before, gently handed it back to me, our fingers grazing slightly as we made the exchange.

"I look forward to seeing you again, Liv," he said

before leaning in and planting the softest, sexiest and quickest kiss on my forehead.

It was like the man was determined to make me squirm with a thousand people as his witnesses.

"Same here, Thomas."

He winked at me once more and then slipped away into the thick of the crowd. By the time my legs gave from under me, he'd disappeared into a sea of dancing people, all bouncing and rapping along with Saweetie and Doja talking about riding with their best friends in a Tesla. Thankfully, Reagan was there to catch me as my knees literally buckled from the weight of the swoon pulsing through my body.

"Damn, girl!" she shouted out. "I'd say Mr.— Wait, what's his last name?"

I straightened myself up and took in a deep breath before responding to her, scoping the area to make sure he wasn't still snooping around as Keisha and Giselle joined us. The last thing I needed was for him to hear what I was sure was about to be a discussion all about him.

"I don't know it yet," I replied, cringing at the implication.

"He's got you sprung like that, and you don't even know his full name?" Keisha asked. "That's some powerful juju right there."

"He does not—well, he might—but don't worry, it's not going to be like that going forward. He already knows my plans for this year, and falling for him is just not in the cards."

I looked around wistfully, suddenly remembering how incredible his lips had felt on my forehead. What an inconvenient flashback to have while I was protesting my case.

"Please," Giselle chimed in. "Don't let Keish make you feel bad about anything here. The way that man was looking at you the whole time he was with you… Shoot, if he's not in your plans, you need to reevaluate those plans!"

I laughed and took a big gulp of what was left of the drink in my hand.

"In other news, does anyone else need a refill?" I asked, waving my empty cup in the air. "Because I could surely use one right now."

"I bet you could!" joked Keisha. "But I'm definitely down."

"Me, too," added Reagan.

"Same here," Giselle said, lifting her cup in solidarity, too.

"Okay, great. I'll get this round at the bar. Does everyone want the same thing?"

"Yep," they replied in unison.

"And I'll come with," said Reagan. "It's a big difference between carrying three drinks and trying to maneuver through the crowd with four."

"Oh, true. Thanks—I appreciate it."

"You bet. Plus," she said, her voice turning to a whisper as we began walking toward the bar, "I need to hear more about what all just happened."

"Well, first, can you tell me how you knew it was him behind me?"

"Oh, that's easy. The look he had on his face was so obviously that of a man drawn to you—and not just because he thought you were cute. Like, you could see there was more there. And then the way he was awkwardly trying to pose behind you…it just was no question. That was a man excited to see the woman he'd invited show up."

I laughed, trying to envision exactly what they'd all seen. I could only imagine the spectacle from their perspective—going from that awkward exchange to me damn near falling over as he'd left. What a show we'd put on!

"If it's any consolation," she added, "the way things went down were even better than the devious plans I had cooked up. So maybe that should tell you something right there."

"Tell me something? Like what, that the best things can happen outside of your plans?"

"You said it, not me."

"Hmm. I get that, but it's just really not how I live my life, Rae."

"Oh, I know."

We squeezed ourselves through the crowd in front of the bar and, within a few seconds, got the bartender's attention to order our drinks.

"I'd like one whiskey ginger, a vodka tonic…oh, do you know how to make a Tom Collins?"

"I sure do," he replied.

"Okay, so a Tom Collins, and wait…" I turned to Reagan as I realized I didn't know what Giselle had been drinking. "Do you know what Gigi would want?"

"Oh yeah, get her a gin and orange juice."

"What? You're kidding me, right?"

In my head, I immediately started hearing the chords to the chorus of one of Snoop Dogg's most known rap songs. That was not what I would have expected from the friend with the *Girl Power* tank top on.

"I know. You can take the girl out of Southern Cali but not the Southern Cali out of the girl."

"Okay," I replied with a chuckle, and turned back to the bartender. "And lastly, a gin and orange juice."

"All right—coming up. Anything else?"

"No, that's it. Thanks!"

I turned back to Reagan and saw the glimmer in her eyes as she stood there waiting for me to speak again.

"Okay, now that that's done, give me the tea! How was it seeing him, dancing with him, everything? You've had me waiting far too long for this."

"Oh, Rae, it was…" I sighed "…far too dreamy and confusing and exhilarating for me to even put into words."

"Don't I know it, *cher*. We could see that from where we stood just a few steps away," she said with sympathetic eyes. "But try."

Chapter Seven

Thomas: I never said I didn't like the episode. Just that I think it's mad wild Dwayne Wayne waited until Whitley was in her dress, down the aisle and getting ready to marry another man before he finally stepped up and said something.

I laughed to myself after reading Thomas's text message. Since the party, we'd been having just these kinds of debates on almost a daily basis, covering everything from sibling-order personality traits to the benefits of registering as a Democrat or Republican and not Independent, plus our ongoing '90s-versus-2000s R&B battle. In each, I learned something new about him, not the least of which was that he was the oldest of three boys; a voracious reader, especially of politics and economics; and willing to die on the hill that the 2000s had been as important to R&B even though that era didn't get the same hype as the '90s. I'd even finally learned his last name: Wright.

Today's conversation was on whether or not the most iconic episode of *A Different World* was as romantic as it was remembered or a massive display of reckless intentions and selfish behaviors. This was something we'd been going back and forth on for at least twenty minutes while I played double duty, shopping with Reagan and Jake to make my flat feel a little more like home.

That's true. It was bloody late on his part. But ultimately, he fought for his girl, I texted back. That's where the romance comes in.

Thomas replied a couple minutes later, just as I was wheeling my trolley out of the cashier line.

But at what cost? he asked. You're telling me that this incredibly intelligent man—with an engineering degree, at that—didn't recognize he might actually be losing the woman he loves until right at the moment Whitley's about to say I do? He didn't know while she was dating Byron, or even once she got engaged?

Oy, you're right. But I think it's less about him not realizing it until the wedding date and more that his need to fight for her became extremely urgent, I retorted. He did go to her the night before, remember?

Thomas: And stopped short of saying what he really wanted to, which was I love you. Don't choose him. Pick me.

Me: He did.

Thomas: I just don't think that's romantic. Now, I'm no one's expert on love—I haven't even really been interested in a serious relationship for a while now. But I know that if I were in love with someone, I'm not waiting until they are walking down the aisle to marry someone else to tell them that. That's an incredibly high risk, low reward way of doing things. Not to mention, it's rooted in everything being about him. If it was about her, there were plenty of other, better opportunities to achieve the same result.

I paused and reread his latest text, not knowing exactly where to start with my response since he'd sufficiently packed a lot into one message. Most intriguing, of course, was his admission that he hadn't been looking for a relationship for a while. But that felt like a trap I should stay far away from. After all, I had yet to take him up on his "non-date" date anyway, so what did it matter to me?

The only problem was the gulp in my throat I immediately felt upon reading that admission. I breathed in deeply to release the tightness that had suddenly developed in my chest and decided to simply address the main topic at hand. Just call me Olivia "Avoidance Queen" Robinson.

What's the alternative then? I asked. He doesn't fight for her at all, and she marries Byron? That would have made for an awful outcome.

Thomas replied back almost immediately, but I blacked out my screen before I could read it, suddenly realizing that I'd been texting with him nonstop even while shopping with Reagan. And although I never wanted to be that person who spent all day on their phone while out with friends, I'd found myself caught up, too fascinated by the workings of his brain to disengage. It was Reagan's voice as she called for Jake to join us at the store exit that provided the interruption I'd needed to jolt me out of my trance.

"Did you find everything?" Jake asked as he strode up to us wearing an all-royal-blue casual-wear ensemble from Polo combined with a pair of white-and-blue Nike Air Maxes.

"Oh yes. I think we've done enough damage in T.J. Maxx for the day," she replied, pointing to the shopping trolley full of rose-gold and silver knickknacks and necessities.

"Okay. Well, let's drop these bags off at the car so we can keep the party going."

I watched them with interest as I rolled my trolley behind them and out onto the sidewalk. Reagan gently grabbed Jake's hand and pulled him close to her, then melted into the side pocket of his eager and awaiting torso. It was a small gesture, but as an outside observer, I could tell she was clearly letting him know she didn't take him being with us today for granted. Jake might not have been directly by our sides the entire time—vacillating between strolling three or four aisles away to give us uninterrupted girl time and joining us right when we needed him to help pick up the heaviest of the items—but my girl hadn't forgotten he was there by any means. The smile on Jake's face as he bent his body slightly to meet hers revealed that he appreciated the act and all debts had been paid.

Reagan and Jake were a marvel, really. The stories I'd heard about their breakups (and makeups) would put Carrie and Big to shame. But in person, all I ever saw were two people who cared deeply for each other and showed it through simple acts of kindness—a far cry from Jake's previous reputation as a selfish, manipulative man who'd broken her heart too many times to count and Reagan's as a woman on a mission to do everything by the book, perfectly, and never let a man get too close to hurt her again. I was bloody sure, for example, that Jake had plenty he could have been doing on a Saturday afternoon besides hanging with us, and yet there he was—shopping the likes of Target, HomeGoods and T.J. Maxx on the Upper West Side just in case we needed his help. That had not been on my bingo card.

I briefly looked down at my phone and noticed that Thomas had now sent me three messages back-to-back, definitely igniting my curiosity to read his replies. But I was also determined to try to stay in the moment with Reagan and Jake as we walked to his car just a block away. In the time we'd spent in T.J. Maxx, the temperature had dropped significantly—New York's way of reminding us that it could still get chilly in the fall—so, I was immediately thankful we'd found a place to park nearby as we walked out into the cool air. And while the wind tried its best, it didn't make it past my black-and-tan ankle-length coat and light mauve sweatpants set. That, plus the hoodie on my top, which had a satin interior made to protect Black women's hair, was all the coverage I needed in case the November breeze grew to be too prickly once the sun set on our shopping spree.

Jake began expertly unloading my shopping bags into his trunk as soon as we arrived at his car, making sure to leave room for whatever we bought in the remaining stores. To help, I grabbed the next largest bag on top of my trolley, momentarily forgetting that it was packed with a box of champagne flutes, two extra-large coffee mugs, a small rug to lay next to my bed and a hair dryer to replace the one I'd blown out despite the power adapter I'd tried to use my first week in the city.

"Oh God," I cried out, trying to get my bearings so that I didn't drop the bag onto the ground.

"You okay?" Jake asked, immediately springing to action and trying to wrestle the heavy bag out of my hands.

"Mmm-hmm," I said, doing my best to tighten my grip on the bag, walk the few steps from the trolley to the trunk and drop it off quickly but gently. "'I am woman, hear more roar' or something like that."

"'Or something like that' is right," Reagan chimed in, laughing from where she was perched beside the passenger door of the car with her gray full-length jacket and its turned-down collar casually blowing in the wind.

"Wait, why are you laughing?" I turned to ask her.

"Because literally the whole point of Jake being here is to do what you just did. And you know this but still couldn't stop yourself from picking up the second-heaviest thing in that cart and almost falling on your face with it."

"I know, but—"

I stopped myself before I could continue protesting. It didn't seem like my rationale about not wanting him to feel used or as if he was always my butler when we were together was going to be received well...or at least not without another round of laughter.

"But what?" she asked with a smile, gently egging me on.

"Nothing. You're right," I admitted. "It wasn't the smartest idea."

"It's not about it being smart, Liv," Reagan replied, finally leaving her spot by the passenger door and bouncing her way up to me with her white scoop-necked T-shirt and gray skinny jeans showing underneath her coat.

When she was close enough to me so that she could whisper, she finished her thought. "It's about not feeling the need to jump in and grab the first thing you see so that you don't feel helpless or as if you're not always in control, you know?"

"You got all of that from me picking up a shopping bag of items *I* purchased?"

"You didn't?"

She gave me a wink and turned her attention back to Jake, who had successfully finished packing everything else from the trolley into his trunk while the two of us had debated about my contribution to the effort. As he closed the trunk door, she planted a soft kiss onto his cheek and then grabbed the trolley to bring it back to the entrance of T.J. Maxx. Another small gesture between the two of them. Clearly, they'd gotten something right that I hadn't quite figured out. It made me think of my debate with Thomas and how desperately I wanted to see what else he'd had to say.

"You all right?" Jake asked as he pressed the lock on his keys to secure his car.

"Yeah—nothing a good stretch won't cure."

"Well, it's a good thing Rae has at least two more stops on deck for you today. That should help."

I chuckled that Jake thought of shopping as stretching. Then again, the app on my phone said we'd already walked five thousand steps, so maybe he was onto something.

"We're going to HomeGoods next, right?" he asked while checking his watch.

"I think so, yeah."

"Okay, good. You should definitely be able to find the pillows and the kinds of mirrors you were looking for there. T.J. Maxx has some of those, but HomeGoods will have more options you can choose from."

"Wait, how do you know this?" I asked, amused at the thought of his extensive decor knowledge. "Are you frequenting HomeGoods on random Saturdays or something when Reagan thinks you're at the gym?"

"Don't put me in a box, Liv. I'm an evolved man," he joked back with me. "Plus, who do you think helped Rae gather all that stuff for her customized bedroom? She couldn't stay out of that store, so that meant I didn't, either."

"You know what? I didn't even think of that. I guess you're a 'Jake of all trades,' hee-hee."

"Cute," he said with a playful roll of his eyes. "But honestly, I'm no one's handyman. I'm just good at picking up on things, you know, like the fact that you've been dying to check your phone since we walked out of the store."

"Huh?" I asked, completely caught off guard that he'd noticed that small of a detail even while I'd thought he'd only been focused on my bags and Reagan's ass. "I don't think that's true…"

With nothing else to say in protest and probably the worst poker face known to man, I closed my mouth shut before I could finish my sentence and simply nodded that he was right.

Jake smiled in response and shrugged his shoulders. "Like I said, I'm good at picking up on things."

He paused to see if I'd take the hint and unlock my phone to respond to whoever he assumed was on the other end waiting for me.

"It won't bother me if you check it, you know. Reagan, either."

"I know."

"Okay," he said with another shrug.

Reagan soon came bouncing back up to us, buoyed by her crisp white Nike Air Force 1s and her zeal for more shopping. The look on her face showed that she could sense she'd missed something important, but instead of probing either of us about the details, she playfully squinted her eyes at us and then grabbed our arms to lead us to our next destination.

"All right, Liv," Reagan said as we stepped into the interior of HomeGoods, with its white tile floors, wood-laminate walkways and rows and rows of everything from dinnerware to actual furniture. "Jake will attest that I've gotten so much of my decor from this store alone, not those fancy boutiques down in SoHo that your coworkers wanted you to go to. I mean, yes, they have great stuff, too, if you like spending your entire paycheck on a rug, but *this* is the real golden goose."

"Ha ha, he may have mentioned this was your go-to spot," I replied.

"Oh, did he?"

Her previous suspicions now at least somewhat confirmed, Reagan turned to her boyfriend and squinted her eyes at him again, waiting to see if he'd spill any further details.

"In a good way!" I offered with a laugh.

"Mmm-hmm. I just bet it was."

I stepped back to grab a new shopping trolley while I watched the two lovebirds as they jokingly argued about whether Jake had ratted her out to me. Their playful dynamic as an expression of love was almost enough to make even the most measured person smile from a place that they didn't know existed at first. At the very least, it inspired me to stop being stubborn and finally check my texts from Thomas, even as we began scoping the store for the decorative throw pillows I'd been promised.

Of course not, he'd replied in the first of four texts I'd missed.

Thomas: He should definitely have fought for her, but months before.

Thomas: To me, the wedding just showed his emotional immaturity. And ultimately, it put the woman he loved in a horrible position—run to him and humiliate the other man she was in the midst of pledging to spend the rest of her life with, or say no to him, the man she loves, begging for her at the other end of the aisle.

Thomas: You think that was fair?

Damn. It was easy to see how he'd made such a name for himself at his law firm. I couldn't exactly argue against him advocating for honest communication as the more romantic of the options. That said, I felt there had to be some nuance in between his all-or-nothing reasoning.

You're right. It wasn't fair to Whitley, I texted back. But surely you understand that everything isn't always black-and-white. I think we can agree that he should have fought for her earlier, but in the absence of doing that, he had to take drastic measures to make sure he didn't lose her before it was too late.

Thomas: Yes, exactly! And that's why it's an example of poor planning more than anything else. It shouldn't have ever even gotten to that point.

Wow, how had he managed to flip this back to his side of the discussion? I wasn't going down without a fight, however. Quickly, I typed back, hoping to get in one more reply before Reagan and Jake noticed my attention wasn't on them.

Me: But then we'd never have gotten the cultural zeitgeist of Dwayne begging her to come to him. You'd take that away from all of us just so he can be...logical? Tuh!

Touché, he replied with a wink emoji. I can't argue with that.

"Yes," I whispered to myself, proud that I'd finally stumped the charming attorney who had been beating me at our debate game all week.

My victory was short-lived, however, as I looked up and saw Reagan standing in front of me with yet another suspicious look on her face.

"And just who have you been texting all day, Olivia?"

She stood with one hand on her hip as she awaited my response, but I was like a deer caught in headlights. I'd barely had enough wherewithal to blacken out my screen before she tried to swipe my phone out of my hand.

"You know who she's texting," Jake interjected.

"Oh, of course I know, but I want to hear her say it."

My cheeks grew hot as I hesitated to confirm their assumptions but ultimately knew there was no use in trying to cover it up.

"Just Thomas," I said, trying to at least make it sound as casual as I could.

"Oh, *juuust* Thomas, huh?" Reagan asked, raising her eyebrows at me.

"Yes." I laughed.

"And how long have you been 'just texting Thomas?'"

She punctuated her last three words with air quotation marks, as if I didn't already know that she wasn't going to believe a word I said in protest.

"Since the party, I guess."

I shrugged my shoulders to suggest this wasn't that big of a deal and we could all very much move on to the next conversation. Neither of them took the hint, however.

"Wait, that was weeks ago, right?" Jake asked.

He was clearly enjoying what he thought might be turning into another one of Reagan's friends' dating stories.

"Yes." I laughed again in return. "I suppose it has been weeks."

"Hmm. And have you taken him up on his offer for—what was it you called it—a non-date?"

I wasn't quite prepared for the two of them to be tag teaming me in their questioning, but I continued brushing it off in an attempt to assure them (and maybe myself, too) that nothing had dramatically changed since we'd seen each other at the party. A bunch of texts really and truly didn't amount to much.

"No, definitely not," I replied. "I've been so busy at work, and he's been very respectful of that. Plus, his job keeps him pretty active, too."

"Uh-huh. Do you know what this sounds like to me, Jake?" Reagan asked, turning to face him. "Excuses."

"Mmm, yeah, we know them well."

"Don't we? Ugh. But why is Olivia making them, do you think?"

I was apparently in yet another situation where the people around me were having a conversation about me as if I wasn't there but also clearly directing their comments toward me. I enjoyed this one about as much as I had the instance at the day party—which was to say, not at all.

"Guys." I stepped in to try to stick up for myself.

"Oh yes, hi, Liv," Reagan said, turning her body back toward me. "Would you like to respond as to why you're making excuses?"

"I'm not making excuses. I promise," I said, chuckling at how ridiculous this conversation had become. "If you recall, the man said I could take him up on his offer whenever I was ready…"

"I'm fairly certain he didn't expect weeks to go by," Jake replied.

"Especially not if y'all have been texting the whole time!" Reagan added.

"You don't even know how much we've been texting," I said, my voice raising slightly as I continued to protest my case.

"Olivia, look at me," Reagan replied, her once playful expression turning very serious toward me. "Do you really think I don't know? The smile on your face as you talk about him tells me everything I need to know."

I sighed heavily. Maybe Reagan was right and Thomas hadn't thought he would be texting me daily for this period of time without me bringing up our non-date again. But everyone seemed to be forgetting one thing: despite appearances to the contrary, Thomas was also the man who'd now told me on multiple occasions that he didn't want to date me. *What am I supposed to do other than take him at his word?*

"You know what? Hold whatever thought is going through your mind right now," Reagan added as she pulled out her phone and smugly began pressing a few buttons before I heard a familiar voice on the other end.

Robin.

"Hey, Rae! What's up?"

I could hear her booming voice through the phone almost immediately.

"Hey, Rob, you busy?" Reagan asked.

"Not really—just getting dressed to meet up with Craig for dinner."

"Oh, good. Well, we won't keep you long. I just needed your help real quick with the other Robinson sibling."

"Wait, with Liv? Why—what's going on?"

"Nothing too crazy. She's just over here denying her feelings for this guy who clearly likes her—I saw it for myself, Rob. He couldn't control himself even if he wanted to—and who she can't stop grinning about to the point that I think her cheeks should be tired by now."

"Oliviaaaaa!" Robin screamed out loud, admonishing me from thousands of miles away.

Reagan swung her phone around so that Robin could lay her eyes on me as she continued to speak. It was almost as if she'd called my mum on me, except for the fact that even though she was my good girlfriend, Robin was also four years younger and dating my brother. So maybe the more accurate feeling was that she'd called my little sister to have her chastise me. *I think I might have preferred my mum.*

"That's not exactly the whole story," I replied.

"It kind of is," Jake chimed in softly from the sidelines. *Now all three of them are ganging up on me!*

"It really isn't," I said calmly, flashing him and Reagan looks of fire before turning my attention back to Robin.

"Wait, is this the airport guy?" she asked.

"It is," we replied in unison.

"I didn't realize he was still around! Good for him."

"Except that Liv seems intent on stopping herself from seeing what things could be with him because he wasn't part of her grand New York plans."

I stared at Reagan, tears threatening to fall from my eyes because I didn't see how I could make them understand that they were right and wrong at the same time. Yes, meeting Thomas hadn't been in my plans, but beyond that, I just didn't have the time or energy to put myself out there for yet another person. Time and time again, I'd been disappointed by men who'd either wanted me to be less ambitious for them or who'd stopped liking me once they'd gotten to know the real me. So, it was easier to just be his friend—that way I knew I couldn't end up hurt again. And that was the last thing I needed when, yes, I had big plans for my time in New York.

"Is that true, Liv?" Robin asked.

"Partly, Rob," I said with a sigh. "But it's so much more than that. Honestly."

"Okay, well, I'll just say this—you were the voice I needed to calm me down right before my first date with your brother. So, should you decide to go on a date with— What's his name again? I don't want to just call him Airport Boy."

"Thomas." I laughed.

"Right. So, if you decide to ever go on a date with Thomas, I'm here. And if you don't, you might have to hear from Rae for a bit, but that'll be okay, too."

"Thanks, Rob," I replied, passing the phone back to Reagan.

After we all said our phone goodbyes, Rae grabbed me and wrapped her arms around me, squeezing me tightly.

"I just don't want you to miss out on something that could be amazing because you're scared you didn't plan for it so you can't control it," she said.

"I know," I said, leaning into her embrace. "And I'm not trying to. I just—"

"Need some more time?"

"I think so, yeah."

"Okay. I get it. No more pressure from me, then."

As the two of us unwrapped ourselves from each other, we saw Jake coming down the pillow aisle carrying a six-foot-tall mirror wrapped with a wooden frame that had a gold metallic finish. I hadn't even noticed that he'd walked away while Reagan and Robin had been talking, but clearly he'd thought he could be more useful elsewhere.

"Jake, OMG."

I watched in awe as he drew closer to us.

"I know, right?" he said, gently placing it down.

Immediately we noticed it was one of those mirrors that was able to stand on its own at an angle if you wanted it to. I stepped up to it and looked at myself in the mirror, already starting to imagine where it could go in my flat.

"This is beautiful," I said, still marveling at the craftsmanship of the mirror but also that he'd found it so quickly and known it would be the one I'd like. I guess he was right after all—he was good at picking up on things.

Reagan stepped up behind me and put her head on my shoulder as we looked into the mirror, both admiring the women we saw before us, who had in different ways taken on a new adventure, coming to New York with hopes for the future. A few seconds later, my phone began vibrating in my hand, jolting us out of our moment of reflection.

I knew who it was without even needing to look.

"Tell Thomas I said hi," Reagan said with a wink before she left me to walk over to where Jake was standing.

Once she was gone, I unlocked my phone and beamed from ear to ear.

In other news, have you heard this new song by H.E.R.? he'd texted with a link to "Come Through."

Clearly he wasn't content with our conversation ending for the day, and neither was I.

That's not new! I replied. It's been out for a while now.

Thomas: Oh damn. Well, I guess it's just new to me.

Me: Ha ha, I guess so! But it is fire. I'll give you that.

Thomas: And maybe also instructive?

Me: Hmm. Maybe.

I blackened out my screen before I got caught smiling too much again and ran back up to Reagan and Jake to keep our shopping spree going.

"Well, I think we have the mirror," I said. "It's just the pillows left, yeah?"

"Yep," they replied, now both giving me Reagan's signature suspicious look.

"So you're not going to tell us anything more about whatever has you grinning right now?" Reagan asked.

"Nope," I replied quickly. "But I will say, I think there's more to come."

"Okay," she said, jokingly throwing up her hands. "I'll take that for now."

Part 2

"Always go with the choice that scares you the most, because that's the one that is going to require the most from you."

—Caroline Myss

Chapter Eight

Bryant Park in the winter was even more enchanting than any photos I'd ever seen of it, especially as small snow flurries crisscrossed in the night sky, lightly dusting the Christmas decor all around us. It wasn't just the village of shops and snow that made it special, however; Bryant Park was also beautifully designed to give its patrons both a clear view of iconic New York structures like the Empire State Building, statuesque even from afar, and a feeling that they were in a small sanctuary away from all the chaos of the city. At least that was how I felt as I waited for Thomas to return with our drinks as we officially made good on our first non-date. It was in that moment of silence that I had a chance to marvel at my surroundings and really take in the beauty before me, up to and including the giant Christmas tree that towered over the entire area, lighting up the open space with hints of purple, red and silver everywhere you looked.

"Okay, I promise you're going to love this," Thomas said as he walked back up to me and handed me a glass mug of hot chocolate topped with whipped cream and a giant red, green and white funfetti–covered marshmallow.

His presence quickly jolted me out of my thoughts, and I smiled in return—happy to have him near me again so we could experience the magic of the evening together. Looking down at my mug, I noticed that the color of the funfetti perfectly complemented the emerald green scarf I'd chosen as the accent to my outfit for the evening—a black knee-length wool coat, patent-leather black oxfords and a black Yves Saint Laurent cross-body purse. Thomas, who had his own mug of hot cocoa but topped with an Oreo-covered marshmallow, stood in front of me just as handsome as the first time I'd seen him, dangerous dimples and flawlessly coiffed beard intact. This time around, he wore a tan winter coat that popped off his gorgeous skin tone and a light blue jean shirt with dark blue jeans underneath. It was almost as if we'd purposely switched our outfits from the day party, just with some winter clothing added to the mix.

"It looks amazing," I replied, still in awe as I clutched the warm mug with both hands.

"It tastes even better."

Thomas waited for me to take my first sip as the sun set on the beginnings of what he'd promised would be a fun-filled Christmas mini tour through the city, starting in Bryant Park, where the winter treats included a free ice-skating rink, a festive market filled with more than one hundred seventy shops and an après-themed area called The Lodge that offered specialty cocktails and remarkable views. But while the decorations and the Christmas lights twinkling the sky above the park were stunning, one thing was clear as soon as the first taste of it touched my lips—the hot chocolate was the star of this show.

"Wow, this is incredible," I said, savoring the warmth as it flowed throughout my body on the chilly early December evening.

Thomas winked in reply, instantly sending a shiver down my spine that even the hot drink couldn't cure.

"And we're only just getting started," he added. "Come with me."

Before I could respond, he grabbed me by the waist and gently pulled me toward him, leaving barely any space between our bodies as we started walking through the winter village. With anyone else, that would have seemed like a harmless move, but with Thomas—the man I was desperately trying to just be friends with—it was the kiss of death to my resolve. He'd effectively put me right into the best position to snuggle into his frame if I wanted to, allowing his arm to wrap me in his embrace as we continued on our tour.

I took in a deep breath and did my best to maintain my composure, hoping that as we continued walking in and out of the dozens of glass-encased shops filled with handmade jewelry, purses and more, we'd inevitably find our friend groove and the tension between us would lessen. In the meantime, however, I knew I had to do something to bring down the heat factor ASAP.

"Tell me something about you that most people don't know," I asked him as I took a few tiny steps to the side and then filled my mouth with another steamy sip of the hot cocoa.

"Oh, all right, Ariana Grande. You want to know all my creep shit, too?"

"I mean…" I shrugged an implied yes and laughed at the fact that, of course, Thomas knew the reference to her song "Imagine."

He'd yet to stop surprising me since the very moment we met.

"Listen, she's got the right idea. The best way to get to know someone is by divulging some things between the two of you. So…spill."

I playfully bumped the side of his torso and bit my lip when he looked back at me as if he was ready to devour me and my hot drink all at once.

"You think we don't know each other yet?" he asked.

"I think we're still getting to know each other."

I looked back at him, my eyes wide, waiting for him to play my new game. It was my best shot at getting the two of us to loosen up since we'd met up forty minutes before. In that time, there'd been nothing but deep and longing stares, unconscious lip bites, and undeniable sparks any time we even slightly grazed the other. That would have been fine if this were a normal date, but it wasn't, and I missed the ease in which we connected as friends—who maybe flirted more than they should have.

"Okay, okay," Thomas said, resigning himself to the fact that I probably wasn't going to let up. "Definitely none of my boys know this, so don't laugh. But when I've had an especially long day at work or one of the clients is getting on my last nerve…"

He stopped before he could finish his sentence and

looked me in my eyes again, almost as if he were trying to see how much he could trust me with his truth. That deeply intense look had almost ruined me previously, but this time, I didn't back down or let the butterflies in my stomach stop me from staring right back at him and making it known that it was time to give me the goods.

"Yesss," I said, egging him on. "Come on with it."

Prolonging the inevitable, he sighed deeply and then sipped a long gulp of his hot chocolate before continuing on. "So, the best way for me to decompress after that kind of day is to blast Rihanna in my headphones and go out for a run."

Thomas said the last few words in his sentence incredibly fast, so fast that I might have missed it if I hadn't been paying as close attention as I was. But I'd heard every word and absolutely loved his very sweet and innocent admission.

"Wait, what?" I said, unable to control the glee spilling out of me. "That's your deep, dark secret? That you listen to Rihanna when you run?"

"Now, hold on. I don't think you're supposed to laugh when someone reveals something to you that they've never told anyone else. Not too many grown, heterosexual Black men are out here bumping Rihanna on their own, Liv."

"You're right," I said, pressing my lips together to try to contain my giggles. "I'm sorry… But I mean, she's Rihanna! Who doesn't love her music?"

"Don't get me wrong, most men absolutely respect her, and we'll be the first to say she's got some undeniable hits, but it's not the same for you as it is for me. I'm supposed to gravitate to Moneybagg Yo or any of the other popular rappers out right now when I need to de-stress—that way no one can question my masculinity."

"Well, Bagg is cool, too, but he doesn't have 'Pour It Up' in his catalog," I offered as a concession for my previous unrestrained laughter.

"Exactly. Or 'Loveeeeeee Song.' 'Talk That Talk.' The list goes on. All I'm saying is when I need to zone out, I either want joyful dance music or trash talk that has been backed up in real life—and in both areas, not too many people are besting her."

"Okay! Let me find out you're literally in the Navy!"

"I'm telling you," Thomas said, letting out a chuckle as he nodded his head to the side.

I clutched my mug tighter and smiled as I listened to him gush over his secret Rihanna fandom. I could understand what he was saying now and was actually bloody grateful he'd chosen to open up to me about something he thought made him seem less cool. That was a lot coming from the smooth-talking attorney who'd charmed me into my first-ever non-date. He may have started off embarrassed to tell me, but as he kept talking, I could see the joy flowing all over his face. And I was suddenly really happy I'd asked the question and he'd engaged me in it, even despite his initial reluctance. In truth, Thomas's love for Rihanna had only served to endear me to him even more—something he was becoming all too good at despite our attempts to stay just friends.

"Well, now I need to put this to the test. Are you telling me that I could begin singing any Rihanna song and you'd know all the words?"

"Every single one," he replied confidently, almost daring me to try.

"Tuh! Well, challenge accepted, Mr. Wright."

I thought about it for two seconds, and then, once again using my cup as my microphone, started rapping the first few bars of her verse in "Lemon." With my love for hip-hop, it only made sense that I'd choose a song she actually rapped on. Plus, I kinda wanted to stump him and figured only her biggest fans would know all the lyrics to that verse.

To my continued unsurprising shock, Thomas didn't miss a beat, jumping right in as if we were duet partners. Before I could even finish the second line, he grabbed my hand so he could rap into my mug as well and then expertly finished off the entire verse without skipping a word.

I stood beside him, impressed and in awe as he pretended to drop an invisible mic and raised his eyebrows to me with pride. I wondered if that was how he'd felt watching me in my zone at the day party. If it was, I could understand exactly what had drawn him to me because I felt like I was getting a sneak peek into a part of him that most people didn't get to see, and I was sure that the sparkle in his eyes could have rivaled that of the Christmas tree behind us.

"Okay, that…was…fantastic," I said, trying to find my words as I described the feeling of watching him in his element.

It was more than just fantastic, though. It had also been exhilarating, tons of fun and oh so swoony, being let into this inner circle of his brain that few could ever dare reach. Fantastic felt like the safer description, though.

"So you believe me now?" he asked, staring deeply into my eyes again.

"Yeah, that's kind of hard to deny."

"Good, good. Well, now that that's settled, it's your turn, love."

Thomas took my free hand in his and spun me around in the middle of the village walkway, landing me right in front of his face after two twirls—once again, whether he'd intended to or not, removing any space between us. Standing before him, suddenly without motion and giggles distracting us, I could see his chest rise and fall as we locked eyes and desperately tried not to lean in for a kiss.

"What's something most people don't know about *you*, Liv?" he asked, his breath so close to me that I felt it on my forehead.

I thought long and hard before responding, looking up at all the festive surroundings while I pondered just how real I was going to be and whether I would choose Door Number Two again?

"Honestly?" I started and then hesitated a bit, trying to get my bearings before I divulged my own deep, dark secret.

"Always," he replied, waiting for me to proceed.

It was something about the way that he looked at me that truly made me believe him, as if there was nothing that I could say that would affect his opinion of me. And maybe it was also the fact that he'd been so vulnerable with me, but whatever the reason, suddenly the choice became as obvious as it had been before, just with a different conclusion this time.

Mimicking his move from earlier, I took in a deep breath, closed my eyes and let my lips move before I could stop them.

"Probably...how scared I am that I'm going to fail this year," I admitted.

"You? Fail?"

"Yeah," I replied, opening my eyes again and linking them with his. "Literally every time I walk through the atrium of my office building, I feel this deep sense of fear. Like everyone's waiting for me to either soar or fall on my face and they'd be perfectly fine with either because at least they'd get the show out of it, you know? And there I am, the little Black woman from London, all dressed up, trying to act like I know what I'm doing when, truthfully, I'm deathly afraid of disappointing everyone around me all the time."

I held my breath and dropped my chin after divulging my secret, waiting to see how he would react to it.

"Liv, wow. First of all, thank you for being honest with me," Thomas replied, lifting his free hand to my chin so that he could raise my head to look at him.

The motion upward permeated through my body so that before I knew it, I was also standing on my toes just so I could be closer to his face.

"I hate that you've put that kind of pressure on yourself, though. Especially because you're already doing things that probably astound everyone around you. The fact that you could ever disappoint..."

He stopped himself before finishing his thought, leaving me to wonder what he was holding back, even as I tried to stop the tears from falling out of my eyes just from the relief of sharing something so intimate with him and not having it used against me.

"Listen, I can't tell you how you should feel. All I know is I am amazed daily by you," he added.

"Thomas..."

"No, I'm serious, Liv. You're a boss. Anybody who's around you for more than two minutes knows that. Hell, I saw it from the moment we met on the airplane."

"When I couldn't even bring my own luggage down from the overhead bin?"

"Yes!"

I thought about that first interaction of ours, recalling how helpless I'd felt, which had only been reinforced by Thomas swooping in to save me. Not my finest hour, by any account. And that could have been the end of our story—the damsel in distress saved by the handsome knight—except he hadn't let it. For some reason, he'd kept popping up by my side, wanting to know more. And now, here we were, rapping to Rihanna together in the middle of a Christmas-shop village. Life was so interesting because who could have predicted that? Certainly not me.

"You did say that you believed I could do anything," I said with a nervous giggle.

"Exactly. And the only way that's changed is that my belief is even stronger now. You are the smartest, most capable and most beautiful woman I've ever met, Olivia."

Well, that's it. There's no way to get around just how swoon worthy that was.

I stepped down from my tippy toes and closed my mouth that was now desperate for his lips.

"Thank you, Thomas, truly…for listening to me and seeing me," I said, nibbling on my lower lip, which had an annoying mind of its own and was trying to propel me toward him.

"There you go with the thank-yous again."

"I know, I know. But really, I'm grateful for our friendship."

"Me, too," he replied, and then bumped me on the side of my hip again.

It happened so quickly, but I could have sworn I saw just a flash of disappointment appear on his face before he replaced it with his signature grin.

"Shall we continue our holiday tour?" he asked. "We still have to go to Lillie's so you can experience what it's like to have every single Christmas decoration known to man strown throughout a bar, then there's the Union Square holiday village, too, and finally we have to get you some dumplings from The Bao, though that part isn't about Christmas—it's just a great spot for the winter, and we're going to be starving by then."

"Wow, you've really thought tonight out!"

"Yeah, I had to. I can't half step when it comes to you."

"Duly noted," I said, biting my lip again to keep her from doing things I might regret in the morning.

"Just one thing before we leave…" he said with a bit of hesitation and then a huge smile.

"Yes?"

"You have a wad of whipped cream on your right cheek. You might want to get that before we hit up the next spot."

"Wait, what?"

I swiped at my cheek and stared in horror at the large dollop of cream on my fingers. It was massive, like a big freaking cloud burst onto my hand.

"Oh my God. How long has that been there?"

"Well…"

"And you're just now saying something?"

"I mean, I thought you could feel it. It was so big!"

Thomas curled his body over in glee, laughing so hard I could see tears starting to well up in his eyes.

"Wow! I've just lost all trust in you," I said through my own set of giggles. "That quickly. Our friendship's now over."

Thomas stood up swiftly, and with the silliest grin still on his face, he looked me dead in my eyes, once again holding me in that sort of trance he had when he wanted to.

"That's not possible, Liv. I'm sorry to have to be the one to tell you, but you're stuck with me now."

Three hours later, I'd learned more than I'd ever thought I could about Thomas Wright in such a short span of time. First, he liked to dabble in a little photography, often joining up with a walking photog group uptown to capture various parts of the city when he wasn't in the UK for work. He also thoroughly enjoyed linking up with his friends in what he called "Black NYC," hopping around to events like the day party he'd invited me to. On that list was everything from Trap Karaoke parties to rooftop get-togethers in Brooklyn, but no matter where the spot, according to him, it was always a "Black-ass good time." One other crucial detail I learned was that, if nothing else, he was not a liar. In fact, everything he'd hyped up before our non-date had actually exceeded my expectations, including the massive display of Christmas decor at Lillie's and the best dumplings I'd ever had at The Bao.

By the time we rolled ourselves out of there at around 9:30 p.m., I was stuffed to the brim with every kind of dumpling known to man—crab, shrimp, wasabi, chicken, even chocolate, to name a few—and I could barely think past climbing into my bed and curling up to get the best sleep of my life. The tricky part, however, was that as much as I wanted to get home, I wasn't quite ready to end our outing yet. That was one other thing I'd learned actually. I could probably spend all day with Thomas and not be knackered.

That realization didn't exactly bode well for all my "focus on your career during this year abroad" plans.

"You know, your place is only about a fifteen-minute walk from here," Thomas said, once again jolting me out of my thoughts as we re-bundled ourselves up in the cold night air. "I could walk you home…if you wanted."

It was like he could read my mind, which was both a good and a bad thing.

"Oh," I replied with just the slightest hesitation. "You're not too full to walk? Because I might be!"

"Nah, this is exactly when you should walk. Get that food moving in your digestive system."

"Okayyy," I replied with a forced smile. "Let's do it, then. But only if I get to ask you some more questions."

"Damn, woman, are you an undercover reporter?" Thomas laughed and stepped closer to me so that I could see him playfully eyeing me suspiciously. I also noticed that crinkle growing on his nose again.

"Nooo, I just like getting to know you," I admitted softly.

I felt my cheeks rising on their own accord and desperately tried to stop them from making a fool of me. It was of no use, however. I was sure that my face beamed as bright as a traffic light when I looked at him.

"Well, that smile of yours might just be my kryptonite, so I guess we've got a deal."

Thomas bumped the tip of my nose with his pointer

finger and then grabbed my arm to swing me around to what I presumed was the direction toward my flat. Clearly he'd noticed said mortifying smile, but ultimately it had convinced him to let me keep quizzing him, so I was going to take the win.

"You know how to get to my flat?" I asked before we started walking.

"Oh yeah, I know the East Village well—so don't worry, I got you."

I wanted to tell him that that was the least of my concerns, but I shut my mouth before I did or said anything else embarrassing.

"Okay, then great. I guess I'm following you."

Arm in arm, we began walking down St. Mark's Place toward Second Avenue. Under the night sky, the tree-lined street and rows of different-colored brick buildings interspersed with various shops, restaurants and bars almost looked majestic and unreal—like I was on a film set version of New York City. I could see how people came here and instantly chose to make this city their home. It was just something about the energy that flowed out from the concrete and the people that made you want to throw caution to the wind and just try anything you'd ever wanted to go after.

"What's your favorite British TV show?" I asked Thomas as we neared the end of the block and suddenly reached the bright openness of Second Avenue.

"What makes you think I have one?"

"Oh, I know you have at least one. You travel to London multiple times a year at this point. And you're too calculated of a person not to think of immersing yourself in some of the language and traditions. What better way to do that than through media, yeah?"

"Fair, except we already discussed how some shows don't always present the real-life experience of living in America. I assume it's the same for you all."

I stopped walking and stared at him with a quizzical look. Was he serious or avoiding the question again? I wondered.

"Is this another Rihanna situation?" I asked. "Are you embarrassed to tell me?"

"No." He laughed sheepishly. "I just don't want you to think you know me already. I'm a mysterious guy, Liv. People always tell me that I keep them on their toes about my moves, my interests, etcetera. And I generally like that, except now there's you—"

"Ohhh, okay," I interrupted, playfully rolling my eyes at his foolishness. "I'll try to remember this next time. Now, will you stop avoiding the question, please?"

"*Starstruck*," he answered quickly, and then started walking again, forcing me to catch up to his long stride.

It was reminiscent of when he'd given his Rihanna reply, except this time his feet were moving fast instead of his lips.

"Wait—I'm sorry, did you say…*Starstruck*?"

"I did."

"The BBC One show?"

"Yes. Well, I saw it on HBO Max, but yes."

"The one where the main character isn't even British?"

"See, this is why I didn't want to tell you."

"No, I just…didn't expect that to be your answer!"

"You don't like the show?"

"I love it, actually. Jessie and Tom forever," I said, laughing. "But the main character is from New Zealand!"

"Yes, but she's in London and everyone around her is British."

"So, if someone were to make a show about my life right now, you'd call that an American TV show?"

"I certainly wouldn't call it a British one."

"Wow, wow, wow. Okay. Now I see that *I'm* actually the one who needs to have you over for a British TV marathon. I mean of all the shows—not *Fleabag*, *I May Destroy You*, *The Crown*, even bloody *Peaky Blinders*!"

"All I'm hearing you say is how much you want me to come over to your place," he said, flashing that insanely gorgeous grin of his to distract me.

"Ugh. You're insufferable, you know that?"

"So I've been told."

Thomas swung his left arm around my shoulders as we passed by a mural featuring purple, green, yellow and blue galaxies floating in a black sky with a woman's blue lipstick–covered lips as the focal point. *What a New York thing to casually walk past*, I thought as I once again found myself resisting a strong desire to snuggle into his five-ten frame, especially as the intoxicating mixture of his body scent and his Le Labo cologne wafted into my nose. In some ways, the whole scene kind of reminded me of home since Brixton was filled with murals randomly scattered all around the neighborhood. Maybe Thomas did, too.

"So what else does Monie Love want to know?" he asked as we turned the corner and began walking down First Avenue, just a few more blocks before we arrived at my flat.

"I think only one more thing for tonight."

"Oh, okay. Now I'm really intrigued. Seems like you saved the best for last, so hit me with it."

I smiled at his excitement and burrowed my face

closer to his torso while simultaneously looking up at him so he could hear my next question.

"What's one thing you *think* I already know about you?" I asked.

"Huh. Like something I haven't explicitly said but should be obvious by now?"

"Yeah, or at least you think it should be obvious."

Thomas took in a deep inaudible breath. If I'd been farther away from him, I probably wouldn't have even noticed it, but as I was so close to his body, I literally felt his chest rise and fall as he contemplated his response. I pondered what he was thinking of in that moment. Was he having his own door-number-one-or-two dilemma? Or maybe he was wondering what the heck kind of question this was that I'd just asked of him?

"Honestly? Probably…how irresistible I find you and how much I can't stop picturing what things would be like if we were together," he finally replied.

Whatever I'd thought he was going to say, it definitely wasn't that.

Instinctually, I jumped almost an arm's length away from him, creating space between us while I processed the grenade he'd thrown into our happy little friend-like non-date.

"I'm sorry, what?"

"Are you telling me that hasn't been obvious? We're literally on a date right now."

"You called it a non-date! That's what we agreed to. That's what—"

"C'mon, Liv, don't be that obtuse," he interjected.

"I—I mean…" I stammered my way through my words, unsure of exactly what to say. "I'm not going to lie and say I haven't felt anything between us. Of course

I have. We talk every day, and let's not even get into *that* dance at the party. But you...you've been adamant from the beginning that you didn't want to date me."

"I haven't wanted to date *anyone*...for a while now. But that had nothing to do with you. It's just that I like the life I've built for myself. My career is where I want it to be, I don't have any obligations outside of work, the partners at my firm entrust me with high-value clients here and overseas, so when I need to travel to the UK for work sometimes, I don't have to worry about missing anyone or checking in. It's the life, actually."

"Exactly. So how does that translate to—"

"To me wanting to be with you?" he asked, interrupting me again.

"Yes."

"Well, I guess I realized both things can be true. I haven't been interested in a relationship, but I also never expected to meet you, an incredibly tenacious and driven woman whose opinion I want on basically everything and who makes up the best part of my day every day. You just hopped into my world and disrupted everything I thought I wanted."

I listened to Thomas speak, stunned silent as we continued walking and running every interaction back in my head, trying to see where I'd missed the clues. I wasn't dumb, so obviously I'd felt that we were drawn to each other, but I also got the sense that he was a man who once he made his mind up about something, rarely changed it. I could relate to that, in fact, and it made things less complicated. Indeed, it was all bloody black-and-white. Neither of us wanted a relationship, so, despite any flirting or lingering looks that might have occurred, we were never going to be anything more, I'd assessed. And at the end of the year, I'd go back home with a cute story to tell about the American boy who I had a slight crush on. He was ruining all of this with his latest admission.

"That said," he continued, "I genuinely haven't wanted to be the guy who makes the precious time you have in the city about me. It's just that…well, you've messed me up in the head quite a lot… I can't believe all this hasn't been obvious?"

"Well, I don't know, Thomas," I replied, finally regaining my voice. "I'm not exactly used to men telling me that they don't want to date me but expecting me to know that they really do."

"That's fair. And all of this is new to me, too, to be honest. Even up to just now, when you asked me that question, I wasn't sure if I was going to say something because I didn't…"

"Because you didn't want to ruin what we have?" I offered, again understanding him more than I cared to admit.

"Yeah. Exactly."

We turned the corner onto my block, and Thomas stepped toward me, closing the gap in between us once again.

"So, now that you know how I feel, are you really going to tell me it's just me?"

I watched as his face, genuine and sincere, waited to see if I was going to crush his heart or make it flutter. His eyes, kind as the day we'd first met, looked back at mine, relaying a sense of urgency I hadn't yet seen in them before…and damn me, combined, it all worked to conjure up a sensation in my spine that threatened to have me laid prostrate on the ground if I couldn't muster up some strength in my calves and knees.

"It's not just you," I admitted. "But—"

Before I could finish that thought, Thomas's lips were on mine, soft and tender at first but then filled with a passion I'd never experienced. With his right hand now on my back, we clung to each other, our lips and tongues intertwining like our very breaths counted on it, like we'd been waiting for this release for years. I instinctively arched my back and stood on my toes to get closer to his face, never wanting to let his mouth go even as he alternated between tracing soft bites along my lower lip and sucking it in whole, a combination that sent continuous shivers throughout my body.

His lips, somehow soft and gritty at the same time, tasted like the sweet chocolatiness of the last dumpling we'd eaten mixed with the mint he'd slipped into his mouth right as we'd walked outside. I did my best to hold my own, standing tall as wave after wave of a pending orgasm crashed over my body as we licked, sucked, bit and pulled at each other's lips for minutes. When we finally came up for air, the softest moan escaped from my mouth, betraying just how putty I was in his hands.

"I told you the first day we met I was a pretty straightforward guy," he said, locking eyes with me once again.

"That you did."

"I don't know if I can be more honest than that, Liv."

I took in a deep breath and contemplated everything that had just happened in the past twenty minutes or so. Somehow, we'd gone from our fun playdate to Thomas blowing up everything I'd thought I knew to be true, even though he'd claimed that was what I'd done to him. And yet that kiss… Oy—if I could lock myself in a chamber of his kisses for hours, I probably would. I didn't know what to do. I didn't know what I wanted. I just knew I didn't want him to leave…not yet.

"Do…do you want to come upstairs?" I asked, stammering through my words, completely overtaken by the moment.

"No," he said, still holding me close to him. "I interrupted you—and I'm sorry about that, by the way—but I heard you. You were getting ready to say, 'But something,' am I right?"

I stared at Thomas in disbelief again. *What the hell kind of roller coaster is this?* He was right, of course. Once again. But God help me, I was more confused than ever now.

"And that's fine. Really," he continued. "But the thing is, when I do come upstairs, I don't want there to be any hesitation in your mind that you want me. That you want to be with me and you want me to please you—mind, body and soul. So, I'll wait."

"Wait?" I asked softly.

"Yeah, wait," he replied with a sly grin. "You know, that thing where you delay an action—even when you're eagerly anticipating it—until the time is right."

"Oh, right, that."

I tasted just a tiny bit of blood as I nibbled on my lower lip again and stepped down onto my heels. This man was literally trying to drive me crazy; that was the only conclusion I could realistically come up with.

"I guess waiting can be good," I said.

He laughed heartily as I tried not to squirm in front of him.

"But you should head up," he replied. "Because I

really want to kiss you again, and if that leads to you asking me to come up once more, I don't think I'd have the willpower to say no next time."

"Okay," I sighed, untangling myself from his grasp and slowly turning toward my front door. "I'll talk to you later?"

I looked back at him over my shoulder as I unlocked the door to enter my building.

"Of course. I already told you, you can't get rid of me now."

I turned my head back toward my building and walked through my front doors, desperately trying not to let him see the ocean-wide smile on my face. *Damn*, I thought as I closed the door behind me and watched him slowly walk away. *What the hell did I just get myself into?*

Chapter Nine

"Whoa. How did you stop yourself from melting right into his arms?"

Robin was mid-throw as she tossed a new set of clothes into her overnight bag when she paused to stare into the FaceTime camera, stunned by my recount of the night before. Technically, she and I were on a five-person video chat to talk about Jennifer's upcoming bachelorette weekend in Palm Springs, but when each of the women had noticed and pointed out a particular glow on my face fifteen minutes in, the conversation had suddenly become about the night before.

Try as I might, I hadn't been able to convince Reagan, Robin, Jenn or Rebecca that they were seeing things, probably because my stupid cheeks wouldn't fall down. So, after much consternation, I broke down and told them everything—word for word, from the linger-

ing looks and laughs to the inevitable kiss that had literally taken my breath away. Well, not everything—one
thing I didn't include in my story, and never would, was
how I'd been playing H.E.R. and Daniel Caesar's "Best
Part" on repeat since I'd fallen onto my bed last night.

"Honestly, I literally don't know," I replied.

"Well, I'd like to just throw out there that I told you
there was no such thing as a damn non-date," Reagan
chimed in.

"Oy! Guess who doesn't need I-told-you-sos right
now?" I asked her.

"You're right. My bad."

Jennifer, who had always been the more sensitive one
out of their friend group, giggled off to the side as she
kindly let the news of my non-date that actually was
a date take over her scheduled call. I was grateful she
didn't consider it rude, but in truth, I probably didn't
have that to worry about. Ever since I'd announced I was
moving to the States for a year, all of Robin's friends
had taken me under their wing in different ways. Jenn
immediately started sending me inspirational messages
every morning, almost as if she was my own personal
Rev Run—this despite the fact that I was moving to
New York and she lived in the District. And while that
might've sounded funny on its surface, somehow each
time she'd sent one, it had been at the very moment I'd
needed a reminder that what I was doing wasn't crazy
and I had it in me to succeed. I thought it was some kind
of intuition she must have possessed and then perfected
as a dean of students at an elementary school. As our
friendship had quickly bloomed, she'd also graciously
invited me to her bachelorette weekend, knowing, of

course, that I was going to be in America anyway and it might be fun for me to come out and have a girls' weekend in Palm Springs. That was the kind of person Jenn was—never selfish and always down to support her friends no matter what.

"Have you heard from him since then?" she asked.

"Yeah, he let me know when he got home."

"Okay, that's good," Robin interjected.

"And I woke up this morning to my normal set of Sunday morning texts from him."

"Wait, you all have texts that are typical for the days of the week?" Rebecca asked.

"Okay, when you say it like that, it sounds cheesy. But on Sundays, he usually gets up pretty early and reads different newspapers online, so by the time I wake up, he's already sent me a bunch of links to stories that he wants my opinion on. That's all."

"Wow," they all replied in unison.

"He's a keeper," Jenn added. "And you know, engaged lady over here should know."

She flashed her ring into the camera with a big grin in a cute attempt to win me over, but I was still too out of it from all that had transpired in the past twenty-four hours to join them in their pure glee. Yes, this super charming, incredibly handsome man had just told me that he thought about us being together, but I didn't get the sense that any of them understood just how much that had blown up everything I'd considered safe about him.

"Well, he's not mine to keep just yet," I replied.

"Oh my gosh. Reagan, why aren't you two in the same location right now so we could ask you to either hand her a drink or shake her silly?" Rebecca asked.

"Because clearly she needs something to remind her that all of this is a good thing. Do you hear that, Liv, a good thing?"

"Honestly, I was wondering the same thing myself just now," Reagan replied. "I should have taken the trip downtown."

I chuckled at Rebecca and Rae's interaction, mostly because Becs was almost eight months pregnant, so all her solutions had become alcohol based lately. Needed to decompress? Have a glass of wine. Just came back from a run? Quench your thirst with some bourbon. Had your new best friend admit that he found you irresistible? Wash that realization down with a nice cocktail! It was almost as if she needed us all to be perpetually tipsy for her since she still had another few more months before she could partake in any spirits on her own.

Also, I'd learned a lot about her since their first trip to London in April. Rebecca and I had initially bonded over the four (me) and five (her) years we had on the other ladies, plus the fact that we were the two who hadn't gone to college with them, but our shared love of all things *Housewives* with no judgment whatsoever truly made our friendship something I'd come to cherish. Her no-nonsense takes on those shows lined right up with her input today.

"I have a martini right beside me," I said, still laughing. "That doesn't make up for the fact that this has changed everything."

"Okay, okay, we hear you," Robin chimed in.

"But what are you so scared of, *cher*?" Reagan asked.

"Right, because I've never seen you look this happy about anyone. Not even when you told me about David that night that we went out for our first drinks. And definitely not during the times when we were all hanging out together."

"And that's what makes this so scary, Rob," I said, clutching my almost-empty martini glass out of sight of the camera.

Maybe Becs has the right idea after all. I might need more drinks to truly keep having this conversation.

"I was with David for two years and never felt like this about him. But that was okay because I knew if we ever broke up, it wouldn't hurt as much. And I was right. For whatever break or breakup David and I are on right now, I've been relatively okay about it. With Thomas, it's only been a few months and yet I'm scared that if I let myself like him as much as I could, I'm just setting myself up for failure."

I blinked my eyes a few times to stop the tears trying to fall out of them and took the last gulp of my drink before I carried on.

"You're all in relationships now, so maybe you can't relate, but my track record with men hasn't been that great. The few times when I've actually liked them and dared to open up and let them get a taste of the real Olivia Robinson—not just the perfect image of a girlfriend that I know how to play when I want to— they've run away so fast they could have battled Usain Bolt. Even David…he stuck around for a while, sure, but he found a way to let me know I was a lot of everything he didn't want in a partner. I don't know if I have it in me to go through that again, especially not with Thomas. It just…it would be too hard of a thing to come back from. Besides the fact that even if none of that were true, I'm leaving in less than a year. How many international romances do you all know that have worked out?"

Robin zipped up her overnight bag and plopped down onto the lavender tufted trunk in front of her bed just as I got up to walk to my kitchen so I could make myself another martini.

"Can I jump in since my relationship is less than a year in?" she asked, and briefly paused until she received my silent head nod to continue.

I'd just put my glass on the counter and grabbed the jar of olives out of the fridge when I heard the break after her question and realized it wasn't exactly rhetorical. She didn't need much beyond the head nod, however, because she quickly jumped right back in as I began pouring the gin into my jigger to measure out the right amount for my mixture.

"You know I get how scary it is to open yourself up to someone when you've experienced nothing but disappointment in your past. But Thomas is a new person, first of all, so I encourage you to do what you asked of me when Craig and I first started dating—give him a chance without putting all the pain from others onto him. You've already acknowledged how different it's been with him, where the two of you have gotten a chance to really learn each other before jumping into anything super fast. Annnd he's not rushing you! I'm still amazed that you both stopped yourselves last night. Craig and I were on each other like white on rice the night of our first date!"

"Rob, eww, that's her brother. C'mon!" Jenn screamed out, interrupting Robin's giggles down memory lane.

"Sorry! I'm just saying…the fact that *he* was the one

to say no last night because he could tell you still had your reservations tells me how much he cares about you. And maybe, just maybe, the man likes you precisely for all the reasons those other guys haven't. It's kind of hard to keep everything that makes you special under wraps as much as you all have been communicating nonstop."

"Now, Rob is right about that," Jenn added. "I know we're all thankful we've gotten to know you as more than just Robin's friend. Maybe give the guy some credit that he knows what he's getting into and he likes it?"

"Oy, I'm great with friends," I said, sitting back down in my drawing room, my new martini in hand. "That's where I shine. And what I thought he and I were."

Reagan pursed her lips and eyed me suspiciously through the camera. "Did you, though? Because from the moment you told me and Jake about him, you couldn't stop grinning. I don't look like that about any of my friends."

"Rude!" Rebecca jumped in. "You better glow when talking about us."

"Well, y'all are different. You know what I mean, and she does, too!"

"Okay, so friends who find each other attractive," I admitted.

"Mmm-hmm. That ain't friends, *cher*. That's denial with a splash of fear. And if Chrissy were on this call, she'd tell you, *mana*, we don't do *vidas cautelosas* around here."

"Yeah, she would!" Robin shouted out, punctuating her statement with a loud clap.

"And then she'd use that booming, raspy voice of

hers and force Reagan to get down to the East Village ASAP and bring some tequila and nachos with her," added Jennifer.

"No lie," Reagan admitted. "That is definitely what she would have suggested."

We all laughed in unison, and I watched them as they remembered their friend fondly. I had no idea what it was like to mourn a close friend and wasn't looking forward to learning it anytime soon. But I was amazed at how they kept her alive in their conversation and their interactions regularly. Indeed, while I'd been spending more one-on-one time with each of the ladies lately, any time we were collectively together, Chrissy's name inevitably came up—and always in a good way. It was as if their union wasn't complete without her. This reminded me that I owed Nneka and Tracy some returned calls, too. *I might do that later when I order some food for the evening*, I thought.

"Okay," I said, throwing up my hands. "I will certainly take all your points into consideration. Now, I don't want to take up much more of this call for my drama. Can we get back to talking about Palm Springs? We've only got a week before we all see each other, and I've never been to California, so I need to know what to plan for ahead of time."

"Oh, that's easy," Reagan said, chiming in. "Think casual chic. Pack light. Basically bring bathing suits and club attire—wait, do you have that with you, or do we need to go shopping?"

"Lord, Rae—you're always looking for a reason to go shopping." Jenn laughed.

"What? I'm just offering my services if they are needed."

"I actually could use a small shopping trip," I said meekly. "I brought one swimsuit with me from London, but it sounds like I need more."

"See?"

Reagan stuck her tongue out at Jenn, who rolled her eyes off to the side in response.

"Reagan never misses a shopping trip, but she is right about packing light," Robin added. "We're having all the bachelorette decorations and other little treats shipped there, so no one has to worry about that. And you know, we already purchased the tables for when we go out on the town. So there's not much else to prepare for, really."

"Well, it's California, so prepare yourself for the cultural difference," Becs chimed in. "Palm Springs is nothing like the UK. But other than that, you should be good."

"Okay, all very good to know! I'm actually really excited for this trip," I said, turning my attention back to Jenn. "I can't thank you enough for inviting me."

"Please," she replied. "I couldn't have you in America and not be there with us. What kind of monster would that make me? Plus, I already know we're going to have such a good time, and you being there with us is just going to be the icing on the cake. It also sounds like we'll need some real face time, and not the virtual kind, to make sure you're not messing things up with our new best friend Thomas."

"Wait, how did we get back onto him?" I asked.

"Get used to it, *cher*," Reagan interjected, laughing. "This is how things go in this friend group. Once they know fear is the only thing stopping you from going after what you want, they will wear you down until you give in. Ask me how I know."

"And you're living the life with your man and your fancy job that was made just for you, so no complaining, missy," Robin replied.

"Yeah, yeah. I'm just saying. They are relentless."

"I think you should be using the word 'we' here," I said, amused at how they'd all effectively flipped the conversation back to Thomas despite my best efforts to re-center Jenn and her trip. And of all people, it had started with the bachelorette herself!

"Who, me? You think I'm relentless?"

"You made a plan to get us together after only hearing about our first interaction in the airport," I replied.

"Oh, well that's just being a good friend, no?"

I stared back at her with a *girl, now you know what that means* look on my face, and she giggled in return.

"Well, whatever, I guess I stand with my girls, then. We…firmly believe in 'what's the best that could happen,' and *we*…make no apologies about that."

"Say it!" Robin chimed in.

"Are you going to see him again before Palm Springs?" Jenn asked.

"I think so. This morning when we were texting, we started talking about meeting up after work one day this week."

"Wow, way to bury the lede!" Reagan screamed out.

"It's not in stone," I protested. "It's just an idea we floated."

"Mmm-hmm."

"Well, I, for one, am very excited about our next round of story time," said Rebecca. "Let's make sure we have time in the schedule in Palm Springs for that, please."

"Done and done," Robin replied.

I drank another sip of my martini, shaking my head at the women who I'd come to all call "friend." Robin had warned me just how much this group was always at the ready to cheer their people on. That had been a warm welcome when I'd needed the boost of confidence to say yes to my year in New York. But now that it was about something that didn't have to do with work or my career, I had to admit, I was a lot more uncomfortable with it. Still, I could appreciate a friend group filled with lots of strong opinions and love, and it seemed like I was stuck with them in the same way Thomas kept saying I was stuck with him.

"All right, ladies, before we sign off, can we make a toast to the fiancée of the group and this banging-ass trip we've got planned for her?" Robin chimed in, interrupting me out of my thoughts.

"Yes, yes. A perfect idea," Rebecca replied as she lifted her cranberry-spritzer mocktail into the camera.

One by one, each of us did the same, until all you could see in the chat were glasses filled with different colored drinks and some faces melting into the background.

"To an amazing upcoming weekend in Palm Springs," Robin began. "We're all so so happy for you and Nick, Jenny. And while we can't wait to stand up with you to celebrate your love on your wedding day, this weekend is our chance to cheer on the incredible woman Nick is soon going to get the privilege of calling his wife."

"And let me tell you, he's got a baaaaad mama jama on his hands, okay!" added Reagan.

"She's right," Robin continued. "So, here's to a real one. To the heartbeat of our friend group and the woman who taught us all how to bloom where we're planted. Palm Springs is going to be so litty!"

Chapter Ten

Even though I was head down on the latest portfolio proposal that needed my review, I knew it was on or about 5:30 p.m. as soon as I heard the all-too-familiar hustle and bustle from the cubicles near my office. Over the past couple months, in fact, I'd learned all the telltale signs of various hours in the day at my job, never even needing to look at the gold, sunburst-style wall clock that hung near the canvas image of me symbolically waving goodbye to London.

Around 8:30 a.m., I'd normally hear the rush of people walking onto the floor, telling stories about their evenings and sighing about all the work they still needed to accomplish. At about 10:00 a.m., the floor would seem eerily quiet, but only because most of the staff had inevitably either started congregating in the kitchen area for their morning coffee breaks or were in various meetings throughout the building. No later than about 1:00 p.m., I usually heard puttering footsteps as groups of people decided if they were going to eat lunch somewhere in the neighborhood or simply heat up whatever they'd brought from home. And somewhere around 5:30 p.m. usually signaled the time for the mass exodus, leaving only the few masochists like me and Walter to close down the floor each day.

Every once in a while, I stepped out of my office during these daily interactions to partake in the activities with the rest of the teams—feel like I was actually part of the portfolio crew. But more often than I'd like to admit, I spent my time like a working Sleeping Beauty, enclosed in my glass office until someone (usually Wendy or Julie) burst in and forced me to take a sanity break.

The last of the telltale signs was the sound of Walter's feet as he stomped down the hallway toward my office anytime between 6:00 and 6:30 p.m.—something that had become a sort of regular routine for him, especially in the last couple weeks. The first time I'd heard him clobbering around, I'd thought it to be an indication of his anger, but no. He just seemed to have a heavy walk, which was quite interesting considering he was maybe one hundred sixty-five pounds wet and probably no taller than five foot nine. But Walter did almost everything big—commanded the room when he walked in, paced up and down in his office during calls and stomped throughout the floor when he was simply walking from one office to the next. It was a far cry from the meek and mild man I'd met on day one, but then again, I'd also learned by now that our first interaction had been more of an anomaly than the norm. Walter was the man in this office, and he knew it.

Since that first day, he and I had actually formed a pretty great thought partnership. Not to say we were the best of friends—he was still my boss, obviously— but he'd meant it when he'd said that he wanted my hands on and ideas represented in most of the proposals and strategy briefs by the time I left New York. And because Walter expected mountains to move when he said so, he'd really only given everyone about two or three weeks after my start date before he'd begun consistently asking anyone who'd sent him something to approve if I'd seen it first.

"Did Olivia see this?" he'd ask, straight-faced with serious eyes and hands tucked into his pockets until he received a yes.

If he got a no, his answer was simple: "She sees it before I do."

Within a week, he never had to say those six words again.

It was a great testament to his trust in me. It also meant I had a lot of work on my plate all the time.

Just like clockwork, I heard Walter's feet coming toward me. *Must be about 6:00 p.m.*, I theorized, looking up just in time to see him standing at my door with a big grin on his face. That usually amounted to one thing—at least a few more hours of work for us both. Instinctually, I grabbed my phone to get ready to text Thomas that I might have to cancel our date.

"Olivia, my favorite," Walter said, sauntering in and plopping down into one of the chairs facing my desk.

"No, Walter, you can't butter me up today," I replied.

"I have plans. I know it's hard to believe, but I really can't be here with you until nine o'clock tonight."

"Oh, perfect—this is exactly what I came in here to talk about."

"My plans?"

"No, Olivia, do I look like Wendy to you?" he asked, clearly taken aback by my suggestion.

I laughed at his confusion, but he wasn't alone. I was equally curious about where this conversation was going.

"Of course not," I replied, trying to hold back my chuckles while a quick vision of Walter with bright red hair flashed before my eyes. "Please continue."

"Thank you," he said, leaning back into the chair so that he could sit in a wide stance comfortably.

It was something I noticed a lot of American men did—white, Black and otherwise. I could only guess that it made them feel powerful somehow.

"You know, I've been loving the work coming across my desk lately, and I attribute that all to you. I think you've been challenging our teams to listen to their clients and not just deliver proposals and updates that seem tried and true, but ones that are tailored to their unique needs and have proven results in other spaces."

"Thanks, Walter. I really appreciate that—"

"But that's not what I came in here to talk to you about," he said, interrupting my interruption of him. "I wanted to talk to you today about work-life balance."

"Excuse me?" I asked, now even more confused about what he was blubbering on about.

Still seated in the chair across from me, Walter leaned toward me so that his elbows were almost to his knees. I wasn't sure if this was his way of trying to indicate closeness without being *too close*, but it was an odd thing to look at, mostly because he didn't exactly seem like the kind of person one would want to have this conversation with. Data. Numbers. Winning. That was Walter's MO. But work-life balance?

It felt far-fetched, and even he seemed uncomfortable bringing it up. I also suddenly noticed that he'd rolled up his sleeves to about halfway up his forearms before coming to my office in some sort of odd attempt at trying to portray an "everyday man."

What is going on?

"Work-life balance," he repeated.

"What about it?"

"Well, my fiancée reminded me this morning that I needed to be doing a better job at it, and I realized when I didn't see you leaving with the rest of the office, you probably do, too."

"To be fair, Walter—"

"I know, I'm usually the reason for your late-night stays, but not tonight. Tonight, I want you to go home, or I guess to whatever plans you have on a Wednesday night."

"It's a date," I replied, laughing at how uncomfortable even the littlest bit of gossip made him.

I could tell he was holding back another quip about not being Wendy, and it made me laugh that much more.

"Well, good for you," he said awkwardly. "So, this is me…telling you to go, you know, do that."

I eyed him as he squirmed in his seat, clearly ready for this conversation to end now that I'd taken it from just big, bold Walter giving me permission to take some time for myself. I also knew he was waiting for my silent head nod before he would inevitably jump out of the chair and go plodding back to his office, but I had one last question before I gave him what he wanted.

"Okay, Walter," I said. "I'm curious, though. Fiancée? How do you have time for that kind of commitment?"

I half expected him to fall out of the chair when he processed my question. Instead, I saw a fire in Walter's eyes that I usually only caught when he received confirmation that someone had exceeded their fundraising goal.

"Oh, that's easy," he said, perking up in his seat. "I got lucky and found someone who has no desire to change me or lessen my ambitions. She gets that some nights I'm going to be working late, and she doesn't judge me for it or question whether I love her because of it. And to make sure she knows I appreciate her, every once in a while, I actually leave the office before 6:30 p.m. and surprise her with something special. Tonight, it's tickets to her favorite Broadway play. She's watched it probably eight times now, with multiple different people. And yet she cries like it's her first time any time she sees it."

"Wow," I said, listening to Walter in awe. "That's special. And rare."

"Maybe. But I think people like me—and you—need someone like a Sarah in our lives. She keeps me balanced and challenges me in all the best ways."

Walter paused and nodded his head toward me.

"Do you think the person you're going on a date with tonight has the same potential?"

"Hard to know, really," I replied with a deep sigh. "It's only our second date, or really first—I don't know. But if precedent has anything to do with it, my chances aren't good."

"Well, if you'd told me a year ago that I would be talking to my senior consultant about work-life balance, I would have laughed in your face. Things change sometimes. Unexpectedly."

"That they do. You're very right."

"I'm always right, Olivia," Walter said with a wink, finally rising out of his chair. "Now, close that computer down and get to your date. I insist."

"Aye, Captain," I joked as he walked out of my door, stomping his way back down the hallway.

I turned my phone onto its back and unlocked the screen, noting to myself that it was now 6:10 p.m. If I hurried, I could make a quick outfit change in the bathroom and still make it to Thomas before our 7:00 p.m. class began. All I really had to do was freshen up and change into the dark blue jeans I'd brought with me, along with my classic Tommy Hilfiger shirt. I'd purposely chosen my double-breasted plaid oversize women's blazer to wear to work, figuring that it would make for a great work-to-date transition—same with my green velvet Taro Ishida slingback heels that were adorned with gold metal studs plus a gold ring and gold leaf embellishment on the pointed toes.

Hi! See you at 7, still? I typed as quickly as I could while walking to the restroom.

Thomas instantly replied.

Thomas: Yep. You'll know it's me because I'll be the guy with the smile that won't go away when you walk up.

Me: Please! I'll know it's you because of the way I can't stop smiling when I see you.

That, too, he replied.

I'll see you soon, I texted back, unsure of what else to say and in a desperate crunch for time anyway.

Thomas must not have known what to say, either, as he simply liked my reply with the thumbs-up reaction, letting me know he received it in the most millennial way possible.

As soon as I walked into the ladies' restroom, I practically threw my phone onto the counter, rushing to make my switchover happen in less than ten to fifteen minutes.

You got this, I said to myself while looking in the mirror. *Or something like that.*

Exactly forty minutes later, my Uber pulled up to the Great Jones Distilling Co. at 6:53 p.m. The first thing I noticed was how regal the exterior of the building looked with its three and a half stories of all-black paint and gold fixtures. Flanked by two grayish-tan skyscraper buildings, the facade stood out immediately, making for the kind of grand appearance that Manhattan's first whiskey distillery since Prohibition would necessarily demand. The second thing that caught my attention was Thomas, already standing outside, waiting on me with his matching all-black outfit and a fifty-thousand-watt smile.

"You look amazing," he said as he gently took my hand and helped me step out of the car.

I was instantly struck by the fact that I could somehow still see the muscles in his forearms underneath the thick black wool coat he was wearing. These were the kind of forearms that were made for scooping a ready-and-willing woman up and carrying her to his bed.

That, of course, sent flashbacks running through my head of how crazy good it had felt when he'd gripped me tightly while we kissed under the moonlight just days before, and I instantly felt myself grow wet.

In truth, I hadn't stopped thinking about how Thomas's lips had felt as they'd enveloped mine since then. So I knew I was going to have to work hard to keep my composure on this date. Focusing on things like his perfectly sculpted forearms and how my hand seemed to fit in his, like they were made to seamlessly cup each other, wasn't going to make that easy.

"You look pretty dapper yourself, eh," I replied as I stepped fully out of the car.

"Well, it is our first date, so…"

Thomas's one lone but incredibly intoxicating dimple peeked out as he looked back at me and waited for my reply.

"Is it?" I asked. "So, the Christmas tour through the city didn't count?"

"No, definitely not."

"I feel like if it ends with the kind of kiss that you left me to ponder over all night, that automatically qualifies as a date, no?"

"Ha ha, well, you might be onto something there," he replied, chuckling off to the side. "But to be fair, we had specifically called that a non-date. I want you to be very clear that this is a real one."

Thomas stared at me intensely, holding my attention until I found myself squirming under his gaze. I could barely breathe sometimes when he looked at me because everything in my body felt like it was being tethered to him, and so my lungs were waiting on his to even say *go* before they moved on their own. This was one of those occasions. It just so happened that the last time, I was almost ready to give myself to him in the middle of the street in front of my flat.

"Okay," I said softly, releasing the tension in my body with short, slow and steady breaths. "I am crystal clear."

"Good," he replied. "Now, let's go inside so we don't miss the start of the class. I've been wanting to check this out for a while now."

"Oh, I see! So, I just gave you a good excuse, then?" I joked as we walked through the gold revolving-door entrance.

"Yep, sure did. The best excuse."

We quickly joined the rest of the evening's mixology class as we all oohed and ahhed our way through a guided tour of the distillery, followed by a four-part tasting of their signature bourbon. By the time that was done, we were treated to a few bites from a premade charcuterie board, which included smoked almonds, marinated olives, dark-chocolate pieces and some of the best cheese and prosciutto I'd ever tasted. If that wasn't enough, they also gave us a smoked old-fashioned to sip on while our mixologist for the night led us in a hands-on course on how to make two of Great Jones's house-made cocktails—the Saratoga Julep and the Great Jones Rye Manhattan.

As the kick from the old-fashioned began warming up my insides, I realized I'd worked through my lunch hour earlier, so I was officially surviving off two cups of coffee, a granola bar and the few bites to eat from the charcuterie board. *Maybe that's why the cheese tastes so good?* I wondered. Either way, I knew I was going to eventually need more than that to coat my stomach if I wanted to show up to work at 7:30 a.m. like normal—and without a massive headache.

I finished my first drink and looked toward Thomas so we could toast with the juleps we'd made, giving my best attempt at making flirty eyes at him. To my surprise, however, the next sound I heard was him bursting into laughter and curling over with tears threatening to fall from his eyes.

"What?" I asked. "Did I miss something?"

"Your eyes are so glassy right now," he said. "You never told me you were a lightweight."

"I'm not." I laughed, suddenly understanding what he found so funny.

"The eyes don't lie, love."

"No, really. It's not that. I actually just realized that I didn't eat much today, so, you know, the liquor doesn't have anything to soak it up."

"Mmmm, okay, see now that's good information to know. We'll have to make sure we get you a chopped cheese before you go home tonight. In the meantime, let's try to make sure your eyes focus on one thing at a time so they don't get stuck crossing over."

"OMG, it's not that bad!" I said, playfully slapping him on his broad shoulders.

"I don't know. I wish you could see what I see."

"Oh, really?" I asked. "Well, tell me, what do you see?"

"The most beautiful woman I've ever laid eyes on…"

"Thomas," I interrupted.

"Barely keeping her eyes open while she desperately tries to stay awake to make her next cocktail," he continued, laughing even harder.

"I'm so glad you're enjoying this," I replied. "It feels great to be the entertainment tonight."

"Nah, I just enjoy spending time with you, so the laughs come easy, that's all."

Damn it, there goes those swoony, spine-chilling feelings again. What is it that's holding me back from giving in to them again? I asked myself.

Oh right, I remembered as I took another sip of my drink. I didn't see how he fit into all my plans. That pesky little fact. But I really did enjoy our time together.

"Same actually," I admitted. "Which is why I'm so mad at myself for not eating earlier. I do kinda wish things were a little less hazy right now, to be honest."

"See? I'm glad you're finally telling the truth. I told you the eyes don't lie."

We both laughed as I bumped the side of his hip and licked my bottom lip to keep from biting it—something I was all too aware I did whenever I wanted mine to be on his. Then, just as quickly, we fell back into the rhythm of the class, following along as our mixologist walked us step-by-step through our final cocktail.

"Tell me more about this butchered-cheese thing you mentioned earlier?" I asked as we neared the end of the class.

"A chopped cheese," he said chuckling.

"Right, that."

"Wait, this isn't your first time hearing of a chopped cheese, is it?"

"Is it, like, an American delicacy or something?"

"I mean, kinda!" he said, stepping back shocked with a smirk on his face. "I would argue it's at least a New York delicacy and the best, classic late-night food option in the city. I'm surprised no one's brought you to get one yet."

"Well, that makes sense because I don't often find myself out late at night. You know my bed starts calling my name around 11:00 p.m."

"No, I know. I just figured that you and your girls would have partaken in it by now, especially with Reagan living uptown."

"Nope. We have had a late-night slice of pizza!" I replied, probably a little too enthusiastically.

"Okay, I mean, that's New Yorker 101. But once you've had a chopped cheese, I think you'll find it to be even better."

"All right. Well, I trust you, so I'm down."

The growing smile on Thomas's face after my reply could have lit up the night sky if we were outside, and I made a note to myself just how much I enjoyed being the cause of it.

"It's a good thing I'm here to help you dig in a little deeper," he said.

I smiled back, probably just as glassy-eyed as before, while I watched him down his last drink and call us a car for our next location.

A few minutes later, we were all bundled up again to brave the cold, December air and waving goodbye to all the temporary friends we'd made during the class as we rushed to catch our Uber before the car pulled off. Together, we climbed in, with Thomas right behind me, once again shooting chills up my spine as he lightly grazed the small of my back to guide me in. Once we were both settled into our seats, I leaned my head back and attempted to calm down the anticipation building within my body—of both Thomas's continued touch and this food he'd been bragging about for the past twenty minutes.

"I know this is very out of the way, and you can get a chopped cheese from almost any bodega now," he said, turning toward me as our car curved onto First Avenue and then FDR to make our way to East Harlem. "But if you're going to have your first one with me, it's gotta be from the OG."

Thomas was already right about one thing. We were taking a major detour for this thing, so I hoped it was worth it for us to travel twenty minutes away when we probably could have taken a long walk from the distillery back to my apartment.

"It's okay," I replied, facing him in the back seat of the car, my head still relying on the mounting anticipation to keep me awake. "At this point, you've talked it up so much, I wouldn't want it from anywhere else. I do have to know, though, what makes it so special?"

"To me? Or to New York?"

"I guess both."

"Well, for me, I equate my first chopped cheese with the day I knew I'd make it here," Thomas said, sitting up straight and turning his entire body toward mine. "You know, I came here so fresh and green and got a very quick awakening that life wasn't going to be a straight shot to the top. After about a few months, I'd started questioning whether I had what it took to be a 'New York lawyer,' whatever that meant. The job was stressing me out, I was struggling to make any kind of headway with the few clients the firm had entrusted me with, and I just was feeling really down. But thankfully, a few of my boys noticed, said, 'Bruh, let's go out for some drinks,' and by the end of the night, they had reminded me I wasn't alone trying to navigate this new world on my own. We were also very drunk, though, so they took me to Hajji's. We got some chopped cheese sandwiches—with grilled onions, lettuce, tomato, ketchup and mayonnaise, like you're supposed to— and I swear, every bite felt like it was changing my life."

"Wow," I replied, in awe of everything he'd just divulged—the connection with his friends, the vulnerability he'd shown in telling me this story, the way he made the food sound...

"I'm kind of at a loss for words."

"That's because you're drunk." He laughed.

"Maybe a little tipsy, but you know that's not why."

"No, I know."

We looked at each other with that unsaid understanding we'd had since our first conversation in the airport. That had been the moment I'd realized Thomas got me in a fundamental way that was both scary and refreshing. Now it was my turn. I'd had almost every single emotion he'd expressed (and the ones he hadn't) since moving here, too, so I knew how important that night must have been for him. After all, he was still in the city years later, thriving beyond, what I was sure, was even his wildest imagination. I also knew he probably still secretly had those moments where he questioned if he deserved it all.

"Do you still have moments like that at your firm?" I asked, bracing myself for an inevitable shutdown in his vulnerability tank. That was what every other man did whenever they dared to try to be open with me before.

"Yeah—of course," he said, drawing me toward him. "I psych myself out all the time, thinking today's going to be the day I don't do everything perfectly and it'll give them a reason to elevate the next guy before me. Or sometimes, I'll deal with those kinda gray situations where I wonder if they only put me on a specific file because they needed a Black man on it, or if a client requests a different attorney, there's that small voice in my head that makes me question if it's because they aren't the Black man from Philly, you know. But at the end of the day, it all just makes me go harder. I get to prove all of those doubts in my head wrong every time I show up and excel."

"Yeah, I know."

I leaned into him, snuggling myself into the nook under Thomas's arm and next to his torso. As he wrapped his left arm around me, I took in the deepest, most calming breath, preparing myself to enjoy the security of his embrace as we rode the next fifteen minutes up the motorway. In a perfect world, this could be my existence every night—just basking in the comfort of his presence without any worry for the future. Openly talking about the good and bad parts of our jobs; pushing each other to be the best and to find balance, just like Walter and Sarah. *If only*, I thought, momentarily stopping myself from even thinking the rest of that idea…but eventually, it came to me anyway. *If only women like me got to have that kind of joy, maybe I'd trust this more.*

"I wish you could see yourself through my eyes, too, you know," I whispered as they slowly drifted shut.

"The glassy ones that can barely stay open?"

"Yeah." I chuckled. "And the ones who see just how amazing you are."

Chapter Eleven

"**Y**ou guys finally made it!"

A couple days later and after several hours of flying across the United States, Reagan and I pulled up to the villa we'd all booked for Jenn's bachelorette weekend in Palm Springs. To our great delight, Jenn, Becs and Robin came running out of the front door—drinks in hand—to greet us just as our cab swung into the driveway.

"We're heeeeeere!" Reagan screamed out in response, practically hopping out of the car without any concern that she would trip in her tan three-inch sandals that criss-crossed at her ankles. *"Laissez les bons temps rouler!"*

In awe, I watched as she grabbed her matching tan tote and took off in a short sprint to grab and hug on each one of them. It was like watching an Olympic track racer come off the starting block—if they had chunky heels and cutoff shorts on. Meanwhile, I stayed behind to tip the driver after he'd pulled our luggage out of the trunk to let the original close-knit crew have a moment before I intruded as the person who was still building a friendship with most of them. Sure, I'd been invited on their special trip, but I understood the friendship hierarchy in play and respected it.

If Reagan's all-out run toward them hadn't told me that, then the fact that I'd clearly missed the memo on what they'd all meant by "casual chic" certainly did. To a person, they each looked incredibly elegant, somehow complementing each other's style without any of them dressing fully alike, and there I was—dressed cute, yes, but nothing like them. Reagan, who had paired her cutoff jean shorts and heels with a tan button-down blouse that she'd let casually flow into a one-corner tuck into her shorts was also "casually" rocking a bunch of gold accessories—multiple-sized bracelets, two slender necklaces that dropped down her chest and slightly grazed the only two buttons she'd closed on the blouse, sunglasses that also matched her skin tone and a black-and-gold belt that pulled it all together. To top off the 'fit, she wore a red-and-tan headband, which pulled her long, wavy curls off her face, and matching red nail polish on her hands and feet. But I'd been traveling all day with her, so that wasn't surprising.

It was the way the others matched her *Housewives* swag that let me know I was going to need to step my game up the rest of the weekend. This was why I'd asked about attire when we'd FaceTimed the other night, but I also should have remembered that Robin was the same person who'd shown up to my flat for a girls' night in with a matching two-piece nude-pink lounge set complete with knit joggers and a crop top. So I should have guessed that her best friends would have a similar idea of "casual." True to that realization, the Palm Springs version of Destiny's Child was dressed far more appropriately for a fancy brunch than a day of travel. Like Reagan, Robin was also wearing jean shorts, in more of an acid-washed color that fell around mid-thigh on her, but that was about where the casualness ended. She paired hers with a dark coral blouse that tied in the front but hung loose in the back so that the bottom of it fell past her shorts, along with some gold slip-on kitten-heel sandals that any older Hollywood diva would have absolutely adored.

Rebecca was giving *pregnant holiday chic* with a black satin slip dress that fell about mid-calf on her and showed off her ginormous baby bump in all the best ways. With it, she wore a light jean jacket, bedazzled flat sandals and a tan fedora that actually really worked on her—despite the fact that no one had looked good in fedoras since the early 2000s.

And of course, the lady of the weekend stood out the most, with her flowy full-length white halter dress that literally grazed the ground as she moved and somehow didn't seem to pick up any dirt. The high-necked sleeveless halter cut looked amazing with her dark brown pixie-cut hair, statement earrings and crystal clear heels that had a striking gold stiletto that looked like it could be a dagger if you weren't careful.

Meanwhile, I'd at least got the jeans memo—wearing shorts that were not quite cutoffs but shorter than Rob's, paired with a short-sleeved scooped-neck black blouse and gladiator sandals that wrapped around my calves— but I clearly needed more *oomph* to fit in with these girls. I made a note to myself to do better tomorrow.

As the driver pulled off, leaving me with our bags, Robin came bouncing toward me with two glasses in her hands, followed by Reagan, who presumably finally remembered that she didn't have hers with her.

"So sorry, Liv," Reagan said as she jumped in front of Robin and grabbed her medium-sized luggage with the rollers on it. "I didn't mean to leave you with the bags—I just got so excited to see my girls."

"It's okay—I get it."

"No, it's not," she replied sincerely. "Definitely let me know how much you tipped him, and I got you on half, okay?"

As Reagan began rolling her luggage to the front door, Robin stepped in and wrapped her arms around me tightly, squeezing and rocking me for what felt like a few minutes.

"Livvieeeee," she said, dragging the nickname she had for me out into two long syllables.

After a few more shakes within the hug, she loosened her grip and handed me one of the drinks. "It's so good to see you, friend. London hasn't been the same without you."

"I know this is going to sound bad, but I'm really happy to hear that," I admitted somewhat shamelessly. "I miss it and you so very much."

"Doesn't sound bad to me at all! I'm the one who's been hoping you enjoy your time in New York but not so much that you decide to stay. You know I hear all the rumblings in the office. You're killing it, which I knew you would, but still, I get so worried they are going to make you an offer you can't refuse and convince you to stay."

"Ha! Thanks, sis," I replied. "But you don't have to

worry about that. I'm loving my time in the States so far, but London is home. Brixton is home, you know? I don't want to be too far from there for too long."

"Okayyy, I hear you. I also know what it's like to move to a place and realize it might be your *new* home. Don't forget you're saying this to the woman who moved from America, fell in love with your brother and now can't see herself living anywhere else anytime soon."

"Your situation was very different. You wanted to find love in London—that's not in my plans."

"And yet…that little sparkle that shines on your face when anyone says Thomas's name… I'm not saying it's love," she said, throwing up her hands in defense before I could counter her. "But it looks familiar, that's all."

I chuckled awkwardly and sniffed the glass to try to move us to a different conversation. I hadn't yet told anyone how much I'd loved everything about the date he and I had gone on just two days before and how safe I'd felt in his arms as we'd ridden to and from East Harlem that night, mostly because I wasn't ready to think about what that meant for me going forward. But I knew if I engaged Rob any further, it was going to come up, and I certainly wasn't ready to dissect it with her before I even knew what I wanted.

"Enough about all that," I said. "More importantly, what's in this drink you just gave me?"

"Oooh! So, it's a new concoction I made just for our trip called Jenn's Sweet Treats. It's pineapple and mango juice mixed with white rum and tequila with just a splash of champagne to cut the sweetness."

"Robin! Are you trying to kill us?"

"I promise, no, but just try it! It tastes so good."

She raised the glass to my lips, and as I sampled

it, I knew just how dangerous it was going to be. You could barely tell it had any liquor in it despite the fact that she'd just told me three were in it—a sure setup for failure. With the conversation successfully veered, the two of us began walking toward the rest of the ladies, who were still amazingly waiting outside of the villa's front door.

"Okay, I hope you have lots of food inside," I replied, taking another sip as we neared the others.

"Yes, of course—there's a whole spread waiting on the counter. I don't need anyone getting sick on the first day. I've got too many things planned for this weekend for that to happen."

"Ohhh nooo," Reagan cried out as we came within earshot. "Did I hear Rob just say the dreaded 'plans' word?"

"Don't start with me, Rae." She laughed in response.

"No, c'mon, we all know you can go a teensy bit overboard with trip planning if you're not careful."

"That's true," added Rebecca as she carefully but lovingly grabbed my arms and pulled me into a baby-filled embrace, whispering how good I looked before she continued her comments to Robin. "Do we need to remind you of the itinerary you made when we first came to visit you in London? It was at least fifteen items on your list. I swear, the only reason we convinced you to narrow it down was because I was pregnant. Otherwise you would have had us on a very strict schedule."

"No, you don't need to remind me," Robin replied, rolling her eyes. "And this one isn't as extensive. But we needed *something*, or I know us—we'd just end up sitting around the villa all day, lounging by the pool."

"From my perspective, there's absolutely nothing

wrong with that," Jenn chimed in, peeking her head into the discussion before giving me a long hug as well. "I could use a relaxing break from the students and all their drama."

"All right, everyone, calm down," Robin began in protest. "Of course we're going to do that, too. But it's not a bachelorette weekend if we don't end up dancing on someone's table by the end of the night at least once."

"Okay, now that's true," Jenn admitted. "I do want that, too."

"Of course you do!" Robin replied.

The five of us continued laughing and joking about Robin's tendency to overplan trips as we finally stepped into the villa that was surrounded by the most fantastic mountain views I'd ever seen and yet really only took my breath away once I walked inside. With walls made of floor-to-ceiling windows covering at least three-fourths of the house, it was like our own private oasis complete with pearl-white and light wooden furnishings, a pool big enough to take laps in it and multiple lounging opportunities throughout. There was even a firepit surrounded by five white and wooden lounge chairs and a second dining table located by the pool, perfect for eating at sunset or sunrise.

"I'm down to hear your plans, babes," I interjected, admiring the scene before me while also wanting to stand up for all the overplanners everywhere. That had been one of the reasons Robin and I had bonded in the first place, so while it was fun to laugh with the crew about it, if anyone understood her need to organize the chaos in her mind, I did.

"Thanks, Liv," she said with a smile, and then quickly

took the opportunity to run to her room to grab the stapled set of papers she had at the ready.

"Yes, thanks, Liv," the other ladies repeated sarcastically.

I shrugged my shoulders in reply and waited for her return.

"Okay, it's not as bad as you all think. Just listen," Robin began as she walked back into the sitting room, clearing her throat before she proceeded. "Today, of course, we're all getting settled. I figured we could chill for a bit and have a sunset dinner outside before maybe doing some in-home karaoke to cap off the evening."

"All right, Rob," Reagan chimed in. "That sounds nice and not over-the-top at all. Maybe we were being a bit too judgy."

Robin looked back at her with an *mmm-hmm, I told you so* look and then continued reading.

"So then tomorrow, I thought we could have an early breakfast. If anyone wants to come with me to Joshua Tree, I was thinking we could leave here around 7:00 a.m. That way we're back about ten or eleven o'clock for prime pool time. Then, I figured we could go to one of the resorts that the villa is associated with. They have a bunch of different restaurants, a water park, a spa, even a swim-up bar, so we could hang there for a few hours. Note—if we want to make a spa appointment, we probably need to do that today, though. And then, we come back here and get dressed for our night out on the town, where we have table reservations at two different clubs."

As Robin took a break from reading her list, the rest of us eyed each other, stunned into silence. Now, I was all for planning, but this was even too much for me.

"Uh-uh, see? Now this is what we mean! That's too much!" Reagan cried out.

Her protest was followed by a round of mmm-hmms throughout the room.

"She's right, Rob," Jennifer added. "You know we love you, and I sooo appreciate you wanting to make my bachelorette weekend as epic as it can be, but, like, yes, there's twenty-four hours in a day, but we don't need to use them all. You know that, right?"

"What?" she asked innocently. "I didn't say we had to do *all* these things. I just threw out some sugges- tions for options!"

"*Cher*, the only things I want to do out of that whole list you just read are the pool time, the spa and the dancing on tables. All the rest of that can go." Reagan laughed. "And honestly, I don't even need the spa as long as we keep drinking these cocktails you made."

"No shade, but I agree with what she said," Jennifer added.

"Same here," Rebecca chimed in after having spent the last few minutes trying to hold back tears of laugh- ter. "I mean, did you hear yourself when you said you were leaving the house at 7:00 a.m….while on vaca- tion?"

"Well, that's just because I didn't want it to eat into the pool time! Tell me, how often are any of us going to be this close to Joshua Tree again anytime soon?" Robin asked in her defense.

She turned to me as her one last hope, but this time I couldn't help her out. While she was absolutely my connection to the group, I fully agreed with the rest of the ladies this time and was happy to see I wasn't the only one hoping this holiday would be more relaxing than anything else. I put my head down in my response before Robin could even direct her question my way, hoping it would curtail some of the sting.

"You, too, Liv?"

"Sorry, Rob," I replied softly.

"No, no, don't do that to her," Reagan said, sauntering up beside me and putting her arm around my shoulder. "You can't try to get Liv on your side because y'all met first. She's part of the whole crew now, so she gets to tell you when you're being ridiculous just like the rest of us."

Robin rolled her eyes and sighed deeply before plopping her papers onto the counter in defeat. Meanwhile, I was happy to hear Reagan say explicitly that I was legit part of their crew and have everyone agree. I hadn't realized until being around them all again in person that I'd still needed that validation, but I guessed I had and could breathe a little lighter now.

"You know what?" Rebecca asked as she walked up to Robin with the drink pitcher in her hand. "How about I take that itinerary and you take another pour of what I'm sure is an amazing drink that you've made, huh?"

Robin laughed at Rebecca's continued drinking solutions to everyone's problems in lieu of her being able to partake and grabbed the pitcher from her before complying.

"Fine!" she replied. "But you all are going to regret not going hiking two months from now when you're back home and someone randomly mentions our national parks. Mark my words."

"In what world is that happening, Robin?" Reagan asked, continuing the chorus of laughter in the room.

"Certainly not in any of ours," Jennifer interjected.

"Whatever," she replied, playfully rolling her eyes again as she filled up her glass. "Mark my words."

Robin paused momentarily and looked around the room before raising her glass high into the sky. "I guess now that I have a full glass again, we should at least toast to the start of a great weekend. Is that an okay plan for everyone?" she asked.

"Now that's a plan we can all get down with," Reagan responded.

The four of us gathered around Robin, near the grazing counter, and lifted our glasses high into the air as well.

"To Jenny," she began. "We all love you more than we could ever fully say, and we want nothing but the best for you. I hope this bachelorette weekend shows you even a snippet of that love and also brings us all even closer together."

"Cheers!" we replied in unison, and clanked our glasses together before everyone but Becs took a healthy swig of Robin's homemade concoction.

As Reagan struck up a conversation with Rebecca about what her mocktail consisted of—hulled strawberries, lemon ginger beer and a lemon slice for garnish, from what I could hear—I started making my way through the villa to find one of the remaining empty rooms to settle into. After rolling past two that were occupied, I came upon one that looked like it hadn't been touched yet and had everything I needed—a king-size bed with a white comforter, a sliding glass door that took up the whole back wall and led to the pool, and a soaking tub.

This is going to do just fine, I thought as I rolled my luggage in and sat down for a breather, taking my phone out of my back jean shorts pocket at the same time. Without overthinking myself out of it, I snapped a photo of the view from my bedroom and sent it to Thomas, letting him know that I'd made it safely.

Glad to hear, he replied just a few minutes later. I hope you have a lot of fun with your friends. But don't do anything I wouldn't do. I know how y'all like to get down on bachelorette trips.

Well, I texted back, there do seem to be plans for table dancing at some point.

And what makes you think that's something I haven't done? he asked.

Oh, I'm sorry, let me not put you in a box lol, I replied.

Thomas: Yes, you really shouldn't. I've still got a lot of surprises up my sleeve.

I smiled reading Thomas's messages and thought back to Robin's comment about how my face lit up when someone mentioned his name. If they could see it now, I was sure I'd be getting clowned. I texted back, trying my hand at flirting.

Me: Now, see, if there's one thing I fully believe, it's that. I already told you that you never cease to surprise me.

Good, he answered. And I don't plan on stopping anytime soon.

I clutched my phone in my hand and fell backward onto the bed, my cheeks burning from a grin that wouldn't disappear. *What am I going to do about this man?* I wondered. I guessed time would tell.

Chapter Twelve

The next day, to no one's shock, not a single soul woke up by 7:00 a.m. to join Robin on her hiking excursion. What *was* surprising, however, was when we all crawled out of bed, slightly hungover from hours of karaoke the night before, and learned that she hadn't gone, either. Seated around the grazing counter, we were passing around coffee mugs when Robin walked into the sitting room, still in her pajamas, at 9:00 a.m.

"Robin?" Jennifer asked, stopping in her tracks as if she'd just seen a ghost.

"In the flesh," she deadpanned, rubbing her eyes with one hand while putting out the other so that someone could pass her a coffee mug as well.

"But what happened to Joshua Tree?" Reagan asked.

"Well," she hesitated. "You guys might have been right about me going overboard with that one. Plus, I didn't want to be all the way out there while you all were here. I want to be where you are."

"Awwww, that's sooo sweet," Jenn replied, forming her hands into the shape of a heart and covering her chest to show how much love she was feeling in the moment.

"And the time difference probably got real this morning, too, right?" Reagan interjected with a smirk.

"That, too."

Robin shrugged her shoulders as she clutched her large white coffee mug and walked to the Keurig machine in hopes that it would help to bring her back to life.

"Aaaaand someone might have been overcompensating because she misses her man?" Rebecca interjected.

It was one of those questions that was really more of a statement, but her voice rose up an octave or two higher at the end to make it sound like she maybe didn't mean it definitively. We all knew she did, however.

"Okay, don't push it." Robin laughed. "But maybe a little of that, too."

"Well, whatever the reason, I'm glad you stayed," I said, chiming in after taking a big gulp of coffee. "I've been looking forward to this girls' trip since I touched down in America. And our time in the pool wouldn't have been the same without you. I need as much time as I can get with you before you go back to London and I don't see you again for several months—probably not until Jenn's wedding, right?"

Robin put her hands over her heart to show how touched she was by my admission and then quickly jumped to attention when the Keurig machine alerted her that her coffee was ready.

"Liv is a big mush ball," Reagan chimed in. "I see

why she fits in with us so well. But she *is* right. We would have missed you. Though—paraphrasing the famous poet Future—I do believe it's better to cry in the jacuzzi, so I guess that would have been my plight."

Unable to hold back her laughter from her own joke, Reagan giggled uncontrollably even as she tried drinking some coffee to contain herself.

"Get out of here!" Robin replied, before playfully tossing a big bag of chips at her. "I know you didn't just use the 'You gon' cry in this Phantom or dat Nissan' line on me!"

"Now, don't take your frustrations out on the tortillas, *cher*. These are some prime nacho-making chips. We have plans for these tomorrow, and you know how you feel about plans!"

The five of us continued the morning just like that, giggling and carrying on as if there weren't normally thousands of miles in between us and we saw each other every day, the conversation covering everything from career plans to worst dates ever and always ending with someone curled over in tears from laughing too hard. As coffee mugs turned into champagne flutes and glasses full of Jenn's Sweet Treats, bathrobes turned into bathing suits, and then eventually, by the evening—all of our best outfits for a night out on the town.

Once again, without planning it, they'd all chosen 'fits that complemented each other but still let each woman shine on her own. The difference this time was that I did, too. My black mini crop top and gold-mesh high-waisted skirt with a slit on my right thigh were similar enough to Reagan's white one-shoulder crop top with her burnt-orange floor-length skirt that opened in the front due to her high split, but distinct enough that we could both stand high in our stilettos and command our own attention. The same went for Rebecca and Robin, who each had on a low V-neck top but in vastly different ways, and Jenn, who helped blend us all together with the high slit in her mini skirt and her low V-neck top. Rob wore a dark green, purple, hot-pink, yellow and blue striped blouse with a V-neck that went all the way down to her belly and only snapped closed with the help of the black belt that was attached to it. Her shirt then flared out, the hem landing a few notches above her knees—which made it the perfect complement to her cutoff jean shorts and heels. And Becs, who might have been the flyest pregnant woman I'd ever seen, made quite the statement with her tan bandage skirt and champagne-colored V-neck blouse tucked inside.

By 10:30 p.m., we were all standing around, hyping Jenn up as she climbed onto the table we'd reserved at the first club. Robin had just convinced the DJ to play "Ladies Night" by Angie Martinez, Lil' Kim, Missy Elliott, Da Brat and Left Eye, when Jenn—in all her bachelorette glory—finally decided it was time for her moment in the sun. I was particularly impressed at the fact that she managed to get up there without showing all her goodies to the club, considering just how high the split was in her gorgeous black-and-white mini skirt. She'd paired that with an off-shoulder white satin V-neck, long-sleeved crop top and all the confidence in the world.

"Speech! Speech! Speech!" we all implored as she quickly got her bearings in her clear chunky backless heels.

"Oh!" she said, feigning innocence while scooping

up a bottle of champagne out of the bucket on the table. "You all want a speech? From me?"

"You already know we do, Miss Thang!" Robin replied.

"Yeah, give it to us," Rebecca added.

"Well, if you insist," Jennifer said, grinning from ear to ear and holding her bottle high.

She cleared her throat once before proceeding.

"Ladiesssss!" she screamed out.

"Yessss!" we replied in unison.

"I said, my laaaaadies!"

"Yesss!"

"I love all y'all so freakin' much. This has truly been one of the best days ever. I can't begin to thank you enough."

I watched in fear as Jenn's abounding joy quickly turned to sentimental tears, wondering how I could get her back to her fun place. In a matter of seconds, she'd gone from a '90s hip-hop star onstage to someone with supremely wet eyes, and I knew if I didn't stop her, she was going to have all of us joining in, crying in the club. We could not let that happen.

"Wait, wait!" I shouted. "This speech isn't supposed to be about us. It's supposed to be about you. Try again, Jennifer!"

"Welp, Liv's right," Reagan said with a shrug, and then shot me a quick, silent *Thank you* off to the side.

"Okay! Okay!"

Jenn threw her arms into the air and took in a deep breath before going at it again, literally swallowing her tears up as we all stared her down.

"All day has been amazing! And I know, I know, it's not done yet—but this has been one of the best days ever for me. And when I think about why I'm here, why we're all here tonight," she began. "I have to say that I'm so happy. A lot of that is because of the work I've done over the past year in therapy…and with you all… to get myself to the point where I love me, and my man, and my girls, for who everyone is, all on their own. No comparisons. No fear. Just love."

"I hear that," Reagan interjected, raising her glass up to Jenn, who clinked it with the bottle she still had in her hand.

"And listen, I know this might be controversial," Jennifer continued. "But Nick has literally changed my life, y'all. I'm so grateful for this man. I used to think that was an unfeminist way to think, but screw that—I have a partner who supports me, challenges me, loves me and is even willing to let me throw some pink plush handcuffs on him when I'm trying out something new."

"Yeah, he did!" Rebecca chimed in, holding her belly as she and the rest of us cracked up laughing at the memory of when she'd given Jenn those very handcuffs and learned later just how shocked Nick was when Jennifer had slapped them onto his wrists.

Confused at first, he'd tried it out because that was his girl. I didn't know much about Nick, but I knew one thing—he wasn't perfect, but there wasn't much he wouldn't do for Jennifer Pritchett. I could see why she was so happy with him.

"If you know, you know!" Jenn continued, laughing and pointing at Becs with her bottle. "But seriously, that kind of day in and day out partnership is so clutch. I know how blessed I am to have him, and you girls, in my life."

"Amen!" Robin added, now raising her glass in the air as well.

"Aaaaand," Jenn continued on, "I know Liv said this isn't about you guys, but…it's my speech, so I can add this part if I want."

She stuck her tongue out at me before proceeding forward.

"I'm so incredibly thankful that every single one of you has someone in your life just like that, too—who has shown up time and time again, and whether it's been years or its super new, you can just tell he's the one. So, shout-out to us, and shout-out to Nick, Jake, Oliver, Craig—"

"Ahem, excuse me," I interjected, raising my hand in defiance.

"I was getting ready to say Thomas!" she replied.

"No, no, but you shouldn't. He's not my man! I don't have a man," I protested.

"Girl." Jennifer paused her speech and looked directly at me. "If you don't stop playing around, acting like we haven't seen you texting this man the whole time you've been here."

"Mmm-hmm," Reagan chimed in. "She does that when she's with me, too."

"Of course she does—because she likes him," Robin added.

"And he's good for her," Reagan continued. "Sometimes unexpected things are good, *cher*." She turned toward me, lifting her glass in my direction.

"I do really like him," I admitted. "I don't know how to explain it—just when I'm with him, it feels like finally, I met someone who doesn't need me to change to be the partner for him. Like, he gets me, and he's supportive, and his kisses are what heaven probably feels like…"

I shook my head quickly to stop myself from spiraling down a rabbit hole.

"That's what we've been saying for the longest, *cher*! This is great. I'm just happy you're acknowledging it now," Reagan replied.

"Yeah, but he's also the same man who told me he wasn't looking for a relationship—"

"Until he met *you*, right?" Reagan asked.

I stared back at her in response, simply folding my lips onto each other to keep my mouth closed once again.

"Exactly," she added. "You're focused too much on what's the worst that can happen, *cher*, when what you should be focused on is the way you two look at each other when you're in the other's presence. I've seen it with my own eyes. That mess is seductive! I wanted to get home to my own man after being around y'all."

Jenn, Rebecca and Robin laughed and *mmm-hmm*-ed throughout Reagan's soliloquy, leaving me to just stand there and take my medicine as Robin had the day before.

"Not to mention, I've never seen you this googly-eyed about someone before," Robin added. "When you were in London, you barely mentioned David's name unless someone else brought him up."

"Boo, down with David," Reagan interjected.

"Agreed. I'm just saying," Robin continued. "No one's saying Thomas is endgame—"

"Actually, I did," Jennifer interrupted, still standing high on the table before us.

"Okay, well, Jenn is our sentimental bestie, so she's saying he's endgame. I'm just saying, and I think the rest of us are just saying, that it might be time to stop fighting it and actually give this guy a chance. You never know what could happen..."

"And what would Chrissy ask in a situation like this?" Reagan asked, interrupting Robin's speech.

"What's the best that could happen, *mana*, if you just tried?" Robin replied.

I smiled and rolled my eyes, grateful for the kind of friends who loved me enough to challenge me but annoyed at the same time—because, like, who wanted to be challenged? I'd heard someone once say that you knew someone was your best friend when you could go months without seeing each other and pick right back up where you'd left off when you did. This night made me want to take that a step further. I'd learned someone was your best friend when they told you things you didn't want to hear with love and care and in a way where you could receive it as such. Being around these ladies, I definitely understood exactly what that felt like.

"Okay," I responded. "I hear everyone, loud and clear."

"Oh! That reminds me!" Jenn chimed in. "Before we take another sip, we have to pour out a little something for the homie Christine!"

"Oh my God. Of course," Robin replied as we all jumped to attention and rejoined our focus back toward the center table, where Jenn had begun tipping her champagne bottle ever so slightly to the side to let a few drops fall onto the floor.

After she blessed the floor, we all raised our glasses high in the sky and clanked them with Jenn's bottle, thanking God for this moment and our friendships. And just like magic, the DJ started playing "Friends" by The Carters, almost like it was fate—or more of Robin's perfect planning. Either way, we were all good with the win.

Chapter Thirteen

"So, Julie, I have some exciting news. I just learned that we're launching a new investment fund in the American market, and I want your team to put together a presentation outlining how many clients would be interested in the fund and what the long-term plan for attracting new investors looks like."

Julie sat across from me, wide-eyed and probably more than a little scared, as I gave her the news that she—one of the management group's youngest portfolio managers—was getting the chance to put together a proposal for this new fund. But she deserved it. From my first day in the office, I'd watched her step up and buy-in to the changes that Walter and I were implementing without hesitation. Her team's investment strategy briefs and proposals always had the most research in them, and I saw how she really took to heart the challenge I made to everyone to come up with ideas that would wow our clients. Whether it was an update to the investors about how to think about their overall portfolio, what factors might affect it or how to protect it, I was consistently impressed with the work she developed.

I'd also been in her position before, excited and nervous, not wanting to let the person down who stood before me, offering me this kind of opportunity. So her stunned silence, while slightly comical, was understandable.

"And of course, I want you to work with marketing to build out materials and develop a launch proposal that's going to set this new investment up for success," I continued as I watched her gather herself and slowly come back to Earth.

"Of course, Olivia," she finally replied. "Thank you for the opportunity."

"No need to thank me. You've earned this. And before your brain starts wondering, you didn't earn it because you and I have lunch together sometimes with Wendy. You earned it because of the work you've put in. Walter wouldn't have agreed to this if he felt any differently."

I looked at her from behind my desk and visibly noticed her jaw loosen a bit and her shoulders fall from where they'd been sitting high up toward her ears. She'd needed that reassurance, and I understood that, too.

"Thanks for the vote of confidence, Olivia. Honestly. I won't let you down."

"This I already know," I explained. "Or I wouldn't have picked you to run point here. You got this."

She stood up from the chair in front of my desk and walked toward my door, a smile building on her face that told me just how amped she was. I could still remember the first investment-fund launch I'd had a chance to develop and the way I'd run to the ladies' room right after learning I'd be lead so I could silently shout and dance without anyone seeing. This was the kind of thing I wanted to do more of—empowering the younger portfolio managers around me who deserved it and who needed to know their senior manager believed in them more than anything. Sure, I loved meeting and exceeding fundraising goals, but I was steadily learning this was what really brought me joy. It was why I didn't mind staying up late to offer feedback on anywhere from five to fifteen proposals and investment strategy briefs in a week. If they were going to show up and put in the work, I was going to meet them with that same passion and dedication—sleep be damned.

Out the corner of my eye, I saw the notebook I'd brought with me from London that had all my goals for the year written out in it. It was a simple blue-and-white notebook, unassuming to most but containing some of my biggest hopes and dreams (and by virtue of all that, also my biggest fears) in it. I glanced at my clock and saw that I had another thirty minutes before my next meeting, so I scooped it up and quickly flipped to the pages where the blue ink had outlined everything that I'd set out to do once I got here.

What do I mean when I say this will be my year? I'd written across the top of the page.

I mean the following:

—I am walking into this new office confident and believing I deserve to be there. From the very beginning, they will quickly understand my value as a senior manager.

—I am building a rapport with the portfolio teams so they respect my input and are inspired to develop more creative proposals and more in-depth and researched strategy briefs.

—I am helping to change the culture, even slightly, to one where people take time to think outside the box, even if only by 1 percent, so that they can present tried-and-true ideas but also ones that aren't stale and get their clients and investors excited again.

—I am heading back to the UK after this year ends with a promotion to senior portfolio manager and well on my way to head of the division.

I hadn't looked at that list since my first day in the office, and yet I could already see myself checking off many of my goals. That felt really, really good. But I didn't want to stop at many. I wanted it all.

I closed my notebook with a renewed sense of energy and turned back to the thirty unread messages in my Outlook folder. *No time like the present to keep moving toward my dreams*, I thought.

Just as I opened the first one, however, I heard my phone vibrating in my purse and picked it up to see who it was. Robin probably could have seen the smile on my face all the way in London when I finally unlocked it.

It was Thomas.

Thomas: Hey, I know we didn't have plans tonight, but it's been a pretty stressful day at work so far, and I'd love to see you. Are you free this evening?

I looked at my phone and at the virtual stack of work waiting for me to get to it. It had been days since I'd come back from Palm Springs, and I'd yet to see him, so everything in me wanted to say yes. I also knew that if I spent the night running around the city with him, I was going to regret it the next morning when my backlog of work to get through had doubled.

I'd love to see you, too, I typed back. But I have a lot of work to do tonight. What do you think about coming over to my place? Maybe we can do both. Spend some time together while I get some work done?

Thomas: I think that's a great idea. With one condition. You give me full reign in your kitchen, and I'll cook us dinner while you work. Then, you give me just a couple hours of your time during dinner, and we can call it a night from there if you want.

Me: You just said work has been stressful today lol. The last thing I want is for you to cook for me after a long day. We can order in.

Thomas: Actually, cooking helps me de-stress. And it's not for you. It would be for us. I have to eat, too, you know.

Me: Okay. Then you have a deal, as long as I get to see you in your Rihanna element, too. You did tell me that was part of your decompressing routine.

Thomas: We'll have to see about that, love. You already caught me slipping by getting me to even divulge that one to you.

Me: And it's a top five thing I like about you…and it's

not five. So, c'mon! You know you want to sing some more bangers with me lol

Thomas: We'll see, we'll see lol. Don't forget, you'll be working while I'm cooking anyway.

Me: That's true. But I always have time for a little Rihanna.

Thomas: Ha! I'll keep that in mind.

Thomas: So, what time works best for you?

I looked back at my clock again and saw that it was close to 3:30 p.m. *At the rate I'm going, I'll be lucky to leave here by seven o'clock tonight*, I thought, and that was if Walter didn't come stomping his way over to my office. But he was the one who'd talked about work-life balance, so I was going to do my best to model that, starting with tonight.

Me: How about 7:30? I should be able to get home by then.

Thomas: Okay, great. I'll be the guy with the groceries waiting on you.

Me: And I'll be the one who can't stop smiling when she sees you.

Before I could get too caught up in all things Thomas, I locked my phone again and placed it back into my workbag. With only a few minutes left before my next meeting, I had a feeling I was going to need every second of it to pull myself back together from the pure joy I experienced while texting with him. The truth was I was happiest when I was with him—and the girls had been right; it was high time I stopped fighting that.

I walked up to my flat at just about 7:30 p.m. that night, and true to his word, Thomas was standing there with a bag of groceries on his shoulder.

"How long have you been waiting here?" I asked, once again unable to control the smile on my face that formed as soon as I saw him.

One of the many things I'd been learning in the time we'd spent together was that Thomas was a man of his word. If he said he was going to be somewhere at 7:30 p.m., you didn't have to wonder if he was going to show up. You just knew. I hadn't realized how important that was to me until he consistently did it, whether it was the simple things like calling when he said he would or the way he always seemed to arrive just a few minutes before me whenever we met up.

"Not too long. Maybe a couple minutes," he replied.

"You should have texted me. I could have been running late or already inside."

I grabbed my keys out of my workbag so that I could unlock the building door for us.

"I did actually," he replied, following behind me.

Once I opened the door and let him inside, I scooped my phone out of my bag, too, and saw that he was right. There it was, a missed text from Thomas that read, I'm here. Let me know if you're nearby.

I must have missed it while walking from the train.

"Oy, I'm sorry," I said, walking before him so that

I could guide him up the one flight of steps leading to my place.

"It's all good. You said you'd be home by 7:30 p.m., and you were. No harm, no foul."

"Thanks."

We moved in step with each other as Thomas entered my flat for the first time, taking his shoes off at the front door as soon as he saw me slip my favorite camel-brown So Kate leather pumps off as well. Without a word, he gently placed the grocery bag on the floor as I began unbuttoning my coat, grabbing the back side of it so that he could slide it off my shoulders, revealing the navy blue blazer, white bodysuit and tan trousers I had on underneath. As I hung my coat on the rack in the hallway, he then took his off as well, which I grabbed from him right before he picked the groceries up once more to follow me toward the rest of the flat. It was like we were dancing a delicate tango—no words needed, but perfectly in sync.

Past the entryway, my flat ballooned into an open floor plan with my kitchen on the right and sitting room on the left, complete with a charcoal-gray sofa-and-chaise set, a glass coffee table and the TV I barely had time to turn on most days. As was the case in many a New York apartment, I didn't have a dining table—however, I did have a reading nook next to the window that lit up the entire area during the day. That was a compromise I'd happily make any day. As it was, my coffee table sufficed just fine as a dining table for one on most nights. Just beyond all that were my bedroom and bathroom, my two places of sanctuary—one with the huge tub I often found myself soaking in at night and the other decorated with the rug, full-length mirror and string lights I'd purchased while out with Reagan and Jake.

Thomas and I walked straight to the kitchen, where he began pulling everything out of the bag as I searched for cooking utensils for him to use.

"Can I ask what you're cooking, or is it secret?" I inquired, watching him pile bell peppers, an onion, celery, garlic, chicken, sausage, tomatoes, rice and more onto my kitchen counter.

"No secret. I'm making my dad's famous jambalaya recipe. It's what he would cook for us any time my mom had a long day and needed a break from feeding three very hungry young boys."

"Wow, I'm sure that required a lot of food all the time."

"Yeah, to say the least."

"So, what makes it so famous?"

"Well, famous in my home, I should say. It was always a hit with us. A Louisiana rice dish made with chicken, sausage and shrimp? Some things you just can't go wrong with."

"Okay," I replied, suddenly excited to try his dad's version of what my mum would have called jollof rice. "Let me pull out some pots for you, yeah?"

"How about…you leave me to find my way around the kitchen, and you go work," he replied, placing his hands on my shoulders and guiding me into the sitting room.

"Are you sure?"

"Very. I think I'm capable enough to find some pots. And plus, the whole point of this arrangement was for you to get your work in while I cooked. You can't do that if you're in here helping me."

He smiled back at me, that dimple peeking out again and very much helping to convince me back into his plan.

"Okay, you're right," I said before pulling off my blazer and grabbing my laptop out of my workbag.

"That's what I like to hear."

I plopped down onto my couch and watched Thomas briefly as he walked back to the kitchen, peeled himself out of his own suit jacket and began maneuvering his way around my kitchen like a pro. It was the way he undid his tie right before he started slicing into the bell peppers that almost made me change my mind about working, eating, everything…but after a couple more seconds of silent ogling, I finally forced myself to turn my attention to the work waiting for me on my laptop, opening up the latest investment strategy brief that needed my sign off.

"Stay strong, Liv," I whispered to myself. It was harder than I'd expected to have Thomas mere steps away from me, with a clear view of the way his back arched as he sliced and diced the food he was preparing. But I really did need to finish up some work…and, importantly, he was making it possible for me to do so while still spending time with him. Maybe Walter was onto something about finding the person who got you, ambitions, hopes, dreams, fears, flaws and all.

An hour and a half later, and only maybe twenty or so glances from behind my laptop to see Thomas's body in motion, I turned down my screen and immediately reveled in the intoxicating smells coming from my kitchen.

"Wow, I hope this meal is going to be as good as it smells," I said, stretching my arms wide to make up for the time I'd just spent hunched over my computer.

Thomas turned around in response, his face revealing that he'd likely only caught some of what I'd said, a fact that was proven true when I saw him slide his earbud out.

"What was that you said, love?"

"Just that the food smells delicious… Wait, were you listening to Rihanna…without me?"

I squinted my eyes and awaited his reply.

"Well, I mean, I had to occupy myself while you worked. Plus, it is part of my decompressing routine, as you know."

"I know," I said softly. "I'm just mad I had to miss joining in with you on the fun. I feel like that happens with work more often than I'd like sometimes."

"You know what the good thing is? It's my playlist, so I can always go back to the last song and we can hear it together."

"It's that simple, innit?" I asked with a smile.

"It really is, love."

He picked up his phone and turned off the Bluetooth so that the tunes would play out loud for us both. Then, with a few more clicks, Rihanna's voice poured out of his phone, syncing up seamlessly with Calvin Harris's beats on "This Is What You Came For."

"The best part is…food's ready, too. So you finished your work at the perfect time."

Thomas began moving his arms to the beat as I got up from my couch and joined him, rocking my shoulders and hips from side to side.

"I wouldn't say finished, but I did enough for tonight."

"I'll take it. Besides, I didn't know how much longer I could go on pretending not to notice you sneaking glances while you worked," he added, briefly looking back at me with a devious smirk as he began scooping spoonfuls of jambalaya onto our plates, still dancing perfectly in rhythm with the music.

"Ha! Was it that obvious?"

"Only because I was checking you out, too."

Thomas turned back toward me with both of his hands full, our plates overflowing with the colorful rice dish packed with meats, and I about lost my footing when his eyes connected with mine.

"Good. At least I wasn't alone, then," I replied, quickly averting my eyes before I lost my breath control as well.

Chuckling under his breath, Thomas danced toward the couch and placed our plates onto the coffee table while I pulled out cutlery for us to eat with and poured two glasses of water.

"Would you like something else to drink besides water?" I asked.

"What do you have?"

"All that time in my kitchen and you don't know?"

"I tried not to dig around more than I needed to," he admitted.

"All right, well, I have some Riesling in the fridge."

"That works. Let's do it."

I grabbed the chilled bottle and two wineglasses and walked toward the couch, sitting down dangerously close to Thomas so that our thighs barely had any space between each other. It was thrilling, feeling the heat radiate from off our skin. But also, I was starving and desperately wanted to try the food he'd cooked before giving in to any other kind of temptation. Before either of us could make another move, I stuffed a big forkful of food into my mouth, delighting in all the amazing spices and how they blended together to form quite possibly one of the best things I'd ever tasted.

"Wow," I said, barely having finished chewing. "Now I see why you say this is famous."

"I'm glad you like it. My dad will be proud to hear that the tradition continues."

"It most certainly does. Does he have any other famous dinners that you want to cook for us one day?"

Thomas let out a big laugh before stuffing his own face with a forkful of rice. "You're already making me a househusband, huh?"

"Not quite. This is just…really nice," I admitted. "I'm glad you suggested it."

"To be fair, it was kind of a team-effort suggestion," he replied.

"That's true. I guess it's a good thing that I have a job that sometimes requires long hours," I joked.

We ate more and more bites of our food until our plates were practically wiped clean—a telltale sign that the meal was beyond delicious. But as I leaned back onto the couch, belly full and satisfied, I also remembered the other reason we'd met up tonight: Thomas had admitted to having a hard day at work, and I didn't want to let that just sit in the air without acknowledging it.

I moved in a little closer to him and put my hand on his thigh.

"All right, Mr. Wright," I began. "Did you want to talk about today and what was so stressful?"

"Mmm. Right. I almost forgot about that," he replied, turning toward me and leaning his head into the couch as well so that we were both facing each other, our foreheads almost touching.

"We don't have to if you don't want to," I offered as a consolation.

I knew I wasn't always the most talkative, either, when things bothered me, so I wanted to let him know I wasn't pressuring him to be so, either.

"I just thought it might be helpful to talk about it—"

"No, I appreciate that," he replied before sighing heavily. "Really, it was just a tale as old as time. Sometimes one of the partners I work with will show up and just be on a tear all day. So, despite the fact that I've even brought clients into the firm myself and how many cases I've helped them win over the past seven years, he'll get on this kick where he feels like nothing I do that day is right. Today was one of those days."

"I'm sorry, Thomas. You definitely don't deserve that."

"Yeah, it's not the best feeling. But I also know how much the other partners value me as a senior associate, and I think that might be part of the issue with this guy, honestly. I had one of the other partners approach me recently about taking that next step up, so it kinda feels like it's not a coincidence that today of all days he came in trying to take me down a notch."

"Mmm, I know how that can go—jealous of your rise but also has no clue all the work you put in to get where you are."

"Exactly."

"I went through something similar at my last investment firm. There was this one woman who just couldn't get past the fact that I was a young portfolio manager and from Brixton and doing better than she was."

"What did you do about it?"

"I just kept beating her." I laughed. "Until a better opportunity came around and I left that investment group for my current one."

"I guess that is always an option," he replied, a slight dejection forming on his face.

Oh no, I realized. That was the last thing I wanted him to feel, not when I believed he could move the moon if he wanted to.

"I'm not saying that's what you should do at all," I hurriedly added. "But I do think you will keep winning and you'll keep showing him that he can't stop you."

"Thanks, Liv," Thomas replied, his smile slowly starting to return to his face. "You're right, but sometimes it's nice to hear it from someone else."

"Well, I can be here to remind you of that every day if you want, with balloons and bells and some more of your dad's jambalaya, if that's what it takes."

"Ha ha, I'm not sure I need all that." He laughed, his head cocking to the side in the way that he did when he was sort of teasing me.

What he didn't know was that those were the same kinds of words men had used toward me in the past, right around the time they'd started to realize I was the girl who did "all that" type things for the people in my life. That was usually the signal that the end was near. So, while Thomas was enjoying himself, I silently started to panic, holding my breath and waiting to see if his laugh would turn sinister or if his dimple would fade away into an abyss as he began to chastise me for doing too much.

It never did. Instead, his smile grew wider as he leaned in closer to me, his cologne starting to come into focus and attempting to cloud my thoughts like the times before.

"But I kinda like the sound of it," he said. "Especially the part where you said you'd be here every day."

"That did sound nice, right?" I replied, finally allowing myself to breathe in and out again.

"Yeah."

"To me, too."

Now that my moment of panic had disappeared, I stared into Thomas's eyes, really seeing the man before me—the very same one who'd captured my attention since the moment we met and hadn't let it go. Who'd shown me over and over again that I could trust him with my heart. Who hadn't asked me to be different than who I was or choose him over my ambitions. *So really, what is it that has me scared?* I wondered.

Time passed in silence as neither of us wanted to break the spell we had over the other. But eventually, our hands slowly found their way to each other and our fingers intertwined in the still quiet of the room. I watched with my breath caught in between my lips as Thomas's eyes traced my face, then down my neck, over my cleavage and then returning to my eyes before he replaced the tiny space in between us with one small tug. Like it was always meant to be connected to his, my body naturally followed along as our faces and mouths collided and the two of us frantically sucked our way along the other's lips.

I moaned softly into his mouth, desperate for more and suddenly never wanting to know what it felt like to have his lips removed from mine. A small whimper escaped from me when he did eventually pull away, but thankfully he soon began to follow the path he'd first established with his eyes, tracing his tongue gently along the edges of my jawline, down my neck, onto my collarbone and finally right where the fabric of my bodysuit left just enough cleavage for him to graze the tops of my breasts—sending waves of chills down my spine the entire time.

"I think it might be time for dessert," I whispered as his kisses began making their way back up my neck with one hand grabbing my twists to give him better access.

"Dessert," he repeated, groaning into my ear like a man greedy for more but willing to wait until he heard exactly what he needed. "Ha! Tell me what you really want, Olivia."

Thomas stopped kissing me and looked me square in my eyes, daring me to be bold enough to tell him all the dirty things I'd thought of doing with him when I was alone late at night.

"I want you," I replied.

"How?"

His eyes never left mine as I squirmed under his gaze. I'd never had someone ask me to be this blunt before, and I was all at once thrilled and nervous at the same time. After all, I was the same woman constantly accused of being extra and doing too much, and here he was, imploring me to let go of everything that was stopping me before and do more, say more, tell him exactly what I wanted.

"I want you…" I said, hesitating slightly and then building my courage back up. "Inside of me, on top of me, enveloping me, pleasing me…until we're both spent and satisfied beyond measure."

"Mmm. I can definitely do that," he replied, returning his lips to my body and placing some bites along the side of my neck. "I want to do that. But also, I told you I'd wait until you were absolutely ready. And I didn't just mean about sex. So, do you still have doubts, Olivia?"

"No. Not about this. Not about you. And not about us."

Thomas smiled at me with one of those smiles that makes the other person smile back, and instantly I knew just how right I was. Everything about this man was what I'd always wanted but had been too afraid to even pray for. He was kind, he didn't want to change me, he had his own ambitions and could easily relate to my goals and doubts in my job…but more than that, he'd been presented with an unexpected encounter, just like I had. And he hadn't run away. He'd chosen me over everything he'd thought he wanted before. And that was sexy as hell.

I bit my bottom lip as I waited to find out what he would say or do next.

"Okay, then," he said, and picked me up off the couch, carrying me over his shoulder and to my bedroom.

Once inside, Thomas flicked the switch for the string lights, which I'd placed meticulously throughout my room, wrapping them around the mirror and other items so that it created an almost moonlit atmosphere. Gently, he placed me back on my feet, facing the mirror and, piece by piece, began slowly peeling off my clothes while we both admired our reflection. Standing behind me, he then unbuttoned and unzipped my trousers, following along my hips and thighs with his hands as they fell to the ground. Next, he peeled the bodysuit straps down my arms, grazing my skin as the fabric folded down my breasts and torso until I stood in front of him and the mirror with just my black thong on.

"You're so beautiful," he whispered, staring into my eyes through our reflection in the mirror before grabbing my hair and giving himself full access to the side of my neck down to my chest. He took his time for the next several minutes, building the tension in my body as he alternated between tracing his fingers down my spine and kneading my nipples, causing intermittent goose bumps along my skin and then crystal clear juices sliding down my inner thighs.

"Take your panties off," he finally commanded.

And without another word, I did just as he said, grabbing the fabric at my hips and watching it roll down my legs as Thomas undressed himself behind me and slid a condom onto the meaty penis that I now desperately wanted inside of me.

A few seconds later, I got exactly what I'd been craving as he gently lifted my butt cheeks and slipped inside my vagina, rocking my entire world with each thrust from behind.

Chapter Fourteen

The next morning, I woke up happy, relaxed and basking in the feeling of Thomas's arms wrapped around my bare skin.

It was honestly quite startling how normal it felt, like the spot next to me in my queen-size bed had been waiting for him to occupy it all this time. And finally, after pushing past my fears, he was here, where he belonged—with me. After a quick glance at my clock to check the time, I snuggled in closer to his body, breathing in deeply as he enveloped himself even tighter around my slender frame even as he remained asleep. With at least another hour and a half before I needed to leave for work, I intended to take advantage of every still, quiet minute in his embrace.

As I lay there, eyes now closed again, I contemplated all the times I'd got it wrong before him. How I'd allowed those relationships to make me question whether anyone could ever want me for me. Question if I'd ever know the kind of connection that so many of the people around me had found, even my own little brother, who'd managed to snag one of the women I trusted and admired the most. And yet something about Thomas was easy from the very start. Not that it had been easy allowing myself to fall for him, but that our connection, no matter how hard I'd tried to run from it, had been palpable from the moment we'd met and only continued growing as we'd gotten to know more about each other. That was something I'd never experienced before, and it felt damn good.

I squeezed myself even closer to his chest and breathed in deeply. How had I gotten so lucky, I wondered…and then just as suddenly, did I need to enjoy this time with him while I could? *Because it can't very well last, right?* That was the silent fear still lingering that I didn't want to admit.

"Mmm. Well, that's one way to wake up from a good night's sleep," Thomas said, awaking suddenly and moaning into my ear. "Good morning."

"Oy, I'm sorry. I didn't mean to disturb you," I replied, realizing I'd probably startled him by holding on so tightly.

Before he could do it for me, I loosened my grip around his torso ever so slightly and began the process of removing myself from his grasp.

"You didn't."

Thomas rubbed his sleepy eyes and then, before I could slip out any farther, pulled me back into the nook that had been my sanctuary just moments before. Once I was returned to my rightful place, he stretched his bare, sculpted arms wide and gently kissed me on my forehead—taking the time he needed to loosen his limbs from a full night of sleep before wrapping them all back around me. Even his long legs, like with our hands the night before, found mine under the covers and twisted around each one, so that within seconds, no part of my body was left unconnected to him.

"Did you sleep well?" he asked, that deep baritone voice of his eliciting flashbacks in my mind to the night before and all the ways that I'd never even known my body could experience pleasure.

Whether with simple instructive commands or affirmations of how good I felt, over and over, that same voice had been what kept me grounded throughout the night as he'd encouraged me to let my guard down and open myself up to him. It was also the same voice that had moaned my name softly through staggered breaths as I climbed on top of him and rode his penis until we both climaxed. And then, that voice (and the man behind it) had practically rocked me to sleep while whispering sweet nothings in my ear as I drifted off in his arms. Talk about a sensory overload in the best way.

"I did," I replied, grinning under the covers as I continued down memory lane in my mind. "Probably one of my best nights of sleep in a while."

"Oh yeah? Well, I'll take that as a compliment in more ways than one."

"You should," I said, giggling briefly and then allowing the beauty of silence to overwhelm me as we both stopped our banter to just be present and still in each other's arms.

For several minutes, we lay just like that, no words spoken, just inhaling and exhaling as one, until my internal clock told me that if I didn't get up, I'd never make it out of my flat in time for work.

"Do you want some coffee?" I asked as I once again began trying to peel myself out of his embrace. "I'm going to make some while I get dressed, so…"

"Yeah, that would be nice. I think I'm going to need it to get out of this bed this morning, for sure."

"Same. I kind of wish it were Saturday and we could just be here all day actually. But it's not, innit."

With one last regrettable heave, I fully rolled myself out of Thomas's arms, climbed out of my bed and finally stood up to begin my day. If we were going to be together (*a wild thing to even contemplate, I know*), I was going to have to get used to nights and mornings with him and still getting up and being to work by 7:30 a.m. That was the routine I'd established after all, and I wasn't about to change it now. So, today was as good a day as any to begin the practice.

"How do you like it?" I asked, grabbing my robe and wrapping it around my body before making my way toward the kitchen.

"More cream and sugar than coffee," he admitted with a chuckle.

"Ha ha, okay, noted."

Step by step, I slowly dragged myself away from Thomas and the bed I still desperately wanted to be in, momentarily paused by his large hand that jutted out and grabbed mine as I started walking by him in what felt like one last attempt to get me to come back. I pressed on, however, undeterred from my goal at hand, and made it to the kitchen, where I went about pouring just enough grounded beans and water into the machine for us to both have a large mug of coffee each.

As I waited for the magical brown liquid to begin filling my flat with its sweet aroma, Jhené Aiko's "New Balance" suddenly started playing in my head—another reminder of just how infatuated I'd seemingly become over the naked man currently lying in my bed. It hadn't happened overnight. But it had very obviously been building for quite some time, as evidenced by my friends' comments on our trip. And last night I'd finally stopped fighting it, leaning into the idea that maybe, just maybe, I did deserve someone who saw things in me that even I couldn't—and loved what he saw.

Realizing that I probably needed to multitask while I continued waiting for the coffee to brew, I scooped up my phone from the coffee table in the sitting room, where we'd left it behind the night before.

"By the way," I said out loud as I began scrolling to see if there were any urgent emails I needed to handle before work, "not sure if you remember, but I think I might have said I wanted to be with you—as in, like, us officially be together—last night."

"Oh, is that what you said?" Thomas responded from inside my bedroom. "I may vaguely recall something close to that, but it's the strangest thing, I don't remember those exact words being used."

Amazingly, even without seeing him, I knew he was smiling from under the covers in my bed. Still teasing me even after the way he'd handled my body like a pro last night. Now that was just rude.

"I didn't say those exact words, but I mean—"

"You're right, you didn't," he interjected, suddenly standing at the junction between my bedroom door and the sitting room. "And yet I did, right?"

The smirk I'd assumed he had on his face was now replaced with something different, something more earnest and sincere.

"You did."

"Mmm."

He stood in exactly the same spot, not moving any further toward me but not yet retreating as he waited for me to say more.

"Well, I do want us to be together, if that's still a question in your mind," I answered.

"Good," he replied, pausing his words as he stepped toward me in the dim light. "I wouldn't say it was still a question, but sometimes a man needs to hear it, too, you know."

"Yeah, okay."

With one last step, Thomas reached his destination (me) and once again pulled me toward him, his hands now sitting on the small of my back as I instinctually leaned into him, climbed onto my tippy toes and joined my lips with his. We moaned in unison as I bit his lower lip and used it as my leverage to thrust my tongue into his mouth, which he sucked at feverishly. It wasn't until I felt his penis jumping as it grazed my thigh that I realized we should stop before I lost all control of my senses and allowed him to carry me right back to bed or, better yet, bend me over the coffee table or couch right before us.

"You," I said breathlessly, laughing and stepping down onto the heels of my feet. "You and your best friend need to go back over there so I can get myself together."

I pointed toward my bedroom to emphasize my point.

"You sure?" he asked, those gray eyes once again staring daggers into my soul.

"Yes!" I exclaimed, trying to convince myself just as much as him.

"Okay, okay—but I don't have to be happy about it."

"Well, neither do I, but you still need to do it."

I giggled silently as I watched him dramatically turn around and walk back toward my bedroom door, his firm butt cheeks threatening to distract me once again. I quickly cleared my throat and pulled myself together, turning back to my phone just as a new message came through from Walter.

Olivia, I have great news, it read. I'm probably not supposed to tell you this, but I've been talking to some of the C-suite brass, and you are most definitely on their radar. In fact, apparently the head of the UK portfolio division is looking to step down as early as next year, and after what they've seen from you in just a few months here, plus what you were doing in London, I think they might be interested in offering you the top position. You get what this means, right? You're on the precipice of everything you've wanted, and even earlier than you expected.

I read Walter's note in shock probably six times in a row before anything he'd written was able to really sink in. Was he for real? I questioned. Was it all just right here all of a sudden? The dream I barely had enough courage to say aloud except for one late night when Walter and I were working at the office, and he'd randomly asked me what I wanted to get out of New York. I'd hesitated at first, but after some proper cajoling, he'd gotten me to admit it all—my whole kick-ass list down to the ultimate goal.

I smiled deeply as the joy finally replaced the shock and washed over my body. Sure, I still had some time before it was final—but it was here! I'd done it. The young Black girl from Brixton had grown into a woman who was on her way to being head of her management group's UK portfolio division. *My God!*

I messaged Walter back saying that he'd already made my whole month and the sun hadn't even come up yet, then swung myself around, throwing my head back, and fully took in the news. I only paused briefly from my swing fest so that I could read the note once more. *You're on the precipice of everything you've wanted*, he'd said.

I sure in the hell was.

Seconds later, I heard the coffee machine switch off, and suddenly dread washed over me. *Thomas.* Sweet, unaware Thomas was waiting in my bed for his cup of coffee while I received what was equally the best career news ever and the thing that spelled impending doom for us. Sure, he'd been understanding last night, I thought, but how understanding would he be when I told him that there was no way I'd be staying in America now. And even though he hadn't yet asked me to, that conversation of where we both lived was always going to eventually come up, right? Months down the line, the only thing that would change was that it would hurt more, but I was always going to have to say goodbye.

This was what I'd been avoiding. This was why I'd tried to keep choosing Door Number Two over and over again, so I wouldn't get lulled into a false belief he might be the one man who didn't mind how important my career was to me. And yet I'd ultimately failed— falling for the man who looked at me with sincere eyes and who'd chosen me over his own comfort level—and now I was going to have to shatter both of our hearts. When I never should have given him mine in the first place. I knew better... I knew.

I walked over to the coffee machine and poured out two cups of coffee into the mugs beside it, prepared them individually according to our preferences and braced myself for heartbreak. I needed to tell Thomas now that I'd been wrong and we shouldn't be together, but I really, really didn't want to. With a heavy sigh, I picked up both mugs and walked to my bedroom, trying to figure out the words I'd use to let us both down gently.

"Just like you like it," I said once I'd walked back into the room, handing Thomas his mug as he finished sliding up and then buttoning his trousers.

"Thank you, love," he replied, gently grazing my fingers as he took the cup out of my hand and then kissing me on the cheek before indulging in a large, satisfying gulp.

I took my own sip of coffee to steady my hands and breathing before finally getting up the nerve to broach the topic I was sure would make me want to go cry in the shower after.

"So..." I started with hesitation. "I just got a note from Walter saying that he thinks C-suite wants to skip the senior portfolio manager promotion I wanted and that they're contemplating offering me the division head spot when I return."

I held my breath as I waited for Thomas's response, holding back the tears threatening to fall down my face from the inevitable disappointment.

"Liv, wait, are you serious?" he asked.

"Very."

"That's…that's amazing, babe! Damn, I'm so proud of you."

Thomas sat down his coffee and, in one swoop, scooped me into his arms and held me tightly to his chest. "I knew they would see what I see," he whispered in my ear.

"Yeah," I replied softly, holding on to him for dear life as my eyes began to water.

Once again, Thomas had surprised me, exuding only joy from my announcement. That was the kind of man he was, I realized. The same one who had been concerned about not wanting my time in New York to become about him because he knew only moments after we'd met how important this time was for me. He *wasn't* David. He wasn't anything like all the others who had disappointed me time and time again, really. And yet, as I clung to him, feeling every vein in his muscles on my skin, I knew I was still going to have to say goodbye.

Just not now, I thought. For now, I wanted to pretend that it mattered that he was perfect for me. Even though every bone in my body knew the awful truth.

Part 3

"So maybe it won't look like you thought it would in high school, but it's important to remember that love is possible. Anything is possible. This is New York."

—*Sex and the City*

Chapter Fifteen

A week later, I found myself uptown, in Jake's condo for Christmas dinner, dressed in a winter white sweater dress with knee-high chestnut-brown boots and surrounded by the group I'd dubbed Reagan's New York village—Keisha, Giselle, Jake and his two friends, Brandon and Lucas. For different reasons, we'd all found ourselves still in the city on Christmas Day, so when Jake had suggested a friends' dinner, we all jumped at the chance to spend the day and evening laughing, drinking and eating good food. I was particularly glad not to be spending the day alone, where my mind had time to wander about me and Thomas and the fact that I'd yet to tell him I needed to end things.

Jake's place was just the home away from home I needed and everything that I'd expected from a Harlem condo decorated by an alum of Howard University and the boyfriend of Reagan Doucet. From the moment I walked in, I was greeted with the sounds, smells and sights of American Blackness, beginning with the smell of the soul food he and Reagan had cooking in the kitchen all the way to the Jackson 5 Christmas album playing on his record player as background tunes. On every wall, except the one that had been turned into a floor-to-ceiling bookshelf, were collages of black-and-white photographs of Black luminaries, the likes of everyone from James Baldwin to Josephine Baker. And scattered throughout his place, matching seamlessly with his Williams Sonoma and Neiman Marcus furniture, were various hints of what he obviously found to be most important in his life, such as the coasters on his coffee table that featured *Life* magazine images from Howard University in the 1940s, the Mardi Gras mask that was presumably from Reagan and had been given prime positioning on his bookshelf, and the Alpha Phi Alpha notebook-and-pen set seated on the corner of one of his end tables.

"This food is so good," I said, leaning over toward Reagan from the midnight blue ottoman I was perched on while eating. "I can't believe you eat this every Christmas."

"Thanks, *cher*," she replied with a smile. "It's probably hard to believe, but this is the truncated version of my family's Christmas meal. I couldn't have pulled all that off with just me and Jake."

"Oh, if you guys needed help, I could have come over," I said quickly, suddenly feeling guilty for not just asking.

"No, I appreciate that. But today you're our guest, so don't let your head take that thought any further."

"Oy, okay," I replied, marveling at the fact that we knew each other well enough at this point for her to know I would have started ruminating about whether I was a good friend or not.

I was glad to have Rae in my life—that much I was certain of, if nothing else. And if the company and the prospect of not spending Christmas alone hadn't been enticing enough, the food she and Jake cooked would have lured me uptown all on its own. On their menu, and subsequently stuffed into my belly, were the following:

Seafood filé gumbo

Baked macaroni and cheese

Seafood-stuffed bell peppers

Southern-style green beans

Potato salad

Crawfish pies

Shrimp and rice–stuffed chicken

And each piece of food tasted better than the next.

To my right, Keish and Gigi were just as happy and full as I was but also in the process of jump-starting the next conversation for us to dig into as a framily. Already, we'd covered everything from the advent of "podcast bros" to all the white celebrities randomly admitting that they didn't shower. We'd even had a short-lived deep dive into all three Megan/Meghans—Fox, Thee Stallion and Markle, respectively—until Jake let us know that the lemon pie he and Reagan had made was finally ready to devour. Just as well, I realized, for I was pretty sure that my only commentary about the Markles was going to be that I was glad they'd found their way to America, a statement that in hindsight might have been pretty ironic to all the Americans sitting around me, who still faced tons of discrimination in their own country.

"Okay, so looking a year ahead from now," Keisha began, crossing her legs and putting down her now empty saucer as she garnered everyone's attention, "what are some of the things you want to say you've done by next Christmas?"

She looked around the room, waiting for the first person to jump in with their answer. It took a few minutes, but Jake was the first to take the plunge.

"I want us to be living together by then," he replied, turning his attention to Reagan and effectively breaking the silence in the room.

"Whoa, really?" Lucas asked as the rest of the room oooh-ed in a stunned Reagan's direction.

"Yeah, I mean, I love this woman," he said, pulling her toward him and wrapping his left arm around her waist. "Why wouldn't I want us to start building what a lifetime looks like?"

"Does that mean you're proposing next year, too?" I overheard her ask him quietly as we all screamed and giggled in response to their love.

"Yeah, babe," he responded, and then kissed her reassuringly. "I figured that part was kind of a given."

"It wasn't, but good to hear it's on your radar."

"And in my budget."

"Even better." She laughed.

I watched from the sidelines as the two lovebirds continued their private conversation in the midst of our very public discussion, but then again, that was indicative of everything I'd learned about Reagan and Jake—they somehow found a way to insulate themselves when they needed to even if among a crowd. It was something I admired about their connection. Something I thought Thomas and I probably had, too, but... *Oh, crap. Thomas.*

I bristled at the thought of what I still had to do with him, how I was only delaying the inevitable break of both our hearts, and quickly tried to turn my mind back to the discussion at hand. The one thing that slightly comforted me was knowing he was home for Christmas, and so I at least had until he got back to the city before I needed to say the actual words—that we were over.

"Okay, okay, that's a great start," Keisha interjected, quieting down all our remaining whistles and hoots. "I don't know who's topping that, but someone else, please try."

"I expect to have all my student loans paid off by then," Giselle replied, jumping in as she curled her legs into the right corner of Jake's couch and wrapped herself in one of his plush throw blankets.

"Gigi, that's boss!" Brandon screamed out, leaning over to high-five her before quickly tempering his response back into his seat when we all turned our attention his way. "Sorry, I'm just... I'm just saying that's a big deal. I'm happy for you, friend."

"Thank you," she said, blushing. "I appreciate the excitement. I'm excited, too!"

"That's great, Gigi," Keisha added. "As y'all know, I'm about to take on even more student-loan debt when I start business school this summer, so you just make sure you remember the little ones when you're Navient free, okay?"

"I got you," Giselle replied, laughing at Keisha's sarcasm.

"What about you, Liv?" Reagan asked as she walked

into the sitting room from the kitchen after having sufficiently completed her private conversation with Jake. "Are you still going to be with us come next Christmas?"

She poked me playfully in my side as she sat back down across from me in the chaise lounge attached to the sofa, relaxing into what I could only guess was her normal spot when she and Jake were home alone.

"Actually… I hadn't had a chance to tell you yet, but according to Walter, I might be head of the UK portfolio division this time next year."

"Wait, what?" she screamed out, excitement fluttering on her face. "Oh, Liv, that's amazing! That's like everything you wanted when you took this year opportunity in the city!"

"Yeah," I replied with a strained smile on my face. "Even more than, honestly, because I never expected they would shoot me straight past senior portfolio manager to leading the entire division."

"Well, I did. You're badass, and clearly everyone there knows it."

As the rest of the room joined in with cheers and exclamations of my awesomeness, Rae paused to look me in my eyes, and I could instantly tell she knew there was a *but* to all my exuberance. Her read of me reminded me of the first time Thomas had been able to see through my banter in the airport, but this time, I wasn't sure I had it in me to hold back the tears that wanted to pour out. I could do that with a stranger at the time, but not Reagan. Not after the friendship we'd built over the last several months. Thankfully, the rest of the group turned back to discussing Keisha's plans for business school before they could catch my breakdown starting.

"What's wrong, Liv? Why don't you seem as happy

as we are?" Reagan asked, drawing me into a conversation of just the two of us.

"I am happy," I replied, as one lone tear dripped down my left cheek. "I just… It's everything I've ever wanted—"

"Yeah, it is, *cher.*"

"But it also means, once again, I'm the girl who gets to accomplish her career goals but loses the guy."

There it is. I finally said the quiet part out loud.

"Wait, what?" Jake interjected, sliding next to Reagan.

It wasn't lost on me that they even used the same language to express their shock at something. If I didn't adore them both so much, it would be sickening.

"Take me from the start. How did you jump from this amazing, exciting, thrilling accomplishment to you losing my guy Thomas? Did he say something to make you believe you needed to choose between him and your career?"

"Wait, Jake, before you answer that," Reagan interrupted. "Have you even told him about this, Liv?"

Reagan's eyes trained in on mine, seemingly so that she could determine whether I was telling her the truth. But also, there seemed to be genuine care behind her gaze, like she honestly thought I wasn't giving us a fair shot. She was probably right.

"I did, yes. Right after I got Walter's note."

"And?" Jake asked, leaning toward me as if he was prepared to fight somebody no matter what my response.

"He was excited for me. But… I know how this goes, okay. I just do. And the reality is we've never talked about trying to have an international, long-distance relationship. I'm not even sure that's something I'd want, really. So it just feels…inevitable. This time next year,

I'll be back in London, living out my dream, and he'll be here, without me, living out his."

"Oh, Liv, that's a lot to assume, babe," Reagan replied, reaching out her hand and placing it on my thigh. "Especially if you haven't actually talked to Thomas about it. Who knows what ideas he might have for y'all to make it work."

"You do want to make it work, right?" Jake asked, looking at me earnestly as if that was the simplest question in the world.

It wasn't, of course. Sure, I wanted to make it work. What woman wouldn't want her dream partner and her dream job at the same time? And yet I was intimately aware from every past relationship that that wasn't how life worked…at least not for me. I could understand why Jake and Reagan didn't see it that way, of course. She'd bet on herself, convinced her job to let her move to New York and gotten the man and the job at once. But everyone couldn't be so lucky. My position wasn't available in New York, and even if it was, I didn't want to stay here. I wanted to go back home, where I could see my parents in less than twenty minutes just by hopping on the Tube. Where my best girlfriends since primary school were waiting to welcome me back with open arms. Where I could go to Nando's or Dirty Martini with Craig and Robin and Frank without having to plan an eight-hour trip to see them. It was just that I also wanted Thomas, the unexpected blessing that had come into my life and shaken everything up.

But Thomas, well, he had made a perfect life for himself in New York. A life he loved so much he resisted dating me at first because he hadn't wanted to risk changing it. A life he deserved, and I wanted him to have, after all the hard work he'd put in at his firm—one that was about to make him a partner, for God's sake.

None of those realities changed just because I *wanted* to make things work.

"It's not that easy," I replied.

"Nothing worth having ever is," he answered.

I looked away from them both, with their eager hearts trying to impress upon me a reality I knew simply wasn't true, desperate to hold my composure and not draw the rest of the group's attention our way. But in my attempt at distraction, I noticed—and therefore they also noticed—the FaceTime call from Thomas trying to come through right at the worst possible time. I quickly silenced the call before anyone else could see it and stared Reagan and Jake down to hopefully, telepathically, let them know I didn't want to discuss what had just transpired.

"Does he know yet?" Reagan asked, somewhat taking the hint, but not really.

"Does he know what?"

"That you're giving up?"

Wow, what a gut punch.

I'd sort of expected it since Reagan wasn't one for mincing her words, but hearing it, as blunt as she'd said it, still stung a whole lot.

"I haven't told him that we shouldn't continue seeing each other yet, if that's what you mean."

"And so, he's still calling."

"He is."

"And you're not answering?"

I sighed heavily.

"I'm not."

"On Christmas."

Crap. She had a point there.

"So you're just, what, ghosting him?" Jake asked, now seemingly fired up at me in the same way he'd been ready to go to war when he'd thought Thomas to be the potential bad guy in all of this.

"I'm not… No, that's not…" I fumbled with my words, unsure of exactly what to say. "I just don't know how to tell him yet. Or what to say. I almost thought about writing a letter and leaving it at his flat—"

"Oh God, definitely don't do that," Reagan interrupted. "He deserves better than that, Liv. What you all have built deserves better. You know that."

"Yeah," I replied. "I know."

I slumped my shoulders and wished I could rewind things back to when Reagan had first come into the sitting room, figured out a way to put on a braver face, and then maybe we wouldn't be having this conversation. It was a faulty plan, but it was all I had in the moment.

"Okay, you three," Keisha shouted out, turning to us with her eyebrow raised. "If you're done with your little side conversation now, we'd all like you to rejoin the discussion."

"Sorry," Reagan replied, once again sitting back into her corner of the chaise lounge. "You're right. We're being rude."

"It's all good," Keisha replied. "Plus, you're back just in time for something I know you'll have an opinion on… 'Confessions One' or 'Two'?"

"Oh, that's easy," Jake replied, perking back up after having chastised me for the past couple minutes. "It's 'Confessions Two,' and it's not even close."

"Are you kidding me?" Reagan asked, flummoxed

and turning toward him with her arms folded. "The first 'Confessions' is iconic. All you have to do is play the first few notes, and everyone will start oooh-ooh-ing!"

"Yeah, babe, that might be true, but 'Two' has that bop with it. And I guarantee you most people know all the lyrics to that way more than they know the first one."

"I can't believe what you're saying right now." She laughed, playfully pushing him away from her as they continued on their debate, pulling in Gigi, Lucas and Brandon to defend their points.

I sat off to the side, pretending to laugh and be part of the discussion while silently taking in all that they'd just said to me. It had been very hard to hear, but they'd probably been at least right about the fact that Thomas deserved better than the way I was treating him. Not probably—I knew they were. That didn't make what I had to do any easier.

Turning to the side, I caught Keisha's eyes as she mouthed *You're welcome* to me and winked in my direction. I guess I had a Christmas angel on my side, someone who could tell I'd needed saving from Reagan and Jake's interrogation. I returned the favor and mouthed *Thank you* as I shook myself out of my thoughts and forced myself to be present again—to enjoy the beautiful people all around me, all clad in either warm earth tones or some combination of white or cream fabric. None of us with any stains after having devoured all that food…now that was what I called Black girl and boy magic!

"If it helps," I interjected, finally actively joining in the debate, "from a global perspective, I don't think the first one charted in the UK."

"Et tu, Olivia?" Reagan asked, dropping her mouth in shock.

"I'm just saying," I said with a shrug.

"Well, you can say all you want, but that doesn't mean it's not the better song."

She laughed, poking her lips out at me.

"Nah, let the woman cook. It's her only chance to be right today, so let her have it," Jake replied.

Oh brother. I can see now I won't be living this whole Thomas thing down anytime soon.

Chapter Sixteen

"Time check!" Reagan screamed out from the confines of her bathroom to anyone and no one, briefly startling me, Keisha and Gigi to attention before we each realized we were nowhere near a clock or phone to answer her.

"9:48 p.m.!" Jake called out from the sitting room, seated calmly on Rae's couch and sipping from his whiskey tumbler.

To his left was Brandon, also fully dressed and ready to go, the two of them decked out in their finest attire— Jake with his sky blue trousers, charcoal-gray oxfords and a black-and-silver striped button-down that he wore only half closed, and Brandon with his rust-colored tailored suit that he'd paired with a fitted white T-shirt and a pair of matching white Vans. Together, they sat and watched in awe as we ran around Reagan's apartment, trying to finalize the last bits of our outfits for New Year's Eve.

"Ugh," Reagan cried, finally fitting the last eyelash strip perfectly to her face, then waving her hand over it to make sure it was dry. "We are going to be sooo late."

I looked up from tying the final knot on my silver lace-up heels just in time to catch Gigi roll her eyes in exasperation. I could understand her frustration, as I'd been struggling to wrap the laces around my calves (and most importantly, have them stay there) for what had felt like hours, igniting my anxiety, too, which was only worsened by the feeling of being rushed. This heightened every extra minute it took me to get everything to work. But also, I'd finally got my thing done, so I also had the experience of jubilation that I was at once finally among the ready few. Gigi, beautiful as she was, was definitely not.

"See, this is why I don't like to go out for New Year's Eve…especially in New York City!" she said. "It's too much pressure."

Standing in front of Reagan's full-length mirror, Gigi slid her hands over her dress once more, smoothing down the cocoa-brown fabric to make sure the Spanx she wore underneath didn't show through. She turned to the right and left, inspecting all the angles where her shapewear secret could be exposed, finally spinning in a complete 180 to where her backside faced the mirror for one last check across her shoulders. Once satisfied with her look, Gigi glanced over at me, at first, I thought for my approval, but then her eyes lit up, beaming in a way that felt completely incongruent with her demeanor just a couple minutes before.

"Liv!" she exclaimed, swishing her way over to me. "You're done, right? Can you please zip me up? I could only get it to go so far up."

"Of course," I replied, motioning for her to spin around so I had access to her back. "It's like they make these things as torture devices to remind single women that they don't have an extra set of hands to help them."

"Seriously. But that's why we just end up all getting dressed together, I guess."

"Except Reagan only has one bathroom…and it's four of us." I bristled, reminding myself of why we were all feeling the angst and rush of the moment.

"Exactly. Yet another reason I don't like doing this."

I finished zipping Giselle's dress up and patted her on the back to signal my effort was complete, which she promptly thanked me for and went about trying to find the shoes she'd brought with her to wear for the evening. I knew they were somewhere among the litany of clothes and shoes tossed about Reagan's flat, but I wasn't entirely convinced she was going to find them in the little bit of time we had left.

"I knowwwww, you guys. I know," Reagan called out, seemingly overhearing our conversation while she delicately applied her red Fenty Beauty Stunna Lip Paint.

After she let it sit for a second to not get any on her teeth, she continued her thoughts.

"But you know this is Liv's one and only time to experience New Year's Eve in the city, so we had to do it right. We couldn't just be in Jake's condo, chilling and drinking champagne."

"I mean, but that sounds like a lot of fun to me," Jake interjected.

"Of course it does…to you!" she replied, finally emerging from the bathroom in a bright yellow-gold satin dress, the top shaped almost like a bustier with the straps meant to fall past her shoulders and midway down her upper arm.

The bottom of the dress was equally as fitted, showing off her small waist, with a high slit on the right that exposed almost her full size-ten thighs. Most importantly, she was now done and counted among the growing crew of people ready to leave.

"I want Liv to have a moment," she protested. "There are no New Year's Eve moments happening on One Hundred Thirty-Third in Harlem. That's why we're going to Magic Hour, and we're going to have a great time, damn it."

Jake chuckled and threw his hands up in defeat. If it was one thing he knew, it was when not to try to get Reagan off an idea she had in mind.

"Okay, guys," she said, again to no one and everyone all at the same time. "I'm calling the UberXL. It's almost ten o'clock now, and if we don't get out of here soon, we're going to be in line during the countdown..."

"And that will most definitely not be a moment," Gigi interrupted, joining our ever-growing group in the sitting room.

Pretending to wipe her forehead from exhaustion, she breathed in a huge sigh of relief. "All done," she said. "I cut it close, but you can never say Gigi Lewis is going to be late."

Reagan laughed and pressed Choose UberXL on her phone, knowing exactly who Gigi was referring to—the one person who'd yet to join us in the sitting room. Keisha had a lot of great qualities about her: loyalty, superb conversation skills, drive and ambition...but timeliness was just not one of them.

"We know, Gig. Thank you for that."

"Don't think I don't know that was a dig at me," Keisha called out as she finally came bouncing up to us, her velvet hot-pink dress and diagonal-patterned fishnet stockings stopping everyone in their tracks. "I'm ready, too, now, so there."

"I mean, if the shoe fits, babe." Reagan laughed, rolling her eyes. "But either way, I'm glad we're all ready now, with not a moment to spare."

She paused, checking her phone once again, and then said the dreaded words we'd all been worried would come too soon.

"Car's here."

Like we'd been waiting for the person at a racetrack who shoots the gun to let you know when you can finally start running, we all immediately sprang into action, quickly gathered our purses, phones, coats and other accessories, and began piling out of Reagan's flat. Brandon and Jake lagged a few steps behind us, still calm and unfazed. Clearly they'd got used to the chaos of the crew by now, refusing to let the women they called partner and friend rile them up on occasions such as this.

Must be nice, I thought. Chaos still very much left me flustered. And the night had only just begun.

It was nearly 11:00 p.m. when we finally walked into the winter wonderland rooftop party being hosted at Magic Hour NY in Midtown, just off Seventh Avenue. Once inside, we were immediately greeted by an après-themed pink-and-white explosion of decor, featuring everything from frosted Christmas trees to a sparkly dining carousel with over twenty-five thousand crystals and a pink-and-white winter lodge flanked incredibly by even more iced-out forestry. In the distance, I saw a group of women gathered on the makeshift dance floor, drinking and singing loudly to Pitbull and Ne-Yo's definitive dance song, the ever iconic "Give Me Everything," while others were seated in booths sipping spiked hot chocolate with their dates or posing for Instagramworthy photos.

I guess Reagan was right, I thought to myself. *This, and not Jake's condo, is exactly what a New Year's Eve in New York City should look like—decadence, elegance and iced-out decor, all under the beautiful and lit-up gaze of the Empire State Building.*

The six of us took our time walking through the crowd, making our way to the bar while simultaneously people watching and scoping the scene for who Keisha, Gigi and Brandon might want to kiss as the clock struck midnight. As for me—the only other sort of single person in the crew—I planned to ring in the new year simply sipping on a glass of champagne under the moonlight and trying to forget all the ways I was likely actively hurting the one person who made my whole face smile just thinking about him.

If I could pull that off and spend one night not internally beating myself up for letting Thomas down over and over, well, that…would be a New Year's Eve miracle all on its own.

Since that fated morning after I received Walter's message, I'd managed to do the exact opposite almost every day. To be fair, our random conversations didn't change instantly, but any time Thomas broached the idea of us seeing each other again, I clammed up and made an excuse for why we couldn't. In my heart, I knew I was wrong. But I was paralyzed in a way I'd never been before—hating the idea of having to end things with him and simultaneously realizing I was doing it anyway, but with no real closure. It was the ultimate coward's way out, and eventually, he took the hint. Our calls and texts grew fewer and fewer until we'd barely talked to each other in days.

Tonight had to be different, I thought. If only just for the prospect of truly starting the year off as a new beginning.

After we finally reached the bar and gave our orders to Jake to place, I looked around and let my eyes land on a group of guys standing in a corner laughing. Their faces were filled with so much happiness and exuberance as they slapped each other on the shoulders and curled over in laughter. It was a beautiful sight to behold, men just expressing joy around each other, in their own element and not at all aware of anyone else paying them any attention.

I made a mental note to myself that a few of them seemed like they could be good prospects for Gigi or Keish.

The only thing was, as I stared in closer, it almost looked as if Thomas was standing in the midst of those friends. But that wasn't possible, right? In a city as big as New York, there was no way we'd somehow ended up at the same party. It was just my brain pranking me out of guilt.

I blinked my eyes feverishly to make sure I wasn't making up what I saw before me, but after several seconds of trying, I could no longer deny the truth. There he was. Standing off to the side with a fitted white shirt rolled halfway up his forearms and buttoned about three-fourths up his chest with a pair of gray-striped

plaid pants that seemed as if they'd been tailor-made
for him. And of course, his smile (that dimple!) was in
full effect—bright enough to compete with the Empire
State Building towering over us all.

Caught up in the moment, I couldn't stop myself
from staring. First, I was stunned by his outfit choice,
not because he didn't look great—of course he did; he
always did—but because we had barely talked in the
past week and somehow his outfit managed to perfectly
complement my silver deep V-neck disco dress with its
low scoop back and the silky white oversize blazer that
I paired it with.

Wonderful, I thought. It was as if God and the universe were trying to troll me.

"Reagan," I said, grabbing her toward me. "Is this
what you meant by a New Year's Eve moment? Please
tell me you didn't plan this."

Her curious look told me she had no idea what I was
talking about. So, in my best attempt to not draw attention to us, I positioned her head in direct eyesight of
Thomas to clue her in on what I was rambling about.
Reagan's eyes instantly bulged out as she turned toward me to protest the idea that she had anything to do
with Thomas and me being in the same space tonight.

"Oh, no, Liv, this definitely isn't me. I know how
hard this week has been for you—I promise I wouldn't
set you up like this."

I breathed a sigh of relief. She was right. I knew that
this was beyond what she would go through to put us
together. She might have pushed me to attend that first
party because we'd known he would be there, but she
wouldn't orchestrate an ambush—that wasn't her style.

"You're right. I'm sorry for even asking. I just…

What do I do now? I mean, he's literally standing right there."

Reagan looked at me sympathetically and then turned to her left as Jake tapped her on her shoulder and passed her two shot glasses.

"The only thing you can do, *cher*. Take this shot and hope he doesn't see you."

She passed me one of the chilled shot glasses, and without another word, the two of us poured the smooth white tequila down our throats and then promptly chased it with the limes that had come stuck on the rim of the glasses.

"I may need a few more of those," I replied.

"Uhh, you might actually need a bucket, Liv."

I watched Reagan's face turn sideways as she saw, and then I saw, that any hope I'd had of Thomas missing me was long gone. In an instant, we locked eyes from across the room, his deep gray eyes staring daggers into my soul. Like all the times before, his intense gaze halted any movement or breaths from me, but this time it wasn't because of how turned on I was. It was because I was being forced to face him, after having told him I no longer had doubts and then immediately going back on that word the very next day, slowly and horribly ticking away at us with my inaction. The awful things he must have thought about me.

"Here, take another shot," Reagan said, briefly grabbing my attention as she passed me another chilled glass.

I dutifully took the smooth liquor out of her hands and happily obliged, as if my actions were no longer under my control. Take a shot? Sure. Stand paralyzed while the man of your dreams glares at you from a corner? Why not. There was nothing I could do about it anyway. Nothing I could do except once again pour the white liquid down my throat, suck the lime, ask for another one and repeat.

By the time I downed my fourth one, my glazed-over eyes were finally able to somewhat protect me from Thomas's insistent stares. I still felt them, don't get me wrong, and all the disappointment hidden behind them, but at least I could no longer clearly see just how much I'd hurt him. And that was a win I'd readily take since there seemed to be no others in sight. That look, now blurry despite its persistence, held within it all the times he'd tried to call or text me and I'd made excuses for why I was busy or unavailable.

I continued watching him through my now distorted view, studying his every move as he interacted with his friends but never dropped his eyes from mine for more than a few seconds. Each time he did, I could barely count to the number five on my hand before once again, we were locked in, neither of us knowing what to say or do but somehow understanding the magnetic draw we still had with each other.

"I'll be right back," I said, leaning over to Reagan as the rest of our friends toasted to the pending new year behind us.

"Wait, where are you going?"

"You know where."

Filled with a ton of liquid confidence, I slammed my latest empty shot glass down onto the bar, ran my hands through my passion twists and stepped toward him, one uneasy foot at a time. My entire way there, through the thick of the growing New Year's Eve crowd, my eyes stayed on his, almost begging him to forgive me, still adore me, not hate me. And as I got closer, the pounding of my heartbeat steadily increased, regret beginning to overtake the liquid courage. But I pressed on, knowing that at this point, there was no turning back. That would have been even more humiliating.

"Hi, Liv," he said as I walked up to him, his eyes tracing the length of my body.

"Hi, there. Do you think we could talk?"

I bit my bottom lip nervously, praying that he wasn't going to immediately reject my request. I hadn't thought that part completely through when I'd started on my journey, when I'd decided I needed to speak to him immediately. The ugly truth I didn't want to face was that he had every right to react in whatever way made him comfortable. And I knew that, glazed-over eyes and all. So, I stood there awaiting his response and braced myself for the worst-case scenario.

"Sure," he replied, stepping off to the side and guiding me to do the same with his large hand lightly placed on my back.

"You look really handsome," I admitted with a sigh once we were on our own, just a few steps away from his watchful friends but secluded enough for there to be at least somewhat of a private conversation.

"Thank you. You look stunning, per usual."

His eyes lit up almost uncontrollably and the smirk I'd once been thrilled by slipped out from his face. It reminded me of the look he'd had on our first non-date, one of awe, where he seemed to be asking me *How did I get so lucky?* without a single word. I missed that look. It had at one time made me believe I could have it all. Now it just felt like it came with a lot of unsaid, really sad words and maybe even a heaping load of regret.

Thomas must have felt similarly as he quickly corrected himself and returned back to the stoic look that he'd been giving me since he saw I was there.

"It's been a while, Liv," he said, his deep voice matching the serious expression on his face.

"I know."

"Not cool."

"I know."

I adjusted my stance in my heels as I awkwardly readied myself to receive whatever verbal punishment he wanted to lay on me. I deserved it after all. And lowest of keys, some part of me kind of needed it to feel better about hurting the one person I'd never wanted to let down.

"I definitely wasn't expecting to see you here," I added.

"Yeah, same. But maybe it's for the best, since I think you've been avoiding me, right?"

And there it was. Not a verbal punishment at all, but a truthful acknowledgment. That was maybe worse.

"Honestly, Thomas, I just haven't known exactly what to say," I admitted, holding myself back from drawing in closer to him.

"Is it because of the job back home? Is that why you started pulling back from me?"

"Yeah," I said quietly.

Of course he'd figured it out, I realized. At the end of the day, it wasn't that hard to understand. With me now most certainly leaving, I'd *had* to cut my ties and run off before I got too deep with him, before I allowed myself to believe…

Thomas nodded silently with a full understanding washing over his face. Then, as if he needed the space to process his thoughts, he backed up a few steps from me before continuing. "Did you ever think you weren't the only one whose feelings needed protecting?"

"Yeah. Every day, really."

I locked eyes with him once more, tears threatening to fall from mine, but desperate to cry out to him and remind him how I wasn't an evil person. I'd just been scared. And was that so hard to understand?

"And yet you still…"

"And yet I still… I just—"

"Chose to shield yourself from me, of all people," he interjected.

I stood in silence, once again at a loss for words, watching the man before me admit how my actions had affected him. How in my haste to take care of me, like I'd *always* had to do before—you know, get in front of the pending rejection, focus on my career and my friends, not let it break me down too much—I'd failed to trust him. I'd failed.

Neither of us moved, even as it was clear that the conversation had ended, our legs or minds or both somehow paralyzed into this one position. What else more was there left to say, really? We'd been a thing, a beautiful thing, an unexpected thing for months—but ultimately something I couldn't rely on not to eventually hurt me. And so then, we weren't a thing…not anymore.

All around us, the energy of the rooftop grew exponentially as it suddenly dawned on me that we were nearing the time of the NYE countdown. To my left and right, I saw people frantically pouring champagne into their flutes, getting their noisemakers ready and signaling to their smooch partners they were indeed the one. Behind me, I knew my crew was doing about the same, going through the motions to prepare themselves for the moment

Reagan had promised me...the whole reason we were here in the first place. I knew they were getting their toasts ready, each one with their favorite drink in their hand and maybe a glass of champagne, too. That they were likely watching us from afar, waiting to see if we'd break our gaze in time so I could rejoin them, dancing and shouting my way into the new year.

And yet I couldn't move. Thomas didn't, either. Our feet plastered just a few steps apart, our bodies barely within arms' length, but our eyes remained locked in— refusing, for some reason, to let go, even as we finally heard the crowd begin its countdown.

Ten, nine, eight, seven, six, five, four, three, two... one! Happy New Year!

As shouts of joy filled every speck of the rooftop except one, so did bursts of confetti and the sound of clinking drinks and noisemakers. We'd made it to a new year, spent it together, in fact, but not like either of us had expected.

Thomas stepped toward me, the closest he'd dared to get all night, and finally leaned over and kissed me on my cheek. It was achingly close to my lips and provided me with just enough time to smell his signature Le Labo scent, but it was over in two seconds.

"Good night, Olivia," he said. "I really do hope you get out of New York everything you came here for."

"Happy New Year, Thomas," I replied, my voice barely coming out as it got caught in my throat, a signal that even my body knew it was really, really over this time.

As he walked away, the tears I'd been successfully holding back instantly began pouring out. And my body, once poised and braced for the verbal punishment that of course never came—because that wasn't the kind of man he'd ever been—slumped over with exhaustion, trying desperately to prevent the heaving and wailing I felt coming on.

Thankfully, before I could fully melt down in front of what felt like the world, I felt a small hand on my shoulder and the reassuring voice that had been with me since I'd stepped out of the JFK International Airport months before.

"It's okay, Liv," Reagan said, bringing me into her embrace. "It's going to be okay. I promise."

I didn't have the heart or the ability to tell her how much it wasn't.

"Okay, let's go to the bathroom," she added.

With her arm still around me, Reagan started walking me out of the rooftop toward the hallway where the bathrooms were and holding me up so that if you didn't know the situation, you might have just thought she was helping a friend who'd had a bit too much to drink. We passed by tables and sections of the fanciest-clothed people, all dancing, all happy, all oblivious to the two women trying to get past them so that the one in the sequined minidress could cry her heart out in private. So I could finally release every fear I'd been holding in ever since I'd gotten Walter's message.

When we finally reached our destination and stepped inside, Reagan quickly locked the door behind us and turned to me with sympathetic eyes.

"It's okay, now, Liv," she repeated from earlier. "You can let it all out now."

And I did.

Under the cover of the loud music and the insulated bathroom, I let out the loudest wail and cried and cried and cried until I didn't think I had any tears left in me.

Chapter Seventeen

In the privacy of a Midtown bathroom, Reagan stood by, without judgment, and let me cry until my screams eventually turned to sniffles. Only then did she reach for some tissue to pass to me, somehow knowing that doing so before then would have been a futile effort on her part. Thankfully, after about fifteen to twenty minutes of uninterrupted tears, I calmed down enough to be able to take it from her hand and try—at least attempt—to pull myself together.

"I'm so sorry," I said to her once I felt I could finally get words successfully out of my mouth. "You shouldn't have to see me like this."

"For what? Please don't apologize for having feelings or needing a friend."

"I just don't do this, you know. I don't break down crying in front of people."

I wiped the tissue all around my face, effectively removing the majority of the makeup I'd painstakingly applied just hours before in her flat. But it didn't matter in that moment. I needed to try to start erasing the remnants of this embarrassing situation away, so if that meant my Fenty foundation went with it, then so be it.

"I'm used to being there for others," I admitted. "Not the other way around."

"We all need support sometimes, Liv," Reagan replied, passing me another tissue, but this one she'd wet slightly beforehand to keep me from having pieces of tissue stuck to my face. "Maybe the people who are always there for others even more so. And honestly, if you can't cry with your friends, who can you cry with?"

"Yeah," I answered softly. "I know."

It dawned on me that this was the same refrain I'd had in my conversation with Thomas, and the tears started pouring out again as I recalled the expression on his face as he'd watched me, unable to say anything back to him except a continuous acknowledgment that he was right. I was the bad guy, the villain in our story. *Where can the waterworks still be coming from?* I wondered. *Isn't there a limit to just how much any one person can cry?*

"Do you want to talk about what you're feeling right now?" she asked. "You don't have to, but if you want to, I'm here."

"I appreciate that, Rae. Genuinely."

Through more sniffles, I attempted once again to dry up my tears, breathing in and out deeply to calm down my nervous system.

"And I do want to talk about it," I admitted. "I just don't know if I have the words to fully express everything running in my head right now."

"I know, *cher*," Reagan said, drawing near to me and taking my hands in hers. "But try."

Those were the exact same words she'd said to me at the party in Brooklyn months before, indicative of the kind of unconditional support she offered her friends with just a smidge of challenging when needed. Indeed, with those five small words, she conveyed so much. That she understood the difficulty I was having, that she could relate to my fear and regrets, that she was there for me if I spoke about it or not—but importantly, in addition to all that, she wanted me to give it a shot. Try. Just try. Three little letters, yet they carried so much weight.

"Well, you know I'm not someone who gets swept off her feet," I started up, wiping at my eyelids again with the wet tissue. "I had a plan, Rae! And it was a good plan, a *perfect plan*, one that would set me up for the kind of future I could only dream of as a young girl living in Brixton."

I glanced over at her and saw how attentively she was listening and was all at once comforted and uneasy. Needing to distract myself with something while I spoke, I walked toward the bathroom mirror and began fluffing my hair, as if the curls in my passion twists really mattered at a time like this. Somehow it helped me continue, however; just the act of focusing on something mundane gave me the strength I needed to explain the devastation I was dealing with.

"But Thomas did the thing that never happens," I continued. "He literally came into my life and changed everything. He made me start to believe that I could have real love. That someone might want me for me and not suggest that I had to choose him over my career. That someone would actually desire me, all of me, with all my quirks and my extra-ness. For a brief moment, I thought I could have it all, but we know that's not true. I'm not living in a Disney movie here. And so before I could get hurt again, be disappointed once again…before I got caught up too much…"

I paused to try to gather my thoughts, realizing that I was fumbling over my words toward the end of my explanation as I continued struggling trying to describe the conflict in my head and heart to someone else. I hoped that Reagan could understand the gist of what I was saying…that she could hear me even through my failed words.

"Walter's message about the promotion, it just reminded me what my priorities were supposed to be. The perfect plan. And nothing else," I added.

"So you ended things to prevent yourself from being hurt again?" she asked.

"Something like that. I guess."

Except I never actually said the words to him; I just slowly disappeared before he could eventually disappoint me and turn out like every other guy before him, I thought to myself.

"But aren't you hurt now, anyway, *cher*?"

Reagan's question, while genuine and meaningful, still stung. And it instantly made me pause the fluffing of my hair in the mirror. I turned back around to her and quietly mouthed, *Yes*.

Seeing the way my body slumped over, Rae sprang into action and immediately removed the space between us, grabbing me and pulling me into another one of her warm embraces. At first, I barely allowed my arms to hug her back, but as she stood unrelenting and unwilling to let me go, I slowly gave in and finally squeezed her back. All this did, of course, was incite more tears, but by then, I had no more fight left in me to try to swallow them down or prevent them from tumbling down my face. Instead, I just held on to her tightly and let the tears do as they wished, wetting up her bare left shoulder in the process.

"Listen, you know I know a thing or two about making perfect plans," she whispered, still gripping me tightly. "I mean, I created a list and a rewards plan to finally begin taking risks in my life for God's sake, and even then, it was really hard for me to stop relying on the crutch of perfectionism in the areas of my life where I was trying to mask my fear. So, I get it. I get why you've needed to make your plans and stick to them, because not doing so is really scary, right?"

"Yeah," I replied.

"But here's the thing, *cher*. I would never tell you not to make your plans. I just would ask you to consider how it can actually *be* a perfect plan if it doesn't allow room for you to fall in love with a man who literally makes your heart jump. How is a plan like that really serving you?"

I stood there in silence, still holding on to Reagan and thinking really hard about her last set of questions. The truth was I didn't have a ready response for her. I don't think she actually expected me to. But that, in only a way that a true friend could, her job was simply to toss the challenging thought into the universe and allow me to consider it, to question what it meant that I'd given up hope that my plans made room for love, and the moment I was presented with the opposite—I ran.

After a few more minutes, I finally started releasing my grip on her, allowing my arms and then hers to slowly fall back by our sides. I'd got the strength and the love and the challenge I needed to proceed forward, so now it was time to do so—and at least try to enjoy what was left of the party. After all, we'd come here presumably for me. I'd be letting myself and the others down if I just stayed in the bathroom all night.

I moved back to the mirror so I could reassess my look. From the neck down, at least, I still appeared as if I was a woman ready to party. Amazingly, the straps that were wrapped around my calves were even still intact. And because Reagan had had the foresight to take my white blazer off me as soon as we'd entered the bathroom, that had also been saved from any potential makeup and tearstains. But oh, my face was a wreck.

"Don't worry—I got you," Reagan said as she joined me in the mirror and began pulling makeup essentials out of her clutch, including her mascara, blotting papers, eyeliner, bronzer and red lipstick. "Now, obviously, I don't have your foundation, but your skin is gorgeous, so we won't worry too much about that and just focus on everything else. I do think the blotting papers might be able to help us smooth out some areas where there are tear streaks, so we can try that, too. That, with some mascara and eyeliner, and you'll be brand-new."

"Rae, who are you?" I laughed. "Why do you just have all this stuff in your purse? Not that I'm complaining, but…wow."

"Girl, you know I stay ready so I don't have to get ready. Plus, ever since Jake revealed that a proposal is coming soon, I keep some small essentials with me just in case. Because you know I will be a mess when it happens, and before we take any photos, I'm going to need someone to help me wipe my face down!"

I chuckled along with her, realizing suddenly that

it was the first time I'd laughed in hours and just how much I'd needed it.

"Well, if it happens while I'm still here, I got you, too."

"Oh, I know," she said with a wink. "That's not even a question."

Once Reagan was done prepping her makeup area, stacking up the items in the order she planned to use them, she went about the business of repairing my once flawlessly applied makeup.

Gently, she used a combination of the blotting papers and some damply wet napkins to reduce the smearing that had occurred as a result of my tears, lightly dabbing each part of my face, from my forehead to the areas that creased around my full lips. Then she motioned for me to lift my eyes upward so that she could reapply my eyeliner unobstructed to my lower lash line and then smudge it a bit, allowing my eyes to still pop despite no longer having the sparkly mauve eye shadow I'd previously worn. After that, Reagan moved to the mascara, dipping the wand into its case multiple times before she finally pulled it out and added three full coats to each of my lashes. I legit looked as if I had on false lashes when she was done, which was no small feat since I'd always felt that mine were never as long or as full as I wanted them to be. Lastly, she took the fleshy part of her middle finger and swiped the bronzer onto it, and then circled that around the upper parts of my cheeks.

By the time she was done, you could barely tell that this wasn't my original look. The only slight giveaway was some of the puffiness that remained near my eyes from all the damn crying, but honestly, she'd basically performed a miracle.

"Wow," I said, staring into the mirror in awe. "You might have missed your calling as a makeup artist, babes."

"Oh, definitely not. This was one of those *desperate times call for desperate measures* kind of things. I would never want to do this for anyone else regularly. The pressure alone...no, I'll stick with writing."

"Fair, fair," I replied, laughing with a slight roll of my eyes.

It felt nice to smile again—cathartic, even.

"Okay, now there's one thing left to do," Reagan said as she meticulously began putting all her makeup back into her purse.

"Okayyy," I replied with only a small bit of hesitation.

"When we walk out of here, I want you to strut out of this bathroom like nothing just happened. Pretend you're a nineties supermodel on the runway, for all I care. But you walk out of here with your head held high, your shoulders arched back and your toes pointing forward. For all anyone should know, you came to the bathroom for the same reason we all do—to freshen up or to use it. That's it."

"So what you're telling me," I said with a smirk, already pre-giggling at the TikTok reference I was getting ready to use. "Nobody's gonna know."

"How would they know?" she replied with a wink, and unlocked the door back to reality.

In a flash, I quickly scooped up my blazer, put my arms back through it and walked out just as Reagan had directed—all the way back to the rest of the crew, who had by now migrated from the bar to an open area near the carousel. As we approached them, we were instantly greeted with smiles and cheers, and two glasses of champagne—one for me, and one for Reagan.

"Welcome back," Keisha said, dancing circles around us and cajoling us into joining her party groove as she swayed side to side while Usher's "Bad Girl" played in the background. "You may have missed the first toast, dear Liv, but guess what? The beauty of a New Year's Eve party is that there's always a chance for another one. So, we saved these for y'all because you can't very well start the new year without some bubbly. I won't allow you to jinx yourself like that. Not on my watch. No, ma'am."

"I'm very down for that," I replied.

"Tuh. Say less then, my girl!"

Keisha turned around briefly and grabbed her own glass of champagne, nudging Gigi, Jake and Brandon to join us while I playfully bumped Reagan on her side, silently thanking her again for everything. It took another couple minutes for everyone to have a full glass in their hands, but once the logistics were all handled, there we were, all in a circle, our smiles and glasses lifted high, giving me a new shot at a new beginning without ever needing to acknowledge all the sadness that preceded it.

"Cheers!" we all screamed out in unison, clanking our glasses together and then dutifully taking our individual sips of the sparkling wine meant for celebrations.

It was just the reset I needed after such a hard and draining experience, and I couldn't have been more grateful for this set of human beings if I tried.

I looked around briefly to see if Thomas was still around but never found him again. It was just as well,

I thought. Reagan had given me a lot to consider in the bathroom, and I didn't need to see him again until I could firmly and assertively answer all the questions she'd posed once and for all.

Chapter Eighteen

At approximately 6:15 p.m., with the office quiet and no sign of Walter's stomping feet coming down the hallway, I closed my laptop, put my Slack notifications on Away and set about packing up all my stuff to head home.

This was the new me.

Still Team Extra, still utterly committed to my job, but finally starting to trust myself and the work I'd put in for our management group enough that I didn't feel obligated to stay until 9:00 p.m. every night to prove I belonged there. This meant that if the building wasn't metaphorically burning down, there was no good reason that I couldn't leave out before 6:30 p.m. like everyone else—even, critically, Walter, who'd made a New Year's resolution to spend more nights at home with his fiancée.

To be fair, it was winter in New York City, so I still

wasn't beating the sunset home. But this was progress I was very proud of. Progress that hadn't come about as part of some easy revelation, but one that had come through countless nights of self-examination and finally, at the end, a sense of calm and self-assurance that washed over me. These nightly self-check-ins had started off as just excuses to agonize over Reagan's questions, but slowly they'd begun evolving so that by week three, the whole thing had turned into revelation after revelation about how I wanted to live my life going forward.

And so, in the three weeks since the infamous New Year's Eve party meltdown, I'd come to understand a few important things about myself:

1. I'd never, not once, failed to give something in my career my all. This was the number one thing everyone at work knew about me: if Liv was on the case, she would move mountains before she let you down. And while that meant some long nights and sometimes not having the people in my life understand my dedication, it had also gotten me to where I was right now—on the precipice of everything I wanted. I'd take that exchange any day!

2. Despite this shining example of what happened when I didn't quit staring me in my face, I'd stopped myself over and over when it came to my love life, cutting things off before things got too hard or going numb before I was vulnerable enough with my partner that they could hurt me if they wanted to. That was what David had meant in our last conversation in London, I realized. He was an insensitive idiot for saying I'd chosen my ambition over us, but he'd been right that

I'd checked out on him a long time before that talk and nothing he could have said would have stopped me.

It was in the nightly check-ins that I'd come to understand this was all part of my way to protect myself because I could never count on the men I dated. But what I could always count on was my career going exactly as I planned if I put in the work, and so I relied heavily on that. I was essentially like the woman who didn't consciously understand that the reason she loved shopping for shoes so much was because, unlike with her clothing, she could confidently say which shoes would look good on her and what size worked for her in different styles, etcetera. If you knew that a 40 always fit no matter what shoe store you shopped at, for example, why even deal with the messiness of trying to figure out which clothes fit and looked nice on you when that could vary so much in every store across the UK and America? *Because you still need clothes is eventually what that woman might realize, just like I eventually realized I wanted/needed love, too.*

3. I was a damn rock star! Clearly everyone at my job saw it, and so I needed to believe it, too, instead of constantly taking on more and more work to prove my worth. That was how I'd ended up in New York after all, right? With no sense of what I'd be doing but a belief that if I excelled at yet another thing they put before me, I'd prove once again that I deserved what I'd already proved I deserved.

4. I desperately missed Thomas, and even more than that, I loved him…and that—that realization—had been the most eye-opening. For I'd never really loved anyone like that before, not really. My parents, my brother, my friends, yes…but a man who could get up and leave at

any moment? No. I'd never dared. And so the part of my brain that hadn't been ready for that had needed to run away as fast as humanly possible. But I'd been a fool to let my fears prevent me from just letting him love me back. *What a mess.*

On this day, however, at now 6:25 p.m., I, Olivia Robinson, was not a mess. In fact, more than anything, I was clear and prepared for whatever came next. With my workbag fully repacked, I grabbed my cherry-red coat, tied it around my waist and headed for the door. As I walked past Walter's office, I saw him engaged in a similar fashion, hurriedly closing down his work so he could get out of the building on time. I nodded toward him, and with a simple wink, he reaffirmed my decision.

"See you tomorrow, Olivia," he said, stuffing stacks of papers into his briefcase.

"Have a good night, Walter," I replied, continuing my procession forward, past the cubicles, then to Wendy's desk, to the lifts on our floor and through the atrium once I made it downstairs.

As I walked through the now equally silent atrium— the only sounds being the echoes of my heels click-clacking on the floor—I reached into my workbag and scooped up my phone. I'd followed through on one commitment to myself—now it was time to make good on the second. I clicked on Thomas's name and waited for the phone to start dialing.

"Liv," he said, answering on the second or third ring.

His voice sounded gravelly—his deep baritone piercing through the raspy whisper he was attempting—but also incredibly familiar, like the way it felt to hear my mum's *Welcome home* after a long day of work.

"Is everything okay?"

In the background, I heard the also unmistakable sounds of New York bustling all around him, the way the idle chatter resounded in the walls of the train, the muffled announcement from the conductor probably alerting passengers that the doors were closing and then the whoosh that told me he was on the move again.

"Yes, everything's fine," I replied. "I... I..."

I breathed in deeply, trying to steady my nerves for what I was getting ready to say, and then with a burst of energy, I blurted it out as fast as I could before I stopped myself. "I'm really sorry about the way I handled things with us, but I was hoping we could talk sometime this week if you're free."

Seconds went by as I awaited his response with bated breath, wondering if he'd even heard me, if his phone had cut off on the train or if it had come through loud and clear and he was just trying to figure out how to nicely tell me no.

Finally, after what felt like an hour of torture, I heard his voice saying something into the phone, jolting me out of my thoughts in time to get back present into the conversation.

"Did you want to meet up?" he asked.

"Yeah, I think that would be nice."

"Okay."

He paused yet another set of painstakingly long seconds, and I couldn't help but wonder what was going through his mind. We hadn't spoken to each other in weeks, after all, and here I was, calling him out of the blue. If it were me, I'd be saying, *You barely had any words to say the last time we saw each other, and now you want to talk?* if I even answered the phone.

Thank God he's not like me.

"I can do tomorrow after work if you're free then," he said.

"That would be perfect. Thank you."

"Sure, it's no problem. Are you good to come to my place? Feels like somewhere quiet might be best for us."

"Absolutely," I replied, maybe a little too eagerly. "Does seven o'clock work for you?"

"Yeah, I'll be home by then. I'll text you my address."

"Okay, great. I'll see you then."

"Good night, Liv."

"Good night, Thomas."

And with that, we both ended the call, his voice still reverberating in my ears and making me miss him that much more. The silence at the end of the call was maybe even worse than the pauses as he'd gathered himself throughout, but that was okay…it was just my central nervous system realizing what I already knew, I told myself. Yes, what I was doing was terrifying, but I owed it to myself to do the scary thing in pursuit of love for once.

After a series of deep breaths in and out, I slipped my phone back into my workbag and continued on my walk out of the building, past the maze of wooden benches and perfectly manicured, plush green bushes and out into the cold, damp January air. It was just the bolt I needed to not start overthinking. In fact, January in New York felt a lot like London, with its gray skies, frigid weather and an energy that propelled me forward, toward my train station and then eventually home, where I had only one thing on my agenda for the night: pick out a killer outfit worthy of getting my man back.

* * *

Standing in front of Thomas's prewar walk-up building on West Seventy-Fifth Street in my camel-brown nude sweaterdress with its asymmetrical collar that dipped past my left shoulder, cinched at the waist and then fell to about mid-calf like a proper pencil skirt, I had an epiphany that I was planning to use as my saving grace no matter his reaction.

This might end in failure, I thought, *but I'm not going to let fear talk me out of trying yet again.*

With all the courage I could muster, I made my way up the redbrick steps winding toward the front door and dialed his apartment number into the call box. Within a few seconds, his voice boomed through the speaker, calling out my name as both a question and a response.

"Liv?" he asked.

"It's me, yeah," I replied, trying not to awkwardly fidget before I even saw him.

"Okay, come on up."

He sounded calm—chill, even—which stopped me in my tracks only briefly as I pondered if that meant good or bad things for my prospects. I also knew I had to catch the door before it locked again, so with another deep breath in and out, I quickly pulled the handle and walked into the building. *There's no turning back now.*

Thomas's flat sat on the second floor of the building, like mine, which gave me even more time to gather my thoughts. It was odd even being here, really. As much time as we'd spent together and even FaceTimed while he was home, it hit me sort of ironically that this would be my first time seeing it in person. It was like telling someone you loved them only after you'd broken up.

Oh, right. I'm planning to do that, too, I said to myself. Well, I guess this made more sense than I'd realized, then.

After carefully making my way up the stairs so that I didn't trip in the deep chocolate knee-high boots that fit perfectly under my dress, I turned to the left and saw a door swing open. And there he was, waiting for me. Still somewhat dressed in his clothes from work but far more relaxed, he wore a pair of black trousers that looked like they would have made any tailor proud. He'd also unbuttoned his shirt at least twice and taken it out of his pants, letting it casually fall across his torso.

If I wasn't careful, I could easily see myself getting swept up in all the ways he physically enticed me—that part was easy. But I wanted tonight to be about something deeper, a chance for us to be emotionally honest with each other and experience the type of intimacy I'd always wanted but never believed I could have.

"You made it," he said, holding the door open wide so that I could slide past him and into his entryway.

"I did, yeah," I replied, staring into his eyes as he closed the door behind him. "I said I would."

"Yeah, you did."

His voice dropped to a soft whisper, and it instantly broke my heart because I knew what that meant. I'd also told him I was ready to be with him and had gone back on that statement, so who was I to suddenly have my words believed? He didn't have to say that out loud. He probably never would. But I felt every bit of the sting in just those three words alone.

I cleared my throat and tried to start again.

"Is this a shoes-off place?" I asked him, still standing in his entryway, flanked by two closets that faced each other.

The way the space was set up, he couldn't exactly get by me unless he touched me, whether it was to brush my shoulder or maybe guide me to the side by placing his gentle hand on the small of my back. Part of me wanted to see if he'd try, if he was as desperate as I was for his touch—not necessarily sexually, but in that way that told a person you hadn't completely closed yourself off from them. He waited by the door, however, nodding yes as his reply and then watching me as I gingerly slipped the boots down my legs and off my feet.

"Do you need help?" he asked eventually, maybe suddenly remembering that we weren't strangers and he could, in fact, put his hands on me without it being a problem.

By then, however, I was practically done and slightly deflated that it had taken him so long to offer. "No, I'm good. Thank you."

Now able to proceed further into his place, I walked into the sitting room that somehow looked exactly as I pictured it and also sort of not. There were parts of it, like the double-paned windows, which took up almost the whole wall next to the kitchen, that looked much larger in person. Then there were other things, like his coffee-brown sofa and the matching entertainment center underneath his TV, that were a perfect match from what I'd seen over the phone. In a way it reminded me of us and how I could have been looking at us for so long and while I'd had some stuff very right, some parts I'd had so, so very wrong.

"Do you want something to drink?" he asked, following me into the sitting room and watching me marvel beside him.

"Water would be good, yes, thanks."

God, we sounded like two people who'd never met each other before, still trying to be incredibly polite and tiptoe around each other. *This is not at all what I want.*

Thomas dipped into the kitchen, which was visible from the sitting room via a built-in bar/counter, where he'd added two tan-and-brown bar stools since the last time we'd been on video.

"Are these new?" I asked, pointing toward them as he closed the fridge door and passed me a chilled bottle of water.

"Yeah, they are. I got them as a beginning-of-the-year gift for myself."

"Oh, okay," I replied, cringing inside at the reference to the new year. "Well, that's great, Thomas. They look great."

We both stared into the other's eyes, not really knowing what else to say or maybe having so much to say, we didn't know where to start. Either way, the tension was palpable as I opened up my bottle and gulped down as many droplets of the refreshing liquid as I could without choking. After I finished the water in one fell swoop, I turned back to him and finally pushed the words out of my mouth.

"So, I wanted to…" I began.

"So, you wanted to…" he chimed in, both of us starting at the same time and realizing at once that the other was about to say something, too.

"I'm sorry—you go first," I added…only it was once again at the same time as he tried to tell me the same.

"Wow, we really suck at this," he said, finally daring to smile at me due to the insanity of the moment.

"Yeah, very much so," I agreed, grinning as well.

If nothing else, the absurdity had broken the ice

between us. It also reminded me how much I missed laughing with him.

"Why don't we sit down first?" Thomas offered, gesturing toward his couch. "Then at least we're comfortable and you can tell me what you wanted to talk about."

"Okay," I said, obliging and plopping down onto the brown wool cushions.

Once I got comfortable and steadied my breathing, I looked across the couch toward Thomas and began the speech I'd practiced in my bathroom mirror all night.

"Let me start by saying I know how much I hurt you, and I'm really sorry for that. It's no excuse, but I was scared and couldn't see my way past all my worries that I would inevitably fall in love with you—a man who needs to stay here—while I need to go back home, and by the summer, I'd be a wreck. The ironic part of it all is that I was already in love with you. I just didn't want to admit it because, honestly, everything about us is a disruption to the life I planned for myself. And that's…thrilling in a way that is hard to explain, but it also terrified me to the point where I'd lay in bed all night, chest tight, agonizing about how I got myself in this situation."

Thomas listened attentively as I continued talking, barely moving on his side of the couch, but by his facial expressions, I could tell he was trying to understand me even as I sometimes fumbled over my words while trying to explain my thought process. It wasn't like I was ever really going to be able to fully explain all the fears I'd been experiencing at the time because I barely understood them, but I knew I owed it to him— to us—to try.

"So, anyway," I continued with a sigh, "I don't want

you to think it was an easy decision to back up from us—because it wasn't. One part of me was sure that it was the best thing to do to avoid either of us getting even more hurt than we already were, and the other part was so angry at myself for running away from the first man outside of my family who ever supported me and didn't want to change me and just... You just wanted me for me. And I wanted you for you, but I didn't... I don't know, I guess I didn't know how to handle that when it was in front of me."

"Do you regret us meeting and getting to know each other?" he asked, finally interjecting, and thankfully stopping me before I spiraled down a word vomit rabbit hole.

"No, absolutely not."

"Okay."

His mouth might have said *okay*, but his body language seemed unbelieving still.

I leaned my chest slightly toward his to emphasize my point. "Honestly, I don't. I just wish I'd really been ready for it, for us, when I said I was."

"Hmm."

Thomas sat still on his side of the couch, not moving toward me at all but staring deeply into my eyes and effectively cutting off whatever was left of my speech. Really, I wasn't doing that great of a job anyway, so that was probably for the best. After a few moments in silence, he spoke again.

"Sooo, did you come here tonight to basically say what you couldn't say on New Year's Eve, or..."

"No," I answered, interrupting him this time. "I came by because I miss you, and I wanted to tell you that I loved you...love you...and even if you don't feel the same, I wanted you to know that you're one of the best things that has come from my trip to America. And you're a great guy. And I love you. I..."

My voice broke as I tried to get my words out, pausing each time I admitted my love for him, as the tears started flowing down my cheeks and replacing any last remaining chance that I had at keeping my composure.

"Hey, hey, it's okay," he said, finally removing the space between us on the couch as he jumped toward me in a flash.

Once our thighs were nearly touching, Thomas wrapped his arms around my shoulders and pulled me into him, providing me with the comfort I probably didn't deserve since I was the one trying to apologize.

"I'm really sorry," I said, crying into his chest. "I was an idiot. I didn't fight for us... I was Dwayne Wayne!"

"Liv," he said, interrupting me again. "You weren't an idiot. And you're not Dwayne Wayne because you're here now."

Thomas chuckled softly and then lifted my chin so that I could see his face and look into his eyes as he spoke.

"You were scared. I knew that. I mean, I was, too, for that matter. It's why I didn't pursue anything with you for months, but listen... I've never met a woman like you before. I've never had someone capture my thoughts so wholly and intensely and as quickly as you did. That's the only reason I stopped fighting what we so clearly had with each other. I just got to the point where I was willing to do it scared.

"But I knew... Hear me out, babe. I knew that you still weren't ready even when you said you were. I just really wanted you to be. I wanted you to be willing to do it scared with me."

"I am now," I whispered, slowly starting to wipe the tearstains off my face. "I am now, Thomas."

With regained confidence, I repeated myself, louder this time so that he'd know this was different than the last.

"Are *you* still? Maybe?" I asked.

"I wouldn't have even answered the phone the other day if I wasn't, Liv."

I raised my head again, and Thomas leaned back slightly, tilting his head to the side. It was reminiscent of the first day we'd met, sparking up the smirk that had always forced me to catch my breath no matter our surroundings. That smirk had literally been my kryptonite from day one, but tonight, while still incredibly sexy, it was more than that; it was a glimmer of hope that I hadn't completely blown my best chance at love.

"Does that mean…?"

"It means that I love you, too. And yes, I was hurt, but I never stopped loving you. And I'm here. Now. In the only place I'd want to be, with the only woman I want to be with."

Thomas's last few words came out slowly and intentionally, like he wanted to make sure I heard every syllable, and it penetrated my memory in a way that it couldn't be erased. In response, I leaned back into him, dropping my head onto his chest and scooping my arms around his torso. I squeezed him tightly and, closing my eyes, breathed in a sigh of relief that I hadn't messed up so royally that things couldn't be fixed.

Because he loves me. And he's here, I reminded myself. *Thank God for that.*

In return, Thomas enveloped my entire body, wrapping his thick arms around me and making sure that almost every part of our bodies was connected. Then, with nothing else left to say, he sunk his head onto my shoulder, inhaling me in.

We stayed exactly like that as the next several minutes turned into thirty, holding each other closely in a beautiful silence that was equal parts calming and secure. Eventually, our heartbeats and our breath patterns fell into the same pace, and I realized, in that very moment, that this was what my friends had been trying to talk about during the bachelorette weekend. This kind of elemental connection was rare, and once I'd stopped fighting it, it no longer felt scary at all—it was just…safe.

"You know," Thomas said, his deep and endearing voice sounding like a frog was trying to come out, as neither of us had spoken a word in quite a while, "you never actually asked me if I was willing to move to London when you go back home."

"What?" I asked, lifting my head slightly, unsure if I was confused and had misheard him or if he'd said what I thought he said.

"I said you never asked me," he repeated.

"Well, of course I wouldn't," I replied. "How many times have we talked about you loving the life you've built here? I wouldn't ask you to give that up."

"Yeah, I don't mean it in that way, not as in asking me to choose. I mean you never asked me what *my* thoughts were on it. You just assumed I'd be conflicted, but I'm not, Liv."

"What are you saying?" I asked, daring to actually look him in the eyes for this conversation.

I wanted—no, needed—him to be very clear, and I had to make sure I wasn't just hearing what I wanted to.

"I'm saying that I already work with clients in the

UK. You know this. That's why I was on that flight that day. So, yeah, I'm not going to lie—it would be a big change, but not an impossible one. I'd already started talking to one of the partners I work with, and he was excited about the chance to have me overseas to give more face time to our clients there. But then…"

"I freaked out and started breadcrumbing you."

"Something like that, yeah."

"Wow. I just didn't think you'd be willing to give up all of this…for me."

"I know, but it's you. And for you, for us, I'm more than willing to take that chance."

"Okay," I said softly, and forced myself to let his words once again sit in my spirit.

I didn't want to run away from this feeling. I wanted to just take it in and enjoy it.

"To us doing it scared, then," I added, and then dropped my head back onto his chest, tucking myself into his embrace once again.

Correction, Olivia, I said to myself. *This is what it feels like to be fully and wholly loved for who you are.*

There was no way I was letting it or him go again.

Epilogue

"Are you still in your office, Olivia?"

Thomas's baritone voice boomed through my phone, somehow equally chastising and teasing me at the same time. I could hear his smirk even as he spoke, which made me move that much faster at packing up my tan Chanel tote bag so that I would prove him wrong.

"Yes," I said, hesitantly. "But... I promise I'm leaving now. I won't be late for lunch this time."

"Mmm-hmm. This is what you said the last time."

"I know, I know. But give a girl some credit. You know I'm still getting used to actually leaving the office during the day. But I am because I want to see you."

"And yet you're still in the office," he replied, his laugh bellowing into my ear.

"Because you're still on my phone! Okay, I'm leaving it now. Love you. See you soon."

"Love you, too."

As soon as I ended the call, I slipped my phone into my bag, made sure to silence my Slack notifications and headed out, passed the scores of other staff preparing to leave for lunch, too. I smiled to myself, vividly remembering the days when I'd be holed up in my office, save a welcome interruption from Wendy or Julie, too scared to enjoy lunch like every other person who worked at our company. For months, I'd worked through breakfast, lunch and dinner—always trying to outdo myself, prove that I could excel at the next thing and the next thing…and yet here I was, still excelling *and* making time to meet up with Thomas for lunch. It was nice. I guess Walter was right about his work-life balance motto.

Wendy's desk was my last hurdle to making it on time for my third lunch date with Thomas in two months—which, despite his lighthearted complaints about my tardiness for them, I'd really come to love. Not that Wendy herself was an obstacle, but a) her desk was positioned right by the lifts in the lobby, so you had to walk past her before you left out, and b) if anyone would know that Walter was looking for me or needed me to stay for some kind of emergency, it was her.

I braced myself as I walked up to her, the smile on my face hopefully sending signals that read *Please don't stop me!*

"Hey, Wends," I said, slowing down my stride but purposely not stopping. "I'll be back in a bit. If Walter asks…"

"Please," she said, shushing me off. "Go enjoy your lunch with your very handsome and charming boyfriend. Walter and the work will be here when you get back."

"Thanks, Wendy," I said, my smile growing wider and

wider as I picked my pace back up, hit the button for the down lift and waved goodbye as I disappeared into it.

Moments later, I found myself walking into the cool air that only an early May afternoon in New York City could bring, joining the bustling crowd of people headed to the train. Now that it was officially spring, I'd taken the liberty to brighten up my wardrobe and today had worn a hot-pink sleeveless turtleneck shirt tucked into my rust-orange high-waisted wide-leg trousers. So, between that and the way my skin was glowing under the sun's bright gaze, I knew I was making a statement among the blues, blacks and tans most people still gravitated toward in the Financial District, and I kind of loved it. It was just another way I was enjoying this new version of me. Plus, I'd been taking Reagan up on her offer to see her hairstylist, so my brown-and-blond highlighted passion twists had been replaced by my natural dark brown tresses, which fell right below my shoulders and blew effortlessly in the cool breeze.

It would be another twenty-five minutes before I walked onto Pier 45, my yellow stiletto pumps guiding me along the way, just in time to meet Thomas. It was the perfect middle ground between the Financial District and his office space in Midtown, but it was also known for some of the most amazing views in the city. I looked around the pier, checking to see if I'd missed him or shown up to the wrong place, when he suddenly appeared, handsome as always, and dressed in a navy blue blazer and white button-down that I was going to have to desperately stop myself from ripping off when he came nearer.

"Hey," he said, smiling brightly at me as he walked up to me.

"Hi, there."

I licked my lips to stop myself from jumping on top of him.

"You made it on time," he replied, his gray eyes twinkling under the sun and making my cheeks hurt from how much I couldn't drop them, either.

"I said I would."

"That you did, love. That you did."

As he leaned in to give me a hug and a kiss, his Le Labo cologne threatening to make me weak in my knees as always, I finally noticed the black plastic bag he had in his hand and instantly had an idea for what he'd brought us for lunch.

"Is that what I think it is?" I asked.

His wink told me everything I needed to know. Before he could stop me, I dipped my hand into the bag and grabbed one of the two foil-wrapped sandwiches out of it, claiming it as my own.

"You went to Hajji's and got us chopped cheese sandwiches for lunch?" I asked rhetorically, clearly already having the evidence in my hands.

"Well, you know, we're officially on countdown mode to leave here in a few months, so I figured we should make sure to get in all the bad-good food New York has to offer before we do."

"You're a genius," I said, unwrapping the top part of my sandwich and taking the biggest, most satisfying bite. "And OMG. I'm definitely going to miss this."

Thomas watched in awe, still unable to stop smiling as I savored the gloriously delicious and greasy beef-and-cheese treat. I very clearly enjoyed the decision he'd made and the effort it must have taken for him to go there and come back and still get here at the time we'd said. No wonder he'd been pestering me about being on time. It all made sense now.

"Don't worry," he said with a wink. "I might know a thing or two about how to make them myself. So you won't have to miss them too much."

"What? How have you kept this from me all this time?"

"A man's gotta keep some secrets, Liv. You already know about Rihanna… I can't tell you everything all at once."

I laughed heartily in between bites and then with my free hand, grabbed his so we could finally find our way to a bench to sit down and eat properly.

"I guess you're right," I replied. "But how did I get so lucky to find a man who can cook and who loves me?"

Out the corner of our eyes, we both spotted a couple getting ready to get up from a bench just a few steps away, so before he could respond, we instinctually looked at each other and booked it in our best dress shoes, not wanting to lose the spot. It was like old times' sake anyway, the way we banded together and made magic happen. We'd done that from the very start, as he'd helped me wrestle down not one but two pieces of luggage on that fateful September day. Now we'd bested the busy New York crowd all trying to find an empty spot near the water. What a team!

As we plopped down onto the bench, Thomas finally took his own sandwich out of the bag and passed me one of the bottles of water to wash mine down.

"I guess sometimes the best things come unexpectedly," he said, answering my question from before in such a Thomas-like way, one filled with hope even when I didn't have enough for us both.

But he was right. Everything about us had been un-expected. And yet probably the best thing that had ever happened to me.

"How much time do you have for us today?" he asked, biting into his chopped cheese as he awaited my reply.

"How about a lifetime?" I replied with a devious smile, knowing that he would get that I was only par-tially kidding.

I checked my watch and rolled my eyes at the time. "But also, probably another forty-five minutes."

"Perfect," he replied. "I'll take these forty-five min-utes and the lifetime as long as I get to spend it all with you."

"Deal," I said, and leaned my back into his chest, enjoying the sun on our bodies, the chopped cheese in my belly and the man—my teammate—who I wanted to spend forever and ever with.

If New York never gave me anything else, that was all I ever needed from her and more.

* * * * *

#3035 THE COWBOY'S ROAD TRIP

Men of the West • by Stella Bagwell

When introverted rancher Kipp Starr agrees to join Beatrice Hollister on a road trip, he doesn't plan on being snowbound and stranded with his sister's outgoing sister-in-law. Or falling in love with her.

#3036 THE PILOT'S SECRET

Cape Cardinale • by Allison Leigh

Former aviator Meyer Cartell just inherited a decrepit beach house—and his nearest neighbor is thorny nurse Sophie Lane. Everywhere he turns, the young—and impossibly attractive—Sophie is there...holding firm to her old grudge against him. Until his passionate kisses convince her otherwise.

#3037 FLIRTING WITH DISASTER

Hatchet Lake • by Elizabeth Hrib

When Sarah Schaffer packs up her life and her two-year-old son following the completion of her travel-nursing contract, she's not prepared for former army medic turned contractor Desmond Torres to catch her eye. Or for their partnership in rebuilding a storm-damaged town to heal her guarded heart.

#3038 TWENTY-EIGHT DATES

Seven Brides for Seven Brothers • by Michelle Lindo-Rice

Courtney Meadows needs a hero—and Officer Brigg Harrington is happy to oblige. He gives the very pregnant widow a safe haven during a hurricane. But between Brigg's protective demeanor and heated glances, Courtney's whirlwind emotions are her biggest challenge yet.